# THERE WILL BE
# BETTER DAYS

Flame-haired beauty Chloe Collard watched her mother struggle through life, so Chloe promised herself something a long time ago; she would get a proper education and make something of herself. This vow would carry Chloe through her entire life. When Chloe is offered a job as a personal assistant in a prestigious firm, she finally feels her hard work is paying off. And with romance knocking at her door, a happy and fulfilled life is just around the corner. But all is not as it seems when the decisions Chloe has to make are not as straightforward as they first appear...

# THERE WILL BE BETTER DAYS

# THERE WILL BE BETTER DAYS

*by*

## Elizabeth Waite

**Magna Large Print Books**
Long Preston, North Yorkshire,
BD23 4ND, England.

British Library Cataloguing in Publication Data.

Waite, Elizabeth
    There will be better days.

    A catalogue record of this book is
    available from the British Library

    ISBN   978-0-7505-4143-5


First published in Great Britain in 2014 by Sphere
an imprint of Little, Brown Book Group

Copyright © 2014 Elizabeth Waite

Cover illustration © Ryan Jorgensen by arrangement with
Arcangel Images

The moral right of the author has been asserted

Published in Large Print 2015 by arrangement with
Little Brown Book Group

Magna Large Print is an imprint of Library Magna Books Ltd.

Printed and bound in Great Britain by
T.J. (International) Ltd., Cornwall, PL28 8RW

# Prologue

Liverpool Street station offered shelter to twelve-year-old Chloe Collard as she watched her mother polishing the brass hand rails that ran up the side of the steps of the Great Eastern Hotel. It was a foul day, cold, wet and windy, and the thin layer of ragged clothing she wore did nothing to keep her warm. Her best feature was her long flaming red hair, but today most of that was concealed beneath a close-fitting woolly hat.

Full of the old-world elegance of times gone by, the hotel could boast one of the finest restaurants in the whole of London. Not that Chloe had ever been inside the place, but she often had caught a glimpse of the crystal chandeliers and the glossy leather armchairs in the entrance hall.

Her mum was fat and scruffy but with a heart of pure gold. Nothing ever seemed to get her down. She was a tough, gutsy lady who suffered much pain from rheumatoid arthritis, but her eyes always brimmed with good humour, her lips were ever ready to break into a smile and she was known for the fact that she'd share her last penny or crust of bread with anyone who needed it. The jobs she was called on to do in the hotel were not nearly as horrifying as might be imagined. Joe and Jack Johnson, two brothers with the blood of the East End strong in their veins, representatives of all that was fine in a true cockney, were in charge of the dirty jobs both inside and outside the premises. Jobs that the well-dressed managers of the hotel made it their business to delegate.

Do a good job and the brothers made sure you were paid on time and were never without work. They both held Nellie Collard in great esteem, for when they had been lads at school hanging about outside the Nag's Head in freezing cold weather, with the arse out of their trousers, Nellie had always welcomed them into her basement flat to sit with her own children near her coal fire and eat bowls of thick, tasty soup.

Their own parents had been a right pair, father workshy, mother a slag, and what she'd earned from prostitution she and her husband would spend in the local pubs.

What goes around comes around was an old cockney saying, and so it was with Joe and Jack Johnson. Besides overseeing the nitty-gritty jobs at the Great Eastern Hotel, the two men were part of a gang of porters who worked in the very early hours of the morning at Smithfield, the wholesale meat market. It was the perks from that job and their memories of Nellie's kindness that kept

Chloe and her two brothers not exactly well fed, but a darn sight better than most. Scrag end of mutton, half a pig's head, pig's trotters and beef marrowbones were often popped into Nellie's canvas shopping bag, and being the good cook that she was, Nellie produced tasty meals and pans of soup for her three children.

On this rotten cold day, Chloe watched as her mother picked up her box of cleaning materials and struggled down the great flight of stone steps. Dragging her feet, Nellie set off round the side of the hotel towards the back entrance. Chloe sighed. Poor Mum, her legs must be playing her up again. She wondered if her mother had ever entered that hotel by the front door.

It was at that moment that Chloe made a decision. Telling herself that there had to be more to life than what her mother endured, she vowed that she would get an education or die in the attempt.

'I am not going through life wearing other folk's old clothes and eating well only when I'm offered charity,' she said aloud. 'I'll earn enough money to have a bedroom of my own. That windowless basement room that I share with my two brothers will be gladly left behind.'

That vow that Chloe made when she was twelve years old was to carry her through the whole of her life.

# Chapter 1

Each and every morning when Chloe Collard sat up in bed and reached to pull open her curtains, she cast her eyes downwards and was immediately captivated by the amazing display that stretched out as far as she could see. The vast variety of cabin cruisers, the huge yachts that the locals laughingly referred to as gin palaces, the tall masts on the sailing boats, even the poor man's sixteen-foot cuddy boats all moored in Brighton's Harbour Marina were a joy to behold, and she never failed to thank God for the way her life had turned out.

She was twenty-four years old and she owned this penthouse apartment in one of the tall blocks that had in recent years been built around the busy marina. She also had a fantastic job, personal assistant to Roger McKinnon, who was a director of a firm of diamond merchants. Her vastly different way of life was entirely down to that one man.

Chloe had been born in the East End of London. Her father had been killed in a tragic accident in the dockyards and her mother had lost the will to live and died less than a year later. Chloe felt she couldn't lay any blame at her mother's door. Her parents had been devoted to one another from the moment they had set eyes on each other.

The first four years after they had gone had taught Chloe the meaning of the word poverty. She had been fourteen, and her two brothers – Peter, aged twelve, and Matthew, aged nine – had become her responsibility. There hadn't been much help on offer. The rows, shouting matches and arguments, the tears and recriminations that had followed, had been heartbreaking for Chloe. Money was short; her father had lived for the day, never giving a thought to saving for the future. In sheer desperation, Chloe had given in to the persuasion from their local Catholic priest and had agreed that both Peter and Matthew should be allowed to emigrate to Australia, where, she had been assured, they would have a wonderful life and be given an excellent education.

Left alone, Chloe had greatly felt the loss of her family, but sheer determination to better herself had driven her to study hard. Finally she had achieved the credentials to secure herself a place at university.

Her efforts had paid off. She had landed a job in the call centre of Associated Securities, a member of the National Association of Goldsmiths, dealers in diamonds and precious stones. It hadn't taken long for Roger McKinnon, one of the firm's directors, to notice her, and after six months she had been offered the job as his personal assistant, working with him from offices situated above premises in Meeting House Lane in Brighton. From that day on she had never looked back. She had entered a world that previously had been unknown to her.

Chloe was aware that not only was she well treated, she was well paid. In return, she was a good employee. She shielded Roger from unnecessary disturbances and made sure he kept every important appointment. She also sidelined all nuisance telephone calls.

As she thought about her good fortune, a broad smile spread across her face and she pictured the man who had become her saviour.

Roger McKinnon was a good-looking, broad-shouldered, heavy-featured man in his mid fifties. He still had a good head of dark brown hair, though his sideboards were edged with grey. Thick, bushy eyebrows over dark brown eyes gave a suggestion of the authority that radiated from him at all times. He was always immaculately dressed in well-cut suits and his shoes were hand-made from good leather. He had been born in Guernsey, the only son of a well-to-do family, who had realised early on that he'd been blessed with near genius intelligence.

Chloe looked at her bedside clock. It was seven thirty, time to get out of bed and prepare herself for yet another interesting day.

Having taken her shower and dressed herself in the clothes she had made a habit of laying out the night before – she found it saved her a lot of time deliberating as to what she was going to wear – she drank her usual glass of orange juice and then spent the next twenty minutes applying her make-up. Now she only had her hair to arrange. She smiled as she sat facing her reflection in her dressing table mirror, well aware that her hair really was her crowning glory. The colour of a well-polished chestnut, it was thick and long enough to hang over her shoulders. During office hours she coiled it into either a French pleat or sometimes a bulky bun, which she held in place with decorative side combs. When attending social functions, she always allowed her hair to hang loose; it never failed to attract attention.

Gathering her expensive leather briefcase and her up-to-date black and red handbag, Chloe allowed herself one last look in the full-length mirror that stood in the hall of her apartment. She was well satisfied with her reflection. She was certainly slim, not an ounce of fat on her body, but, she thought, smiling to herself, she did have great breasts, not over large, but taut and pert. As Roger was fond of telling her, he thought of her nipples as his own fresh loganberries.

'Why not raspberries?' she had once queried.

'Because raspberries are an everyday produce. Loganberries are the aristocracy of fresh fruits,' he had quickly shot back at her. Her eyes twinkled at the recollection.

Her dark grey tailored suit was elegant, her white shirt blouse pure silk; sheer black nylons and plain black court shoes with a three-inch heel completed her outfit. You'll do, she conceded as she opened her front door and walked towards the lift.

Chloe didn't have to be in the office until nine thirty, and so, as had become a regular habit, she made for her favourite coffee bar, where she knew Philip Conti would be expecting her.

The whole area was a hive of activity. It never ceased to amaze Chloe just how much had been achieved over the years, and she felt she would always be amazed at the dynamism of this marina. The yacht club was always bustling and the harbour master in his high control tower situated next to the lock was certainly kept busy. Very much more so at weekends, when Londoners came down to take their vessels out to sea.

Besides being a great harbour for the boating fraternity, the marina boasted phenomenal leisure facilities: cafés and restaurants to suit everyone's taste. The Rendezvous

Casino, with its glorious views, offered superb dining in the Reflections Restaurant and also traditional gaming tables. There was entertainment of all kinds to satisfy everyone whatever the weather, which all served to establish the Brighton Marina as the successful enterprise it was today.

Taking a deep breath of the salty sea air, Chloe seated herself at one of the tables set out along the side of the harbour. No better way to start the day than by gazing out over the sea.

Hearing the click of Philip Conti's heels on the tiled walkway, it occurred to her how close she and Philip had become. Even before his arm reached out, she knew he would place her steaming glass of latte on the table before touching her. Philip, his three brothers and two sisters and his Italian parents were loved by the regular customers and even more so by the day-excursion folk. That was the beauty of this marina: it was a place where a multitude of different nationalities had not only established various lucrative businesses but had formed long-lasting friendships. Philip had a gorgeous wife and two endearing little boys; all the same, Chloe knew he was going to touch her – she was waiting for him to touch her. As always, he put his hands on her shoulders, drew her face forward and smiled at her tantalisingly before gently kissing first one cheek and then the other.

It was the same every morning. Just a whiff of Philip's fragrant aftershave and the soft feel of his breath on her face had her tensed, ready for what she knew was only an affectionate endearment, yet when his lips touched her flesh, it never failed to start her heart hammering with slow, deliberate thuds and her knees always felt weak.

'Oh my God, Philip Conti! There should be more men like you in this world,' she exclaimed loudly.

'Your adulation will get you anywhere, my darling Chloe. Meanwhile, your coffee is going cold. So enjoy this beautiful June sunshine before you have to be locked away in that stuffy office. By the way, look across to the shop, Mamma is waving at you; on the other hand, she might be suggesting that I pick up any dirty cups on my way back, and who am I to argue with Mamma?'

Chloe laughed. Mamma Conti was a big fat lady but very lovable, and she made the most delicious coffee cakes. She also ruled her husband, her children and their offspring with a rod of iron. It was families like the Contis that added character to this stunning waterside location.

Chloe was taking her time drinking her coffee. Meantime her thoughts were correcting Philip. Stuffy her office certainly was not. It was spacious, the furniture splendid, and equipped with every modern device to make a person's life that much easier. She was thankful that she had learnt to master a computer. She knew, only too well, that she had to keep up with every modern device and apparatus that came on the market. Today's world had accelerated and she had no intention of being left behind.

Change for her had come about so rapidly, and whether or not the alliance she had entered into with Roger was entirely ethical, she no longer cared. She didn't often question herself these days; her way of life was so satisfying, she had learnt not to make her scruples an issue. However, it never took much thought for her to vividly recall just how Roger had put his proposition to her.

The day's work was over and Chloe had been putting on her jacket, preparing to walk along the sea front to catch a bus up to Black Rock, where at the time she had been renting a bed-sitting room in a house owned by an elderly lady named Mrs Woodman.

Roger had appeared in the doorway of his office. 'Can you spare half an hour, Chloe? There is something I would like to discuss with you. Don't worry about your bus, I'll run you home.'

She had removed her jacket and hung it on the back of the chair before sitting opposite Roger, who was by now seated on the other side of his massive desk.

Chloe was by now well versed in Roger's habits and moods, but this evening he seemed to be perplexed. She felt he was staring deep into her eyes. If she had but known it, she was right. Her emerald eyes were big, wide and glistening, and at that moment Roger would have given her anything. He had thought long and hard about what he was proposing to offer this charming, beautiful young lady.

'Chloe, I want you to fully understand what I am about to say to you. If you decide not to comply with what I suggest, I promise you that our working relationship will not change in any way. As long as you understand that, I will say my piece.'

To this day Chloe remembered how her mind had spun around in circles as Roger had softly begun to speak.

'I still have feelings for Thelma, my wife, but they now edge on pity rather than on true love. Since she fell from her horse she has suffered terribly. To begin with she made herself practically bedridden. Wouldn't allow help from anyone. Now at least the nurses do manage now and again to get her into a wheelchair and take her into the garden for some fresh air. Is my position not understandable?'

Roger's voice had held a distinct plea, but his expression was not enough to let Chloe know what his thoughts were leading up to.

He was such a big man. Not brawny, but definitely muscular and very strong. She had suddenly felt very sorry for him but couldn't fathom what she should do about it.

Roger had pushed his chair back and got to his feet. His movements as he walked about had been slow, and Chloe had felt compelled to ask if she could do anything for him. His reply had been a definite no. He begged her to bear with him and eventually he came to stand in front of her and started to speak, telling her that looking into her big green eyes had a man longing to make love with her. That her full lips were asking to be kissed.

'Chloe, I will not deny I have hankered after you, yearned for you, yes, even craved you, but had my dear Thelma been a wife in every sense of the word, we wouldn't be having this conversation. Through no fault of her own, and none on my part, our marriage has become a deadlock. I am grateful that the first ten years of our married life were blissfully happy. The sex was fulfilling for both my wife and me, though sadly there were no children.'

The long silence that followed hung heavily until Roger heaved a sigh and started to talk again.

'Before I met her, Thelma was well cared for, protected and loved by extremely wealthy parents. Not once but dozens of times her father thanked me for having married his daughter, because I had given her a wonderful, loving, secure lifestyle. And that was true. I wasn't a fortune-hunter; I had enough money of my own.'

Endless silence had followed that outburst.

'I am so sad to hear about your wife,' Chloe had eventually managed to say, and when Roger had remained silent she had blurted out, 'Are you asking permission to have sex with me on a regular basis?' The minute she had uttered the question she'd felt her cheeks immediately flame up. 'Oh, I am so sorry.' Her apology was said in a soft whisper.

'Please, Chloe, don't apologise. Now I can at least come straight to the point. Yes, I am a healthy, fit man and I cannot deny the fact that I have needs. I would like you to visit my house once a fortnight, at least to begin with; perhaps even sit a while with my wife, she sees so few visitors. As to us, I don't need to spell it out. You are twenty-three years old and a beautiful young lady. We can take it steady, maybe not even engage in full sex, but I do need to be able to feel that I am still a red-blooded man. I promise I will always take care of you if you think there's a likelihood that we could seal an understanding between us, a loving pact where no one gets hurt and we both benefit. Moneywise I am well able to help you, and you would be taking nothing away from my wife.'

Chloe had held her breath almost from the minute Roger had started to speak again, but now she had no option. She swallowed hard until she got rid of the knot in her throat, then she drew in a deep breath and let it out slowly. Her heart had still been thudding nineteen to the dozen.

It was at that moment that she felt an urge come over her. It was an urge to mother this man, to wrap her arms around him, soothe and comfort him, but in a maternal kind of way. She was no fool. She knew exactly what he was proposing. She had known from the moment that she had come to work for him that there was something that set this man apart from his contemporaries. An elusive ruthlessness lay beneath the sophisticated exterior, an inherent masculine vitality with a concealed sexiness. He might be well into his fifties, but there was a whole lot more to him than fine tailoring, hand-crafted shoes and glimpses of his gold ring, tie pin and Rolex watch.

There had been one occasion when they had used the Brighton swimming pool at the same time and the image of his unclothed body had taunted her. He had a lean waist with no sign of any beer belly, broad hips, a tight backside, and long, powerful legs. Since then she had often let herself wonder what it might feel like to be held close to him, to feel his lips on hers. Even his big, broad hands were different, with long fingers and well-manicured nails. She had often felt herself shiver as those types of thoughts had run through her mind.

Why not?

For a mad moment she imagined she had spoken the two words out loud.

Somehow she had managed to smile up at Roger but had remained silent. It would certainly be a vastly different experience to those young lads she had trifled with in her late teens.

At that point Chloe knew she had been won over. She hadn't needed a great deal of persuasion.

Roger had asked, 'Do you have a current boyfriend?'

How well she remembered her capitulation. Sounding like a shy young girl half her age, she had said, 'I think from this day forth I might have.'

Roger had got to his feet, gone to his magnificent drinks cabinet and taken out two crystal glasses and a bottle of champagne that he had already had standing in an ice bucket. Between them they had drunk the whole bottle of champagne. Said things to each other that had needed to be said. Tactfully touched and kissed, leaving one another with the promise of good things to come.

Eventually he'd rung for a taxi and had escorted her on the short journey to her lodgings, holding her hand all the way. When the taxi had stopped, he had taken her into his arms and really kissed her. A long, lingering kiss that she had found to be surprisingly stimulating.

She had gone to bed that night with her head high in the clouds.

That episode had taken place more than eighteen months ago. It was still as clear today, and Chloe was smiling as she drank the remains of her coffee.

'No regrets!' she murmured to herself.


## Chapter 2

Chloe was still deep in thought, reviving memories, when Philip signalled to her that her taxi had arrived to take her to the office. She gathered up her bags, reminding herself how lucky she was that there was no more getting on and off buses these days.

Actually she owned her own car, a Mini Cooper; it was the first thing that Roger had bought for her after she said yes to his proposal. She didn't use the car to get to work because trying to find a parking space in Brighton was a nightmare. Roger hadn't let the grass grow under his feet in any way whatsoever. Chloe often pondered the way that having a great deal of money eased many a path and undoubtedly helped towards an even more lucrative way of life. Having a taxi to take her to work and bring her home was only one of the many perks she now enjoyed courtesy of Associated Securities. Roger had also insisted that she must look around for better accommodation. It had come as a complete shock when he had told her he had made an appointment for them both to view a few apartments in Brighton Marina.

A representative from the estate agency had spent the afternoon spelling out just how advantageous it would be to make a purchase at this time.

'This is a new venture and the accommodation surrounding the harbour will in time assuredly increase in value.' The young man was well versed in what he was paid to say. Having seen two apartments, Roger had dropped his biggest surprise.

'Do you have a penthouse vacant?' he had asked, sounding completely matter-of-fact. 'If so, we'd like to view that next.'

It would have been hard to say whether it was Chloe or the young man who was the more thunderstruck. Chloe had certainly been speechless. The young man from the agency had soon recovered.

'Certainly, sir, that type of apartment comes with an allocated permanent garage space in the underground car park and also a mooring reservation within the harbour, which is safely secured by terrific sea defences...'

'Just take us up,' Roger had instructed, and the silence that followed as the three of them rode up in the lift ... well! Chloe had thought it would be a brave person who would dare to break it.

How about the moment she had her first view of the inside of that apartment? Could she remember exactly how she had felt? Of course she could.

Stupendous! It was so high up she'd felt she could almost reach out through the windows and touch the sky. Even now she knew she would never tire of the view.

Roger had arranged a meeting at the estate agent's and within six weeks he had handed the deeds to that beautiful apartment over to Chloe. His miraculous generosity had not stopped there. Together they had acted like a couple of newly-weds, combing places such as John Lewis, Laura Ashley and, of course, Harrods.

The end result was that she owned a simply beautiful home.

She had been living there for two months before she had managed to persuade Roger to stay the night with her. Now he stayed as often as he could, depending on the state of his wife's health.

Chloe had accepted the situation with remarkable ease. Each and every day she thanked the Lord that Roger McKinnon had come into her life. He never ceased to amaze her. He was kind, considerate and his generosity knew no limits. Yet in return his demands on her were not great. It amazed her how quickly she had become attuned to his needs and even more so to his likes and dislikes. So much so that when together in bed she knew each time just where he would touch her, yet she was always thrilled by that touch.

It hadn't been so in the beginning. Their first try had been mishandled. Chloe had known then that she had to reassure Roger, get him to relax. Very different these days, she told herself with a smile. Roger had learnt the contours of her body and now each time they came together he sent delicious sensations through her. The feeling was not one-sided. The joy of being so in tune with each other had done away with the need for words. Now they were able to arouse each other to a depth of passion that Chloe was sure neither of them had known existed.

Monday morning, and for the first time Chloe had arrived at the office thirty-five minutes late. There had been an accident along the seafront. Her taxi driver had indicated to the police that he wished to make a detour.

'You and everyone else that is caught in this hold-up the officer had answered drily. More sirens were signalling the arrival of a second ambulance. 'Shouldn't be long now, sir. As soon as we get those that were injured away to hospital, we'll have the traffic moving again. Always seems to happen on a Monday morning.'

'Thank God,' Roger murmured as Chloe opened the door and walked into the office. Coming round from behind his desk, he took her briefcase and handbag from her before helping her to remove her jacket. She watched him set her things down, then turn around and cross the floor until he was standing in front of her.

He held his arms wide open and she gladly walked into them. This was her safe harbour. He was her benefactor; at least that was how it had started. Now, though, he was so much more than just a provider. His hand slid along her shoulder, down her arm until he reached her hand, where he entwined his fingers with hers. Her heart hammered with heavy thuds and she felt weak at the knees. In the beginning it hadn't been like this; more of a business deal. The sex had been satisfactory but never mind-blowing. With time, how different things had become.

She was prevented from thinking any more by his mouth covering hers. His lips were trembling with utter relief: she was safe, his Chloe had not been involved in an accident. His kisses were urgent, even angry.

'Why didn't you use your mobile, let me know what was happening, why you were going to be so late?' He freed his fingers from hers, sliding his hands under her silky blouse and cupping her breasts. Chloe gasped. Even though his touch was familiar, his fingers never failed to send a thrill running through her body.

'Roger, remember where we are, anyone could come in.'

'Darling Chloe, my darling Chloe, I was worried sick when I heard the sirens so near at hand. God, if you had been injured...'

'Well I wasn't.' He really did care for her, and the very thought sent Chloe reeling. Suddenly his kisses were urgent and her body responded instinctively and powerfully. She found herself answering him kiss for kiss, the worry and anxiety of the past half-hour released into his passionate embrace.

That was how their life was now. Roger no longer needed to prove that he was a man, and Chloe certainly did not think of their lovemaking as a duty. Each time they made love, and it wasn't just once a fortnight, each made sure that both had achieved satisfaction. Roger needed Chloe, craved her, felt he could never get enough of her, and she had come to reciprocate his feelings. For one another they had perfected their lovemaking.

During that morning, whenever Chloe looked up from her computer she saw Roger's eyes on her. In the end she asked, 'Are you not going to do any work today?'

The question had popped out unwittingly; she hadn't meant to be inquisitive. She had always suspected that he was sensitive about his work, yet after they had got to know each other a little better, he had insisted that another desk be brought into his office. She still retained her own smaller office next door, and would retreat there whenever Roger was entertaining significant clients. Roger's office had a safe embedded in the wall, cleverly concealed within the wood panelling, in which specimen diamonds and some jewellery were stored. He held the only key.

Roger wasn't used to smiling, but somehow he had picked up the habit since Chloe had come into his life. Just at this moment his body was telling him that he was much younger than his actual years, and he couldn't keep the grin off his face as he asked, 'Chloe, will you keep the weekend free? I would like to take you to the Channel Islands, to Guernsey, where I was born.'

'Thank you very much, kind sir,' she said, smiling. 'And what kind of clothes should I pack?'

'I'll write you out a list of intended events, then you can decide for yourself. The Saturday evening of our stay I would like you to wear something glamorous; other than that, please yourself.'

This was the part of their relationship that Chloe treasured the most. Roger treated her as an equal. Wherever he took her, be it a business event or a social affair, she never had to stand back; he kept her close to his side and always introduced her by her full name. The days leading up to her first visit to his home had been traumatic, but Roger had been a true gentleman, treating her as if she were a life-long friend who was calling on him and his wife. Apprehension had flooded over her the first time she had set foot in the bedroom where his invalid wife was propped up with several pillows. Roger, having made the introductions, had leant over his wife, taken hold of her hand, then gently brushed his lips to her forehead in a gesture that had torn at Chloe's heartstrings.

It hadn't taken long for Chloe to regard Thelma McKinnon as a friend, though her main feeling towards this slender, white-haired lady, who was still only fifty-two years old, was pity. As the two women got to know each other, Thelma would declare how much happier Roger was since Chloe had started working for him. More often than not she would also say how very much she herself looked forward to Chloe's visits.

Was Thelma aware of the true state of affairs? And if so, why did that possibility suddenly cause Chloe a great deal of pain? She would have liked to believe that Thelma willingly turned a blind eye because of her love for her husband, and that perhaps she felt some genuine affection for Chloe.

In the beginning, deciding what to wear for the various events she attended with Roger had been a problem. However, Chloe had several friends who owned their own businesses in the rag trade. Just one request and they had got together and done Chloe proud. Not that Roger didn't accompany her to the bigger stores, and even to fashion shows. At the latter, a lot of the jewellery that the models wore would be on loan from Associated Securities. Chloe always felt reluctant to openly admire any particular dress, coat or suit, because Roger would insist on buying it for her. Besides, when she surprised him by wearing a creation made by her friends, she loved to see the reaction that would appear on his face. She took great delight in sensing his admiration.

Saturday morning, seven o'clock on the dot, her front doorbell rang. Chloe hardly had the door open when Roger took her in his arms. 'All mine for at least four days,' he murmured when he had kissed her. 'Ready?'

'Good morning to you too,' she said calmly, pointing the toe of her shoe towards her two large suitcases. She had learnt to take clothes for every occasion when travelling with Roger.

'Let's be making a move, then.'

A final check of her apartment: had she got her newly acquired passport? Even for the Channel Islands one needed a passport these days.

Roger collected both cases and called the lift while Chloe locked her front door. They descended to the ground floor. Outside, Roger's regular driver stood beside his well-polished BMW.

There wasn't much conversation during the drive to Southampton, where the company's private plane was waiting. Checking in proved to be a mere formality before they were cleared to board. There were introductions to the flight staff and to Roger's four colleagues, only one of whom had a female companion.

Roger discarded his coat and helped Chloe with hers before telling her, 'The flight to Guernsey is so short there won't be time for a meal, but drinks and nibbles will be served. Hope you managed to eat some breakfast.'

'Yes, I did. Just coffee will be fine.'

'Well I have a couple of matters that I need to check on.' He took his laptop from its case and prepared to get to work.

Roger was well aware that from the day he had been born he had led a sheltered life.

When his uncle had died suddenly, Roger's

father, Patrick McKinnon, had stepped into his shoes, taking over his directorship at Associated Securities. It had been a good move. The firm had developed beyond all expectations, accumulating a fortune for each person who had had the foresight to anticipate that industrial diamonds as well as jewellery would help to develop it into the success it was today.

Being his parents' only child, Roger had had it all, right up until the day of his wife's accident. He sighed heavily now, thinking of poor Thelma as he put the finishing touches to the documents he had been working on. He closed his laptop and placed it back in his case.

Their arrival was smooth, and as they walked across the tarmac, Roger inhaled deeply and exclaimed, 'Clean, wonderful air.' Knowing that Chloe had never visited this island before, he began to explain a few things to her whilst they waited to go through passport control.

'Can you not already feel the difference here as opposed to England?'

Chloe smiled. 'Spacious airport and yet no crowds or hustle and bustle, and everywhere so very clean.'

'It gets busy in the height of the season, but nothing like Gatwick or Heathrow. Wait until you see the countryside, Chloe; we'll hire a car and you can do some of the driving. Top speed allowed is thirty miles per hour, and some roads are very narrow; however, every driver is courteous, and gives way, so a little patience helps. The largest town is St Peter Port. Our hotel is situated right at the top end of Smith Street. The Old Government House Hotel: it is magnificent in every way, you'll see, and the views from up there are truly great, looking down over the harbour and well beyond. You'll love it.'

Cars and drivers were waiting to take the party to their hotel, where, discreetly, Roger had booked two suites. After they had unpacked their cases, he introduced Chloe to more of his colleagues. She was thankful to see that most of them had a female partner with them. They lunched on fresh crab and salad in the restaurant, which was situated high up, giving great views out over the harbour, just as Roger had described.

They decided to depart to their own rooms at three thirty in order to give themselves plenty of time to bath and dress ready for the evening's function, which was due to start at seven p.m. Their suites were spacious and lavishly decorated with beautiful furniture, rich floor-length curtains and carpet that one's feet sank into. There were also walk-in wardrobes and adjoining en suite bathrooms. Wonderful, thought Chloe, even more luxurious than my own apartment, and that's saying something.

She spent a long time getting ready and put a great deal of effort into making sure she looked glamorous. More so even than usual, because it had been a request from Roger.

At twenty minutes to seven, in answer to his knocking, she opened the door and stood back a few feet so that he could see the full effect. The look on his face assured her that he was not disappointed.

She was wearing a long one-shouldered emerald-green dress that looked as if she had been poured into it. It showed off her tiny waist and her shapely bust. She had paired the dress with strappy silver stilettos and a sparkling silver evening clutch bag, and had embellished her flowing silky red hair with green and silver slides. The colour of the dress emphasised her big green eyes.

Chloe was delighted with the reaction she received from Roger, though when he told her in no uncertain terms that just looking at her had aroused him to such an extent that he wouldn't be able to go downstairs for dinner, she laughingly told him that in that case he would have to stay in the bedroom on his own.

'You have become a very hard-hearted young lady,' he moaned. Then it was his turn to laugh as he said, 'I'll make sure you suffer tonight. I'll have you begging for mercy.'

'Really? I shall be interested to see if you

can back up that claim,' she told him brazenly.

My young Chloe has done me proud, Roger was thinking as together they descended the hotel's magnificent staircase. Chloe herself was enjoying the looks she was getting from other men. She needed no telling that she had become a woman of the world, confident and very self-assured, no longer held back by her early upbringing.

Roger turned his head towards her and raised his eyebrows, asking a silent question.

'Why not? I think we can safely agree that both of us are on a promise,' she whispered with a teasing smile.

Her cheeky response brought a gleam of amusement to his eyes before he successfully masked it.

They passed through the open glass doors on to the terrace, where Roger's colleagues had gathered. Chilled champagne, iced water and bite-sized savoury nibbles were laid out on several tables.

'I shall have to leave you for a short while. I'll be back to take you into dinner,' Roger hurriedly told her as he handed her a glass of champagne.

Chloe was wondering if Roger had any idea of the effect he had on her. She sipped her drink slowly. He looked immaculate tonight, but then he always did, even when he had no clothes on. This affair of theirs was never meant to be so meaningful. It had become impossible for her not to be affected by Roger's presence, for no matter how hard she tried, he was always in her thoughts. She just could not imagine a life without him in it; he had become her world, and it wasn't just to do with how much money he lavished on her. He had become a disturbing individual who caused her heartbeat to quicken and left her longing for him to make love to her. Time and time again she told herself not to be so foolish, that it wouldn't do any good. But she couldn't help it.

She watched as this powerful man came towards her to partner her into the dining room, and she smiled. Best to live for the moment, she told herself. We are here in Guernsey for at least three or four days; might as well make the most of it.

During the last twelve months Chloe had become accustomed to dining out with Roger, and every meal had been superb. Tonight, however, she felt she would have to call a halt. There were so many courses, she was struggling. Every delicacy was mouth-watering, from the savoury starters through to the Belgian chocolates and the tawny red port that the ladies drank while the men lit their cigars and sipped a fine old brandy.

It was quite some time before the band struck a chord to signal that dancing would now commence. When several couples had taken to the floor, Roger shifted in his seat and whispered a few words into Chloe's ear.

Chloe felt her cheeks grow red. She didn't have to make any answer because Roger had helped her to her feet and led her out to dance a glorious old-time waltz.

Holding her tight within his arms, he proved beyond any doubt that he was a superb dancer, totally in charge of every step and each individual movement. Pressed up close to him, she could now vouch that the words he had whispered to her had not been an idle boast. She could feel not only his manhood but the sweet sensitivity that was radiating from him.

It was one o'clock in the morning when all the good nights had been said and folk were making their way back to their rooms.

Chloe was bending low to turn the key in the door to her suite when Roger wrapped his arms around her from behind and pulled her up to rest against the length of his body. 'You've teased me enough this evening,' he whispered. 'Don't send me away.'

She felt herself sag into those strong arms. It felt so safe, so right; they needed each other. Somewhere in her head bells were going off, warning her that she was dreaming a dream that could never come true. She shivered. Live for the moment, she reminded herself as Roger opened the door and they entered the room together.

For the next three days Chloe was left very much to her own devices while the men attended to business. Two rooms in the hotel had been set aside as conference rooms, and smaller rooms for seminars. A whole host of businessmen who lived on the island were coming to the Old Government House to attend the meetings.

After breakfast on the Monday morning, Chloe was sitting in the front lounge reading a newspaper when her attention was caught by the arrival of these well-dressed gentlemen. She smiled to herself as she looked them over. Roger had told her that Guernsey was a rich island where the banks flourished and those who were in the know felt the benefit of their offshore activity. She folded her newspaper and watched the businessmen as they entered the hotel. They were a breed apart, speaking on their mobile phones as they walked, each one carrying a leather briefcase and a laptop. She felt she could almost smell the money.

She could easily have chosen to be companionable with the other ladies of the party, but she preferred her own company; too many awkward questions might have been asked. It surprised her just how much she enjoyed driving the hired car and visiting places of her own choice.

The evenings were a different story, each better than the previous one. On Tuesday, their last night in Guernsey, they were to attend a charity ball being held at the St Pierre Park Hotel. Roger and his colleagues had attended a meeting held in a private room at this hotel, and had reported back on the excellence of the hotel itself, which over-looked the sea, as well as the outstanding quality of the food.

For this occasion Chloe chose to wear an exquisitely cut long, slinky black dress with a flowing train. Her accessories were gold. As always, her flaming red hair comple-mented her outfit perfectly.

Roger also looked distinguished, attired in an impeccably tailored black evening suit, white linen shirt and black bow tie. So hand-some! The very look of him set her heart fluttering.

It was certainly a night to remember. Roger proved himself to be a really marvellous dancer again, and Chloe felt she had never spent a better night.

While they were making their way back upstairs in the early hours of the morning, Roger's eyes suddenly gleamed with a wicked look. 'Shall we round off our short holiday in style?' he asked.

Chloe laughingly punched him. His smile was so warm and wicked it would have melted ice. 'Are you asking to share my bed again tonight? Neither of us will get any sleep, and we have to travel home in the morning.'

But it was impossible to refuse him. Besides, she was already thinking how wonderful it always felt to fall asleep in his arms. She agreed willingly. She was going to make the most of the last night of their short holiday.

Arriving back at Southampton airport having spent four glorious days with Roger, it took a while for Chloe to come back down to earth. If only they could go back to her apartment and carry on as a normal couple would. Quickly she banished that thought. You have been given the world on a plate and yet you are yearning for more, she rebuked herself as she walked with Roger towards the waiting car.

She had to constantly remind herself that she couldn't afford to dwell on problems she couldn't solve. She must at all times count her blessings, because if she didn't, the only thing she would be left with would be heartache.

# Chapter 3

How glorious her apartment was. How lucky she was to have such a beautiful place to call home, but how lonely it was. Chloe told herself she enjoyed living alone, but she knew she lied. That wonderful break when Roger had shared her bed every night had made her realise how much she missed him when he wasn't there.

She had enjoyed every moment of their weekend. Now she had to wake up to the fact that Roger did not belong to her. He was Thelma's husband. Much good that did any of them, though.

'Stop it. Stop feeling sorry for yourself,' she loudly scolded herself.

She decided to get something from the deep freeze that she could put into the microwave for her dinner while she watched a movie. When that finished, she ought to get ready for work tomorrow. She'd have to access her laptop and see what e-mails there were. Anything to fill the time. By then it would be time for bed.

The way things had turned out between her and Roger was something that neither of them could have foreseen. They loved each other. They hated being apart. What if he were to put Thelma into a nursing home? He could well afford to find somewhere that would provide the very best of care. Then she and Roger would be able to live together full time.

You are turning into a selfish bitch and that is a very bad thing, her conscience cautioned. Why don't you just count your blessings and get on with your life?

Next morning, nine thirty on the dot, Chloe gave a deep sigh of relief as she opened the doors of the adjoining offices. She was thankful to be back at work; it even felt good to be wearing a business suit again. With that thought a sly grin spread over her face. She must remember to keep her jacket buttoned up, because beneath it she was wearing a beautiful flesh-coloured chiffon blouse. It'd been very expensive, but when Roger got his first view of the transparency of the material, every penny would have been well spent.

As Chloe seated herself at her desk, she saw that the light on the telephone was indicating recorded messages. She pressed the button to listen to them. The first two concerned matters she could deal with later. Then Roger's voice came on the line.

'Chloe, I am in Brompton Hospital, Chelsea. Thelma has had a bad turn, difficulty with her breathing. I've notified everybody

45

that needs to know. I'm sure you'll cope. I'll phone you if and when the opportunity arises.'

Oh dear God! She had been wishing that Thelma could be taken into care! She flinched away from letting her thoughts run any further along those lines, but there was no mistaking that that was what she had been thinking.

Two weeks had passed without a single word from Roger. Chloe told herself that he was preoccupied with Thelma, but she couldn't help worrying. Could his feelings have changed so drastically?

She had been working alongside Lloyd Spencer, another director of the company. Everything had gone smoothly enough, but she'd had to concentrate to keep her mind on her work. She wasn't the least bit sorry that it was Friday afternoon and work was over for another week. What was worrying her was the fact that this would be the second weekend that she had spent on her own. Holly and Barbara, two of the other PAs at the firm, had noticed that she looked down in the dumps and had asked if she would like to join them for a Saturday night out. She had been touched at their friendliness but had asked if she might take a rain-check.

As it turned out, she was thankful she had refused.

46

She was just about to step into her homeward-bound taxi when a courier on a motorcycle drew alongside. 'Package for Miss Chloe Collard?' he said, raising his eyebrows in question.

'Yes, thank you, I am Miss Collard.' She waited until the cab was on the move before she opened the package and read the note inside: *Sorry for the unavoidable silence. I have made reservations for us at the Reflections Restaurant for dinner tomorrow evening. Will pick you up at seven o'clock. RM*

So matter-of-fact. No word of affection. But at least they were to meet, and she found herself heaving a great sigh of relief. There was something small still inside the padded envelope, and she drew out one of the small black drawstring velvet bags used by the company to store and transport small diamonds. 'What on earth?' she murmured, quickly replacing the bag inside the envelope. She didn't dare view the contents until she was safely inside her own apartment.

Having thanked her driver and listened to him wishing her a good weekend, she made all haste to get into the lift. Outside her apartment, her hands were trembling as she struggled to get the key into the door. Dumping her jacket and laptop, she withdrew the small bag from the envelope and laid it on the coffee table, then sat down and stared at it. She was dying to see the contents yet more than half afraid of what she might discover.

Eventually she loosened the drawstring, opened the neck of the bag and shot the contents out into the palm of her hand. It was very small, just a twist of white tissue paper, which she hastened to unwind. A single white diamond and two tiny opals sparkled up at her. She had been with the company for long enough to recognise what they were. She couldn't take her eyes from these jewels, which shimmered and sparkled with various shots of colour as the light caught them. What on earth was she supposed to do with them? she asked herself. It came to her then that there had been an invitation enclosed in the package. It seemed that she would have to wait until tomorrow night before she would be able to get an explanation from Roger.

Chloe had taken great pains to get herself ready for this date. It seemed a bit daft thinking of it as a date, but what else could she suppose it was? She had spent the whole morning having her hair washed and set and her fingernails manicured. She was wearing an exquisite cream-coloured two piece that Roger hadn't seen before. The material had come from Hong Kong, the finest silk, beautiful to the touch. The dress was calf-length, no sleeves, cut straight across the chest, allowing just a glimpse of her rounded bosoms, and gathered into tiny pleats that met at her slim waist. The jacket was long, cut with flowing points that reached to her hips, while the lapels were decorated with amber-coloured rhinestones.

Roger arrived a quarter of an hour early, and the relief that flooded through Chloe's body as she stared at this tall, handsome man who had come to play such an important part in her life almost had her fainting away.

No greeting. Not a word. He just took her in his arms and held her close, and the loneliness and frustration of the past two weeks was forgotten.

It was Roger who spoke first. 'Chloe, you will never know how much I have missed you.'

'Me too,' she whispered, and he could hear that she was on the verge of tears. She pulled herself together enough to quickly ask, 'How is Thelma, is she still in hospital?'

Only half releasing his hold on her, Roger gently kissed her before saying, 'Thelma is never going to be much better. Her lungs have been badly affected, mainly because she insists on spending so much time in bed. She refuses to do any kind of exercise and rarely agrees to be helped into her wheelchair and taken out into the garden, where she would be able to get some fresh air into her lungs. She is at home now; it's where she wants to be. I have taken on a full-time night nurse to give Nurse Reynolds a bit of a break. The care home were wonderful. The doctors suggested she remained there, and I still think it might have been for the best, but Thelma had other ideas and who could blame her? She wants to be in her own home. To be honest, I think she has lost the will to live.

'Anyhow, my darling,' he continued, releasing her, 'stand back and let me have a good look at what I have been missing. There are times when I believe you have reached the peak of your achievements when it comes to dressing, but you always go that proverbial extra mile. You look fantastic.'

'Thank you, Roger, you don't look so bad yourself.'

For a while then there was silence as they kissed long and hard, which left Roger moaning that he should have come earlier, before she was dressed.

'Are you pleased with the reservation I've made?' he eventually asked. 'On our own doorstep, so to speak, and a wonderful setting. We can have a drink and not worry about how we shall get home.'

Chloe's spirits rose. He was obviously going to spend the night here in the apartment. She couldn't ask for more.

Roger thanked the head waiter as he walked them to their table. Heads turned as they crossed the floor. The women were no doubt drawn to Roger's physique, and he certainly looked impeccable. The men were definitely envious of him. Who wouldn't want a woman like Chloe? Her silk dress clung to her finely tuned body, and that long red hair and the swish of her skirt as she walked left many a man feeling breathless.

Roger lowered himself into the chair across from her. A whiff of the sea air coming in from the open French doors was a blessing: they both needed to keep cool. Chloe said she would leave the ordering of the meal entirely up to Roger. Although she lived close by, it was the first time she had actually been inside the restaurant. Right on the edge of the harbour, it had great views of the marina. The lights were low and a live band was playing soft music; who could ask for more?

They had finished their starter and were waiting for the waiters to bring the main course when Roger took hold of Chloe's hand and held it between both of his. 'Darling, you haven't so much as mentioned my gift. Aren't you pleased with it?'

Mentally Chloe rolled her eyes before she blurted out, 'What am I supposed to say? It is unbelievable, but a shock more than a surprise.'

Conversation was put on hold while the wine waiter refilled their glasses.

There was pride in Roger's voice as he began his explanation. 'Chloe, we both know how vastly different our lives have become since we have got to know each other, and I dearly wanted to show you how much I appreciate you. What better way to say it than with a diamond? I have a brochure that the president of our board of directors acquired for me. It will show you a collection of rings that have recently been on exhibition within the trade, both modern and antique designs. You may choose any one and I will have it made up for you using that single diamond as the centrepiece and the opals as dressing. You must also decide whether you prefer to have the shank made in yellow or white gold, or perhaps you'll opt for platinum. Before I give you the ring, I shall have to send it away to Hatton Garden to have it hallmarked.'

To say that Chloe was astonished would be an understatement. Roger couldn't stop smiling. As long as he lived, he would never forget the look on her face when he told her his plans for her ring.

At this moment Chloe wished they were back in her apartment. She wanted to show her appreciation to Roger for all he did for her. This last fortnight she had felt a desperate need for him and had missed him badly. He made her feel feminine and desirable. But now he was going to spend the night with her, and that thought put a sweet smile on her face. He still had hold of her hand as she raised her gaze to look into his beautiful dark eyes and asked, 'How can I ever start to repay you for all you have done for me?'

Roger winked at her, his grin shameless. Lowering his voice he said, 'It will be a long night. I'm sure you will find a way.'

Chloe's thoughts were racing. She had learnt so much about the art of lovemaking. She didn't think Roger could have been as adventurous with Thelma, or if he had been, it was a very long time ago. Once when she had queried this point with him his answer had been that they were only doing what came naturally. Chloe had only really had one boyfriend – George, a boy at college. In the end she had decided that all that fumbling about wasn't for her. In so many ways since she and Roger had got together the whole art of lovemaking had become an intriguing and compelling feature for both of them.

She picked up her wine glass and drained it dry. Her heart was beating far too fast as yet again she thought about the fact that Roger was going to stay the night with her. She would make sure that he would remember every second of every minute of those few hours. Maybe it was the magic of having been given a diamond, but she couldn't remember ever shaking with need or getting flushed all over just from thinking about him staying with her for the whole night.

Chloe had no way of knowing that her feelings were being entirely reciprocated. Roger wanted the meal to come to an end. He wanted to be able to hold his Chloe stark naked. He wanted to see her body, to touch her, to be able to taste her. He put his hands in his lap and clenched them. Not very much longer, he kept reminding himself, but patience had never been a virtue of his.

At last he was paying the bill, adding a generous amount for the staff to the total, and it was only a few minutes before they were walking towards the block of apartments where Chloe lived. Normally they would have taken a turn around the marina, enjoying the sight of the moonlight on the sea, admiring the many boats anchored in the harbour.

Not tonight. They had other things on their minds.

Hardly had they stepped inside her apartment than Roger was covering her mouth with his. Her lips parted and his tongue met hers instantly. Oh! She tasted so good. It seemed ages since he had been so close to her. He tried to hold himself in check, to coax her along slowly, but that suited neither of them. They were tearing their clothes off, leaving them on the floor where they dropped as he lifted her into his arms and carried her into her bedroom. Their enthusiasm for each other knew no bounds. His arms were locked tightly around her, and the feel of her body, her firm breasts and the heat of her, made him hot, heavy and ready to enter her in minutes. As he did so, her drawn-out sigh was like a balm to his soul. She had needed him as much as he had needed her.

Hours later, Chloe lay in his arms, sleeping peacefully.

Oh, how he wished that they could live together on a permanent basis. He had tried so hard to come up with a strategy that wouldn't hurt his Thelma but at the same time would allow him and Chloe to lead a normal life together. There had to be a solution, but by God he was having a hard time finding it.

Chloe moved within his arms and he tightened his hold before gently kissing her forehead. She moved again and sighed sleepily. 'Oh, Roger.'

Roger suddenly felt good. Very good. There was no way either he or Chloe could call this evening disappointing.

That had to be enough for now. Who could ever tell what the future would hold?

# Chapter 4

It was a beautiful morning, Chloe noted as she looked down at the marina from her bedroom window. The sea was calm, gentle waves lapping at the secure walls of the harbour. She opened a window and felt the slight breeze whispering in from the sea with its faint salty tang. So very different from London, where she had been born. But then her early life bore no comparison with what she had now.

Roger was still sleeping; he was to be with her for the whole weekend. She had to stop herself from wishing that their lives could be set on a more permanent footing. Try counting your blessings, she admonished herself once again as she walked naked to her en suite bathroom, where she turned on the switch that operated the shower head and then stood beneath the sharp spray of hot water. The perfume from her shower gel filled the air as she spread it over her skin. She did so enjoy having a shower; it had been an unheard-of luxury where she'd grown up. She was about to rinse herself when the glass door slid open and Roger stepped in. She couldn't help but smile, his early-morning look was so funny. His thick mop of hair hadn't seen a comb and his unshaven chin gave him a menacing look.

She did love to see him unclothed! He looked very different from the successful, well-dressed businessman that she worked with every day.

'If you've quite finished staring, will you please move and make room for me.'

Chloe had to laugh. She'd been admiring his physique, which for a man of his age was exceptional. 'I'll get out and leave you to it,' she said, more calmly than she was feeling.

'Oh no, you don't get away from me so easily he told her as he took hold of the bottle she'd been using and began smoothing the shower gel over her back with gentle strokes. 'Would you deny me this pleasure?' he asked playfully. 'You may return the favour and do my back when I've finished.'

She knew it was sheer madness, but she always felt a degree of reserve at moments like this, which was daft really given the intimacy they regularly shared.

Meanwhile Roger's thoughts were way ahead as he turned the water off, grabbed a towel and began to rub Chloe dry before attending to himself.

He intended to see that matters pertaining to Chloe's future were put on a more permanent basis. Recently Thelma's health had deteriorated, and in his mind that fact was largely down to Thelma herself. He truly believed that his wife had lost the will to live. He and Chloe had discussed the situation endlessly. They both had great sympathy for Thelma and yearned to help her, yet their discussions never resolved anything. In the long run it boiled down to the fact that Thelma had given up hoping she might regain strength in her limbs, and if she was determined not to help herself, there was little that even the doctors could do for her.

Roger slid open the doors to the shower, reached out and took down two towelling robes, helping Chloe into one before donning the other one himself.

'I'll make us some breakfast, and while we eat we must decide what we are going to do on this beautiful Saturday morning.'

While Roger had been speaking, Chloe had been running a comb through her long chestnut hair. Now, with a flourish, she laid down the comb and tossed her tresses over one shoulder.

Roger had been watching and he couldn't resist saying, 'You really are a terrible tease, Chloe, you know that, but this morning it won't work. It is almost a month since you chose a design for your ring, and today we have a private appointment in Hatton Garden–'

He was stopped from saying anything further by Chloe, who was acting like an excited five-year-old, flinging her arms around him and jumping up and down.

'Stop jiggling and make a pot of tea, or do you want coffee this morning?'

'Oh Roger, how can you act so calmly? A private meeting in Hatton Garden on a Saturday morning just for me! Oh, and by the way, you should know by now that for breakfast I only ever drink tea.'

He watched as she sipped her tea. She looked so happy, and it struck him afresh that they really did love each other. It wasn't a one-sided affair; what had started out as a business proposition had certainly changed for both of them.

'Chloe, will you please finish your breakfast and get dressed. Although no definite time has been set for our appointment, I would like us to get into London somewhere around midday.'

'It is still only just turned eight o'clock,' she pointed out.

'I didn't see the point of spoiling my chauffeur's weekend by taking the car into London. I've ordered a taxi for nine o'clock to take us to the station; plenty of fast trains to Victoria and we'll use taxis while in town.'

'You think of everyone and everything,' she said, smiling up at him. She really meant what she said.

'Just so long as you approve. Now will you please get yourself dressed.'

Later, when the intercom buzzer sounded and a voice said, 'Mr McKinnon, your taxi is here,' they walked to the lift each lost in their own thoughts. Roger, as always, looked impeccable in a dark grey suit, pale blue shirt and navy blue striped tie. Gold cufflinks peeped from his wrists, as did his expensive watch. His hand-made black leather shoes were as highly polished as ever. Chloe was looking a little more frivolous, in a navy blue silk calf-length dress with a matching jacket, the sleeves of which had a row of twelve mother-of-pearl buttons reaching from elbow to wrist. The style was so simple: simply cut, simply beautiful. A mother-of-pearl brooch was pinned to her lapel.

'Perfection personified,' Roger murmured as he scrutinised her from head to toe.

They were comfortable in their first-class carriage, reading newspapers, and the short journey to Victoria passed quite quickly.

They had to queue before they got a taxi, and that fact didn't sit too well with Roger. The taxi driver took them through Holborn Circus and into Clerkenwell Road. When he finally dropped them at the far end of Hatton Garden, Chloe felt a moment of panic. What exactly had she got herself into? Hatton Garden was the centre of the diamond merchant trade, she was well aware of that; it was a moneyed part of London in a class

60

of its own.

As the driver held the door open for her to step down and Roger took money from his wallet, the door to the premises ahead of them opened and two well-dressed men came out and stood at the top of the flight of stone steps that led up to the entrance. It was obvious that Roger was expected.

'Roger McKinnon, how are you? Great to see you.' One of the men, who was about Roger's age, had his hand outstretched as he walked down the steps to meet them.

'Great to see you too.' Roger grinned. 'May I introduce you to my PA, or as I prefer to call her, my right arm, Miss Chloe Collard.' He turned to Chloe and drew her nearer to his side. 'Chloe, meet my long-term friend and business colleague Theodore Walsh, though when we were at Cambridge together he was always known as Teddy.'

Smiling broadly Theodore Walsh took hold of Chloe's arm and began to lead her up the steps. 'We are hoping you will be more than pleased with your visit to us. Meanwhile may I introduce you to another of the members of this corporation, Stuart Bartholomew.'

Stuart waited until Chloe had reached the top step before he held out his hand. 'A great pleasure to meet you, Miss Collard,' he told her quietly.

By now she and Roger were being led into

what looked like a small private sitting room. When all four of them were seated, each with a glass of wine set in front of them, Theodore spoke directly to Roger. 'Would you like to see the finished article before we ask Miss Collard for her approval?'

'No, no need for that at all: Chloe chose her own design. But thanks for asking.'

For Chloe these goings-on had an unreal feeling about them. Perhaps she was daydreaming.

She soon lost that idea as the coffee table that held her glass of wine was moved nearer to her and a large piece of black velvet was laid out on it. Then Stuart Bartholomew unlocked a wall safe and removed from it a small white leather box, which he handed straight to Roger.

Roger held it in his hand for a moment, then sighing softly he passed it over to Chloe and very quietly said, 'I give you this ring as a token of my love and my appreciation for all that you have done for me. God willing, our association will continue to be beneficial to both of us.'

Chloe opened the lid and almost dropped the box. The gasp that she emitted had all three men smiling. She could not find the words to describe the beauty of the ring that lay within the satin-lined box. Several moments slipped by and still she just stared at what must surely be the most beautiful ring in the whole world.

The shank of the ring was gold, as she had requested, the single glittering diamond set dead centre with one sea-misty opal each side. Two platinum hearts had been set one on each shoulder of the ring beside the opals. She continued to stare at this alluring, charming ring, until she could no longer see it. Her vision was clouded by the tears in her eyes.

'Chloe, take it from the box and try it on,' Roger urged.

For a moment she held the ring in the palm of her hand, and when she looked up and saw the love shining from Roger's eyes she was overwhelmed. She didn't hesitate, though; she placed the ring on the fourth finger of her right hand. There was to be no open declaration.

Holding her arm stretched out, she spread her fingers and was pleased at the reaction she got from the two City gents. Everything they said in admiration was true. A flawless ring on an immaculate hand.

'Unbelievable,' was all that Chloe could manage as she turned towards Roger, but the sigh that he gave came from deep within his heart, and as she watched, she saw his eyes brim with tears.

A tray laden with china, a pot of coffee, a jug of hot milk and a plate of savoury bites was brought into the room by a plump middle-aged lady whose face was wreathed in smiles. By the time they had drunk their coffee, said their thanks and got into a taxi, Chloe had just about managed to take her eyes off her very special ring.

'Darling, I suggest that we have lunch here in town. I would like to take you to the Goring Hotel, which is only a very short ride from Victoria station. Does that sound good to you?'

'Whatever you decide, Roger, though I'm not sure I shall be able to eat anything.'

'You will when you see the type of food that will be set in front of you,' Roger told her as he tapped on the window to attract the driver's attention

Everything about the Goring Hotel reflected the best of the English way of life. Once they were seated in the elegant dining room, Chloe looked around at the old-world grandeur as Roger ordered wine from an immaculate waiter.

They had a delicious four-course meal, with the huge joint of beef being carved at their table by the top chef himself. For someone who had declared she would not be able to eat anything, Chloe did remarkably well.

Although the railway station was only a short walk from the Goring, Roger insisted on having the door staff call them a taxi. During the journey back to Brighton, he never once released his gentle hold on Chloe. Now and again he would gently kiss the top of her head as she nestled into his shoulder.

Brighton station was extremely busy, but Roger soon found a porter who was able to persuade an incoming cabbie to drive around to a side entrance rather than joining the rank. This earned both the porter and the taxi driver a handsome tip.

When they finally reached her apartment, Chloe was most surprised to hear Roger say that he was going out. 'I shall not be more than half an hour,' he insisted as she tried to reason with him.

He was actually out for nearly forty minutes, and when he came back into the sitting room, he was laden down with parcels. The smell of gorgeous food filled Chloe's nostrils.

'What on earth...?' she stuttered.

'I didn't want us to settle down all comfortable and cosy and then have to go out again to eat. So I've fetched a few things from the delicatessen. We can put them in the fridge and have them later on this evening.'

Roger never failed to surprise her. She couldn't help but wonder how he knew all the right people and all the right places to go.

She was glad he'd bought the food. It meant they could change out of their smart clothes – 'London always makes me feel grubby,' Roger complained – into their dressing gowns, and settle down for a quiet evening on the huge settee.

By eleven o'clock they were in bed, curled up in each other's arms.

Roger broke into her thoughts. 'If I let myself fall asleep, will you promise to still be here when I wake up?' he said as he lay cuddled up against her back, his arms around her holding her close to him.

'I'm not going anywhere,' Chloe told him. 'In fact I'm afraid to go to sleep in case I wake up to find out that today was all a dream.'

'Darling, it was no dream. Today I've gone as far as I can to prove just how very dear you are to me. Now I think it is about time you closed your eyes and got some sleep.'

'Is that an order?' she asked drowsily.

'Yes, it is,' he whispered softly. And minutes later, when he raised his head to look at her, she was sound asleep. He gently pulled the duvet further up the bed and tucked it around her.

On Sunday morning they had a good lie-in. Chloe was first up, and was carrying a tray of tea back to the bedroom when Roger came out of the shower.

'I didn't hear you get up. I thought we'd have a cuppa in bed,' she told him.

'Don't worry, I'm not ready to get up yet. I just thought I would have a good hot shower before I start the day by making love to you.'

'You said last night that you would like to go for a walk around the marina this morning.'

'Yes I did, and yes we will, but not until we've drunk our tea and made passionate love.'

When she stopped laughing, Chloe set the tray down and prepared to pour out two cups of tea. Roger, looking spruce and wide awake, his hair still wet, got back into bed. Chloe perched on the edge and passed him his tea, saying, 'You do realise that it is Sunday?'

'Of course, and as my father was fond of saying, the better the day, the better the deed.'

Chloe spluttered over her tea and had to put the cup back down on the saucer. 'Roger McKinnon, you are incorrigible,' she said, grinning broadly.

'Yes, of course I am, but then you knew that from the moment you set eyes on me, and you love me no less for that fact, or do you?'

Chloe didn't answer; she picked up her cup and drank the rest of her tea. Then she took Roger's empty cup from him, loaded up the tray and carried it back out to the kitchen.

When she returned to the bedroom, Roger made a grab for her. Like a couple of kids they playfully punched each other, pillows were thrown to the floor and arms and legs became entwined. There were no prizes for guessing the outcome. Chloe's dressing gown and nightdress were flung over the end of the bed by Roger, while she retaliated by ripping off his pyjama trousers. Roger only ever wore trousers in bed, at least since he'd become aware that Chloe loved to rest her head in the hollow of his shoulder and let her face rest on his bare flesh.

The sex that followed was quick and energetic, which this morning obviously suited both of them.

Roger finally dived out of bed and beat her to the bathroom for his second shower of the morning. When at last she did manage to get under the hot spray, she found she was grinning to herself. It was turning out to be a very unusual weekend, and a very special one too.

Little did she know that Roger had another surprise tucked away. He had gone to great lengths to make absolutely sure it was something that would please her. He was planning to take her to America. In his opinion, everyone should visit New York at least once in their lifetime.

He would go to the ends of the earth for Chloe. Before she had come into his life, everything had been put on hold. For years he had lived only for work and for the purpose of making money. What a difference she had made. No amount of money he spent on her would ever be too much.

## Chapter 5

Chloe was sitting outside a café in Brighton's Lanes with Stella, Lloyd Spencer's PA. She didn't make a habit of sharing her hour-and-a-half lunch break with other employees of the company, but today Roger had gone to London to consult with a specialist about the decline in his wife's health. Chloe hadn't felt like lunching on her own and Stella had always shown discretion when the subject of Roger and herself was brought into any conversation.

The waiters at this popular café were always pleased to see these two young ladies, and they certainly stood out in a crowd. Stella's shoulder-length hair was silver blonde in sharp contrast to Chloe's chestnut red, and for the duration of their lunch period they had taken out the restraining clips and side combs, allowing their silky tresses to flow freely.

Brighton's Lanes were famous worldwide, for there was always so much to see and do, and today was no exception. Besides the antique shops and the many jewellers, whose windows displayed huge amounts of gold, there were street artists and hawkers, and a good sprinkling of cafés, whose delicious aromas enticed the day-trippers to loiter.

'Right,' Stella said, 'we've lingered long enough. What do you want to eat?'

'Well, I rather fancy the seafood platter, but it states that it is a meal for two,' Chloe answered slowly, still contemplating the menu.

'That's fine seeing as there are two of us.'

'Are you sure that's what you'd like? You aren't just having it to please me?'

'No, truthfully, that will suit me fine. There is a salad served with it, and garlic bread, so yes, let's have the seafood platter.'

'Right,' Stella said again after the waiter had taken their order, 'let's get down to some serious gossip. Things've been so hectic in the office these past few weeks, I've hardly seen anything of you. For a start, you can tell me why you haven't accompanied Roger to town today. We've all come to take it for granted that the two of you are joined at the hip.'

Chloe took a deep breath. 'You must know that Roger's wife has been practically bedridden for years. Today he has an appointment with a specialist to discuss whether there is any chance that an operation might alleviate her suffering. He obviously doesn't need me to be there.'

'Hold on a minute,' Stella said sharply. 'I wasn't criticising; you'll never hear me doing that. You and Roger are both adults, and every member of the company, particularly those who have known Roger since their days at university, has feelings of compassion and understanding for him.'

Chloe smiled. 'Thanks, Stella, that's good to hear. One thing I have found out is that life is not what you make it, as the saying goes. Life is what you make of the set of circumstances you find yourself in at any given point.'

Thankfully they had both calmed down by the time the waiter came back with the bottle of wine that Stella had ordered. Having been shown the label, she nodded, and he filled their glasses. They toasted each other and were then silent as they did justice to their excellent meal.

'Are we having a sweet today?' their handsome waiter asked, grinning widely.

Both girls laughed and Stella said quickly, 'Don't know about you, sunshine, but we'd both like coffee gateau, please.'

Their gateau was placed in front of them and they dipped their forks into the creamy four-layered cake.

'How come Italians make such wonderful gateau?' Chloe wondered aloud as she scraped up the last morsels.

They both had smiles on their faces as they walked back to the offices of Associated Securities.

Without Roger's presence the office felt empty, and it was certainly silent as Chloe checked the computer for the e-mails that had piled up in her absence. The afternoon dragged, and it was with a sigh of relief that she looked at the clock and realised that the taxi to take her home would be here within fifteen minutes.

All I really want is a cup of tea, nothing to eat – I had more than enough at lunchtime – she was telling herself as she entered the main doors and walked towards the lift. The building seemed so quiet, no one about; that was not unusual, and normally she wouldn't have taken any notice, but having been without Roger all day and not having heard a word from him, she was staring at a lonely evening.

The lift came to a halt. Chloe stepped out and fumbled in her bag to find her key. Turning the key in the lock, she pushed the door half open and immediately sniffed; she could smell cigar smoke.

In an instant her features changed, a smile lighting up her face. Roger was here, in her apartment.

She went straight into the toilet and quickly repaired her make-up and freed her hair, letting it hang loose over her shoulders. She washed her hands, gave herself a quick spray of the expensive perfume Roger regularly bought for her and finally kicked off her high-heeled shoes and wiggled her toes. As she walked into the lounge, her heart stood still in her chest. Roger had heard her come in and he was standing up, arms outstretched. As she walked into them, she felt a burst of happiness like she had never felt before.

'Hello, my darling.' Roger's voice was low and husky, and it sent her pulse racing. 'Have you missed me?'

'More than you'll ever know,' she whispered.

'Would you like a drink before we decide what we're going to do with our evening?'

'Please. I see you have a bottle of wine open; that will do fine for me.' The drink didn't really bother her; nothing did now that Roger was here. From what he had said, she had the impression he was planning to stay the night, and she knew she had so much to be grateful for.

'The fishmonger's van was outside one of the restaurants when I arrived, so I stopped and bought two large fresh salmon fillets. When I put them in your fridge I noticed you had a grand supply of salad. I thought that later on I can dress the salad and while the salmon is in the oven you can make a Hollandaise sauce. How does that sound to you?'

'Perfect, as usual. Meanwhile I want you to sit down and tell me whether your trip to London was worthwhile. Did you learn if anything more can be done for Thelma?'

'Is that really what you want? I had other ideas, more to do with the bedroom,' he told

73

her with a provocative smile. 'I thought perhaps you had missed me today.'

'You know darn well I have, but first things
first. Did you get any answers regarding
Thelma?'

Roger had the grace to look sheepish. 'My
visit to Harley Street was nothing to do with
my wife's health. I am truly sorry that I lied
to you, Chloe. I knew that if I told you that
Dr Mansfold had arranged for me to see a
specialist you would have started to worry.'

'And now?' She knew she was not going to
get a satisfactory reply, but still she pushed
the matter.

'Nothing to tell you except all kinds of
tests have been done on me today, various
specimens are being sent away and all we
have to do is wait for the results.'

'Surely this Harley Street man must have
given you a clue about what you might be
suffering from.' Chloe was frightened at
what Roger was *not* telling her.

Roger decided to put an end to the conversation, at least for tonight. 'You've probably
guessed that there is a chance that I may have
cancer. Now, please, can we change the
subject? I for one have heard enough ifs and
maybes for one day.'

'Oh Roger, I am so sorry, really I am. I
don't know what else to say.'

'Actions speak louder than words, so
unless you are desperate for your dinner, I

suggest that you allow me to make love to you. We can eat later.'

It wasn't really the reply that Chloe had wanted to hear but she meekly went along with it, hoping against hope that she would be able to please him. In the bedroom she settled herself in the one armchair while Roger perched on the side of the bed. She pulled her skirt up to her thighs, crossed her silk-clad legs and held her arms outstretched to Roger.

'Well,' he said, smiling and beginning to unbutton his shirt, 'it looks to me as if I am not the only one who fancies an appetiser before dinner.'

Under normal circumstances Chloe would have matched Roger's enthusiasm, but this was not lovemaking. Roger was treating her as if she were solely responsible for the bad news he had received that day. Even as she murmured a protest, he grabbed at her hair and yanked so hard she gasped. But he only gripped her hips harder and continued to hurt her. Nothing seemed to satisfy him. He wanted to nip and pinch, to abuse every inch of her. She belonged to him now and he was making sure she was aware of that fact. His lips were burning against her flesh, she could feel the heat rolling through her, filling her until at last it burst and left him shattered.

The storm inside him had burned itself out.

He laid his head back against the pillow and closed his eyes. His hands were gentle as he stroked her back.

Tears and mascara ran down Chloe's face.

## Chapter 6

Last evening and the night that had followed had left Chloe drained and anxious. She knew that Roger hadn't told her the full story, and she had to work hard to stop herself from imagining the worst.

They had gone to bed at ten o'clock, and she had not protested when Roger had made vigorous love to her. Although her whole body now ached – her breasts especially had come in for some rough handling – she felt it had been worthwhile, in as much as Roger had finally composed himself and was once again the dignified gentleman she had learnt to love so much.

By mutual agreement they had decided not to go into the office today. Roger had wanted to take her down to breakfast at one of the many restaurants that flourished within the marina. She had declined, and was more than pleased when he offered to go out and bring some food back so that they could spend time making plans.

Left on her own, she tried to sort out in her head exactly what Roger had told her. It wasn't much; he had reluctantly given her the bare details and begged her not to ask any more questions.

He had gone to see Dr Percy Mansfold, who was a friend as well as his GP. On being made aware of the fact that Roger had been suffering pain, Percy had made the appointment with the Harley Street consultant. After three hours of tests, the consultant had been honest. His first opinion had been bowel cancer, but he had advised Roger that it could be very tricky to diagnose and, crucially, to differentiate from other conditions.

Roger's suggestion to Chloe was that they pack a bag and go off on holiday while the doctors studied the test results and made up their minds. America was his first choice; he'd offered her the choice of flying or taking a cruise.

She had tried to reason with him. The USA didn't have a National Health Service if he fell ill, she had protested.

'So what?' Roger had argued. 'Money speaks all languages and I have more than enough to pay for the best.'

Chloe decided to set to and tidy up the apartment while she waited for Roger to return. 'Hope he brings some hot dough-nuts,' she said aloud and then giggled at herself. She should be thinking about what was going to happen to Roger, but that would bring her sharply down to earth and she realised she just did not want to face the prospect of him being seriously ill.

She went into her bedroom. The sheets on the king-sized bed were all rumpled, the pillows on the floor. She moved swiftly, fetching the basket of household cleaners and dusters from the cupboard beneath the kitchen sink. Setting the basket down in the hall, she went back and rummaged for a pair of rubber gloves. It was only two days since she had had a manicure and she certainly did not want to chip her nail polish. This thought had her holding out her hands, her fingers spread wide. I love this shade of polish, she was thinking. Veronica, who always did her nails, had told her it was the latest shade, named Allure. Could she ever remember being so pampered? Certainly not in the years before Roger had taken her under his wing. Who in her previous life ever had money to spare for manicures?

With the bedroom once again looking spick and span, clean sheets, pillow cases and duvet cover on the bed, she tackled the bathroom. There were two showers in this apartment, and how she loved them. Not that the second bedroom had ever been used, but both showers had been put to good use. She and Roger had made terrific love in each of them. The memory had her aroused, but at the same time the thoughts that she had done her best to shy away from came flooding back. Was Roger very ill? Was he going to die? No, he wasn't even anywhere near sixty yet, and as he said, he could afford to pay for the best medical care that could be found.

It had certainly brought her back down to earth with a bump, learning the reason why he had gone to London. Apart from his side and his back aching, he had never once complained of feeling unwell. Please, dear Lord Jesus, don't take him from me now, Chloe prayed. He is my family, my whole life; after what we have had together, how could I possibly go back to being on my own?

She heard his key in the door, and he came in laden down with bags and parcels.

'That marina can supply anything and everything anyone could possibly need,' he laughed as he laid several paper carrier bags on the kitchen worktop. He indicated with a pointed finger two large square cardboard boxes. 'Darling, please stow those in the fridge. They contain a complete four-course dinner for two, which we shall avail ourselves of this evening. First, though, I have breakfast here, and yes, I did remember the jam doughnuts. By the way, I love the apron, and your hair looks great tied up in a scarf. Have you got yourself a cleaning job? Because if you have, I shall require six months' notice; can't find another PA any quicker than that.'

Chloe almost threw a duster at him. He had insisted that she have a cleaning lady come in once a week – he would have paid for one every day had she agreed – and he thought that meant she wouldn't need to do any housework herself. Men!

'You put the kettle on while I put all this lovely breakfast food out on plates.' Chloe was taking hold of the reins this morning.

Roger had been longer than was necessary purchasing the food; he had gone into a bar on the far side of the marina and lingered over a cup of coffee. He was well aware that what he had told Chloe had been only half the truth. Every warning bell in his body was clanging and jangling at this moment, but he didn't care. All he was sure of was the fact that he had to protect her. Never mind the half-promises and the good intentions of the consultant, he knew he was very ill. How long before he died? God alone knew. Chloe and her future was what concerned him the most, for he had known almost from the beginning of their arrangement that he did truly love her.

The attraction that had been between them from the start was amazing. He had experienced an all-consuming passion for weeks just looking at her, and for once in his life he had acted on impulse, made her a proposition. He had never regretted it. She had made him feel like a man again. Really alive.

He loved to just touch her, feel her, knowing that she enjoyed their lovemaking as much as he did. Last night he had felt terrible; the way he had treated her was unforgivable. He'd really lost control. Taking his anger out on her had been totally out of order. Apologising had not been enough; he had to think of another way of saying how much he regretted losing his temper.

He found himself jumping like a cat on a hot tin roof when Chloe nudged him. He had been lost in his thoughts. Without a word, he turned to her and kissed her – her face, her neck, even her eyes. Then, taking her hand, he led her slowly into the bedroom.

They sat side by side on the edge of the bed. He stared deeply into her eyes and saw mirrored in them his own feelings of love and desire. She gently began to unbutton his shirt, and as she took it off him, she saw again his broad shoulders, his tightly muscled arms, and felt how unfair life was being to them.

Then it was Roger's turn. All the anger and hurt of last night had passed and he was as gentle as a pussy cat as he removed her clothes. She stood in front of him, quivering with excitement and longing.

He took his time, letting his eyes roam over her body, and she wanted him then, more than ever before. Gently, almost as if she would break, he pushed her backwards on to the bed and began to kiss her, little biting kisses that were so titillating. She groaned softly. Later she matched his strokes as they moved in perfect unison. Last night he had been hurt and angry. Today he was showing her how true love could be very gentle.

Later they lay tangled together, spent and satisfied, their hearts thudding against each other's chests. For long, quiet minutes they savoured the familiar feeling of one another. Finally Roger leant up on one elbow and kissed her gently on the lips. She looked into his face – the face she had grown to love over the last two years – and did her best to smile.

'Don't leave me, Roger.' Her voice was so low as to be virtually inaudible.

Roger was too choked to form an answer.

They lay together until their bodies became still and the passion that had surrounded them had drained away. Roger kissed her again, staring down at her as if he wanted to devour her. His eyes took in every feature and his brain filed them away, never to be forgotten. Chloe did the same. They were both aware that there was a possibility they were living on borrowed time; that he might not have long to live. Her life would be very different without him to care for her. None of this was spoken of. What they had at this moment was enough for each of them.

It had to be.

'Forgiven, am I?' he asked very meekly.

'Only if you make me a nice cup of tea.'

He got up laughing, and the rich, easy sound of it told her they were back on steady ground again.

## Chapter 7

Percy Mansfold hurried up the steps that led to Roger McKinnon's magnificent detached house overlooking the sea in Hove. His heart was pounding at the realisation that after a wait of three weeks, he was about to deliver the results of Roger's tests.

It was only a week since his latest discussion with Roger, and that hadn't gone at all well. Roger had complained that the pain he was suffering grew worse by the hour. By now he was prepared to hear the worst, or so he had said. It was always hard when one had to deliver bad news. Over the years Percy had become good friends with both Thelma and Roger, and that only made this sad situation more difficult.

Once their cordial greetings were over, Percy explained that had Roger sought medical help when his condition had been in the early stages, much could have been tried that might have been beneficial. Now, however, the secondary stage had been reached and there was little that could be done.

He did not add that in fact the secondary stage was well under way. But if the truth be told, Roger needed no telling.

Roger thought it pointless to ask how long before he died. He made it very clear that he would deal with matters in his own way.

When Percy Mansfold had left, Roger went into the lounge, which had long since been turned into a bed-sitting room for his wife. Most evenings he sat with her, though she didn't always know he was there. Because of the pain, she was heavily sedated.

'Where is Roger? Where's my husband?' she had suddenly taken to asking. Although it seemed she was constantly confused, he persevered, sitting by her bed and holding her hand until she became fretful and told him he was a stranger who had no business being in her bedroom.

A rum old pair we have ended up as! Roger often declared silently to himself.

Roger's housekeeper opened the front door to Dr Mansfold. 'Good morning, Doctor, Mr McKinnon is in his study; he asked that you join him there. He has also asked that I bring coffee. Is that all right with you?'

'Coffee will be fine, thank you, Mrs Burton,' Percy Mansfold told her, though he thought that something a bit stronger

84

might be more appropriate.

The two men were this morning meeting as old friends. The look on Percy's face as he entered the study said it all, and as he put his arms around Roger's shoulders and hugged him close, the need for words was lost.

A moment or two passed in silence, then Roger cleared his throat and said, 'Thanks, Percy. Let's sit down and I'll open a bottle of malt.'

Mrs Burton brought in the coffee tray and set it down on a side table. For once she did not offer to pour for the two men; she too needed no telling that this was a moment when silence spoke louder than words.

Percy dealt with the coffee while Roger poured very generous measures of whisky into two glasses.

The doctor was well aware that Roger had no intention of discussing his own medical condition or the consequences that must surely follow. However, he was also Thelma's GP and he would be lacking in his duty if he failed to raise the question of her future. Having downed half of his tot of whisky, he took the bull by the horns.

'Roger, have you given any thought as to who will take care of your wife?'

Apparently Roger did not share his concern. 'Thelma will be well taken care of, I can assure you on that score.'

Percy was not appeased, but he took into

account the feelings that must be nagging away at his old friend. 'As long as you make sure that you nominate someone who will have Thelma's welfare at heart.'

'Percy, I promise you faithfully that I will spend what time I have left putting my affairs in order. I have long tried to persuade Thelma that she could be really happy in a care home. She knows money does not come into it. She could receive twenty-four-hour care, but she won't hear of it.'

A long silence followed that statement, and Percy drained the rest of his whisky and prepared to leave.

'Percy, how did you get here?'

'I took a cab, I had a feeling we might be having a dram.'

'Great foresight, means we can have another, and then I'll phone you a taxi, make sure you get home safely.'

Three quarters of an hour later, the two men stood at the foot of the steps and engaged in another bear hug. Percy drew away first and got into the waiting taxi. The driver was slightly bewildered. Never before had he witnessed such sad, raw emotion between two gentlemen.

For the rest of that day Roger stayed in his study, spending long hours planning his course of action. He made a telephone call to David Ferris, his solicitor and long-standing friend. Arrangements were quickly made for a meeting to be held in Roger's beautiful home in three days' time.

Roger needed those three days in which to see Chloe.

How much would he tell her? He had no idea. He was going to have to play it by ear. It wasn't talking he had in mind. He just needed to see her. To be with her. To drink in her loveliness, to stroke her chestnut hair, to feel her smooth skin. He also needed to impress on her that what had started out as a business deal had on his part become a real love affair.

Tomorrow he was going to show up at the office. He had several things on file that he needed to reread and a few instructions he felt he should leave. Then in the evening he intended to take Chloe out for a meal.

The last supper! That was a sinister thought.

Roger had been in his office for at least an hour before Chloe put in an appearance. She went first into her own office, where she took off her jacket and rolled back the cuffs of her white silk shirt. A quick glance through her post and she turned to go into Roger's office next door. The light was on; were the cleaners still in there?

Oh, the love that burst up through her veins, along with an overpowering feeling of relief, when she saw him seated at his desk. It had been three days since she had last seen him, and during the whole of that time there had been no communication between them. Now Chloe had to blink away the tears that threatened. She had been holding herself together, clutching at straws and praying fervently that he would have received good news from his consultant.

Neither of them uttered a word. Roger got up from his seat, came out from behind his desk and took her in his arms. They stood there, each oblivious of their surroundings.

'Have you had the results, are you going to tell me?' Chloe's face had straightened and she looked earnestly at her lover who had become her best friend.

Roger shook his head. 'These consultants charge colossal amounts of money for their time and knowledge, but when it boils down to fact-finding, they draw back. Still, my visit to him has not been a complete waste of time. Now how about you? Missed me, have you?'

'Like you'll never know,' she told him passionately, her eyes ablaze with sincerity.

'Good,' he answered quietly. 'Today I have quite a lot of work for us to get through, but this evening I've booked a table at the Grand Hotel, where I shall be taking you to dinner.'

'Oh Roger, are you sure you're up to it?'

Heaving a heavy sigh, Roger said, 'Please, Chloe, don't treat me like an invalid. I have a decent suit and accessories at your apartment; we'll leave the office by four o'clock today, and that will give us a chance to spruce ourselves up. Does that sound all right to you?'

Chloe knew she had been gently reprimanded, but she had to make allowances. 'Not only all right, sounds like a fabulous idea. I shall drag my glad rags out of their covers and do you justice.'

'You always do; you'll have every male in the place turning his head when you enter the room.'

'Oh, you haven't lost your old smoothy touch,' she laughed. 'Shall I make you a coffee before we start work?'

'Yes please, but there is one more thing to put right before you leave this office.'

Chloe raised her eyebrows. 'And that is?'

'You haven't once offered to kiss me.'

'Neither have you,' she protested.

'Well, how about we take that as our first priority of the day?'

Smiling gently, she walked towards him again. It felt strange; three days' absence and matters between them seemed to be on an entirely different footing. That was until his arm drew her close while his free hand gently cupped her left breast. His lips against hers felt soft and warm, yet within seconds his tongue was telling her that he had missed her. The kiss was no longer soft and lingering; it was demanding, a kiss that Chloe knew she would remember for as long as she lived. It was urgent, a longing for fulfilment; it was telling her that no matter what, he loved her with a love that knew no bounds.

As soon as they'd had their coffee, it was a case of all systems go. Roger's mind was alert, his memory faultless and his judgement fair. Chloe, though, found her thoughts wandering.

Had Roger really enjoyed the life he had made for himself, acquiring wealth and status, or had he been hiding his sadness that he had no one to share it with? Having built such strong walls around himself for so many years, why on earth had he suddenly formed a relationship with her? Like all women, Chloe listened to friendly gossip, and from what she had heard, no one in his circle of friends knew him at all well. Certainly no woman could claim any personal knowledge of him. Since Thelma had taken that fall from her horse, the general opinion was that Roger had let nothing and no one touch him. That is, until Chloe had become his PA.

Now she was scared to think what the future might hold for her.

In the end, they stayed late at the office, not arriving back at Chloe's apartment till ten to seven. The lights from the marina below lit the lounge faintly and Chloe quickly pulled the heavy curtains together. No intruders were welcome tonight. In fact if she could have had her way, they would not even be going out to dinner. She wanted Roger to take her in his arms, curl up on the settee with her and stay like that for hours. She needed to know he was here with her; she wanted him all to herself.

Her mind went back to the day that he had first put his proposition to her. He had told her that looking into her big green eyes made a man long to make love to her. A right old softy she had thought him then, and how right she'd been. What she had never counted on was falling in love with him. She knew, without being told, that she wouldn't have him for much longer. And what the hell am I going to do without you? she ranted to herself. He had become her reason for living. Without him? She shook her head vigorously; she had no answer.

It was at that point that Roger came back into the room. He had undressed and was wearing just a white towelling robe. 'Come on, my darling, let's take a shower together before we get dressed to go out.' He spoke kindly, holding out his hands to pull her up.

The sweet passion in his eyes ignited a matching desire in her. 'Don't even think about it. We'll be late,' she protested.

'No we won't. I have booked our table for eight thirty and the Grand is only half a mile along the seafront. Besides, I have promised myself a different session this evening. I fancy some gentle loving, soft and sweet; you can use your baby soap and baby oil on me. I do really need some tender loving care. Please.'

'You great big softy, you could worm your way into any woman's heart.'

'I don't want any woman; just you, Chloe.'

Roger turned the shower spray to warm and switched the power on, then laid two huge towels over the radiator so that they would be nice and warm when they were ready for them. What happened then was truly wonderful. Caressing, fondling, no hurry, unbelievable how gentle they both were, and yet sheer satisfaction was accomplished. They had connected more than just physically, and they slumped lovingly into each other's arms before donning their towelling robes and returning to the bedroom.

As Chloe dressed and did her make-up, she told herself that this was true love, no doubt about it. It had taken time for her to admit it, but all uncertainty had now been swept away.

She chose to wear an elegant fitted black lace dress with long sleeves and a gold-braided hemline that reached to her ankles. The neckline showed just the right amount of cleavage and was also embellished with gold braid. High-heeled gold sandals, a minimum of gold jewellery, and a small red clutch bag with a gold clasp completed her outfit. Last, but by no means least, she withdrew her precious leather box from her drawer and took out the very special ring that Roger had had made for her. She held it close to her face, wondering if there could ever have been a better declaration of his love for her. As she lowered the ring and slipped it on her finger, she was having difficulty in seeing, her eyes brimming with unshed tears.

Roger too had gone to great lengths. His suit was impeccable, showing off his broad shoulders, but he had left the jacket unbuttoned and she noticed he had lost weight. Such a brave face he was showing. She had to force herself to smile as her eyes met his amused grin.

'Last throw of the dice, eh?' he said softly.

The intercom buzzed telling them their taxi was waiting, and Chloe was glad she hadn't had to form an answer.

'The Grand always lives up to its reputation,' Roger told her in the taxi. 'It is large and luxurious.'

This was Chloe's first visit to the hotel. As she entered the reception area, she was amazed at the magnificence of the decor. The floral arrangements alone must have cost a fortune, she said to herself.

Champagne was brought to their table straight away, together with a lavish selection of finger food. That was just the beginning. Every course was presented to tempt the most discerning palate.

Roger had pulled out all the stops.

It was just turned eleven o'clock when Chloe and Roger slid into the rear seat of their pre-ordered taxi. For Chloe there was a sense of relief, and yet her heart was heavy and a terrible feeling of foreboding was growing by the minute. She wanted to wind her arms around Roger's neck, snuggle up to him, kiss him, except she felt such a degree of reservation, which was crazy. Oh how she wished they had spent the evening at home. There was so much she still wanted to say to him.

The taxi drew to a halt outside the entrance to her apartment block. Roger got out first and Chloe heard him say to the driver, 'Will you wait, please? I shall see this young lady safely up to her apartment and then I'll need you to drive me back to Hove. I shall only be a short while.'

'Righto, guv, you take your time,' the cheerful cabbie answered.

Hand in hand Roger and Chloe walked into the building. Going up in the lift, silence reigned.

Once inside her apartment, Roger tenderly took her in his arms. His voice had a distinct tremor as he said, 'Chloe, my darling girl, thank you for every minute you have spent with me. Now you must live your own life and make it a good one.'

He bent his head and kissed her, long, slow and deep. Then he released her and stepped away.

She heard him open and then close the door.

He was gone.

## Chapter 8

Mrs Burton needed no telling as to what was going on this morning. Dr Mansfold was in the room that was now used as Mrs McKinnon's bed-sitting room, and she had just answered the door to David Ferris, whom she knew to be the family solicitor. With Mr Ferris were his personal assistant Sybina Goodwin, whom she had met before, and two well-dressed young men in their early twenties. That meant coffee for at least six people, but her instructions had been not to bring the tray into the study until Mr McKinnon rang the bell. Mrs Burton noticed that the two young men were standing in the hall looking extremely uncomfortable.

'Can I be of any help?' she asked.

'We have been asked to wait outside until we are needed,' the taller of the two replied.

Mrs Burton suspected that they must be here to sign the will as witnesses. She quickly opened the door to the dining room, which was rarely used these days. 'Come along, sit down in here. I'll let Mr Ferris know where you are when you're needed.' She gave them both a motherly smile.

Meanwhile, in the study, the business in hand had quickly been brought to a head. Roger McKinnon and David Ferris were seated side by side behind Roger's large desk. Sybina Goodwin was facing them, her laptop resting on her knees.

Roger had previously written out exactly how his will was to be constructed, and three days ago he had taken the finished composition to the solicitor's office for his endorsement. Now David Ferris looked across at him and asked, 'Are you ready?'

Roger nodded his head.

David took up the document and in a steady voice began to speak. 'Everything you laid out is in good order; there is no need for me to go through each and every item. However, since you have included funeral arrangements for your wife and have stated that you love her dearly and have cared for and protected her to the best of your ability, I have taken steps to make sure that all her future needs come under the jurisdiction of your executors. Do you agree with that proposal?'

'Most certainly.'

When David finally finished speaking, he handed the completed document to Roger, who read it slowly and thoroughly from beginning to end before agreeing that everything was in order.

'Roger, if you are entirely sure that you are satisfied and that there is no need to make any alterations, I will call in the two members of my staff to witness you formally sign the document.'

Completion was accomplished.

'Shall I leave the will here with you, or do you wish it to be kept in our safe back at the office?' David was doing his best to keep this meeting on a business footing.

Roger placed his hand on the solicitor's shoulder. 'Take it with you, and thanks, David, you've been a good friend.'

He rang the bell, and Mrs Burton brought in the coffee.

Later, having seen everyone off the premises, the housekeeper asked, 'Will you be having lunch, Mr McKinnon?'

'Something cold with a salad will suit me fine. I'm going out for a walk but I'll be back before Thelma's night nurse comes on duty, and I shall be home now for at least a full week, so I suggest you have a few days' break yourself. It is no more than you deserve. You have been very loyal, especially since Thelma has taken a turn for the worse.'

'Well I'll not argue with you, sir. My sister has been poorly and I have been promising to visit her. Shall we say three days?'

'I shall be here all the time, so that will be fine.'

'Thank you, sir. I will lay your lunch out ready for you, but I won't leave the house until you get back.'

'Very well, I shall be back within the hour. I just feel the need to get some fresh air into my lungs.'

Roger did not walk far; he just sat on a bench, glad to be alone with his thoughts. His mind was working overtime, but eventually he felt sure that he had everything he had to do sorted into the correct order.

Later, as he opened his front door, he was pleased to see that Mrs Burton had left a small suitcase standing in the hall with her coat thrown over it. Hearing he was back, she came bustling towards him. 'Are you sure you will be able to manage on your own, sir?'

'Please, Mrs Burton, just for once think of yourself. Visit your sister and buy her some fruit and flowers from me.' He held out some folded twenty-pound notes.

'Oh sir, there isn't any need for that,' she said, looking at the money.

'There might not be a need, Mrs Burton, but will you please accept it as a gift from me.'

'Well thank you very much, sir, you are very kind. I have left your lunch ready and Mrs McKinnon is sleeping, still a bit fretful, though. Is it all right if I get off now?'

Roger picked up her coat and held it out for her to put on. 'You have a nice rest and I'll see you in three days' time.' He opened the front door for her and stood watching as she walked down the path. When she reached the pavement, he waved at her before closing the door. One more thing to do before he could begin to set his plan in motion.

He picked up the telephone that stood on the hall table and tapped in the number that he knew by heart. When a male voice came on the line he said, 'This is Roger McKinnon, please may I speak to Nurse Woodbury.'

'Sorry, Mr McKinnon, but my wife is sleeping and I don't like to disturb her. Is it important?'

'Not if you will relay my message. I am going to be at home until further notice and I thought Mrs Woodbury would appreciate a couple of nights off.'

'Mr McKinnon, you couldn't have called at a better time. It is our wedding anniversary tomorrow and I was hoping to take my wife out for a meal, so if you're sure...'

'Quite sure. Your wife has been an absolute treasure. Please ask her to phone me in a couple of days' time. Meanwhile, enjoy your anniversary.' He heaved a deep sigh as he replaced the receiver.

For the next few minutes Roger stood looking down at his wife. She was sleeping peacefully, which was most unusual. Even on a good day she flailed her arms about, never lying completely still.

It was twelve thirty; a long afternoon and evening stretched ahead of him. He fetched the book he was reading from upstairs, then inspected the lunch that Mrs Burton had left for him. It looked really appetising: cold breast of chicken, ham and tongue. With an ironic smile on his face, he said aloud, 'Might as well eat it.' Seating himself at the kitchen table, he unwrapped a granary roll and buttered it lavishly, then dotted mayonnaise, salt and pepper on the salad and started eating. Within minutes he found that he was enjoying the meal.

By two o'clock, Thelma was stirring. Roger heated some milk in a saucepan and mixed it with the powdered food recommended by Dr Mansfold, then proceeded to try and feed Thelma. It was a messy job – she obviously did not like the taste – but he persevered. He repeatedly told himself there was no dignity left for either of them. Their lives had greatly diminished.

'At last,' he said aloud as the ten o'clock news came to an end and he switched the TV off.

In the kitchen he had everything in readiness for what he was about to do. He mixed a huge amount of Thelma's sedative powder into half a glass of orange juice and deliberately, unhurriedly stood stirring the cloudy mixture.

Back at his wife's bedside, he felt very mixed emotions as he raised her head and held the glass to her mouth. It took a long time for her to drink the mixture, but as he gently wiped her lips between each sip, he murmured words of tender encouragement. When the glass was finally empty, he sat beside her holding her hand.

It was one o'clock in the morning when her breathing finally eased and she gave what her husband convinced himself was a sigh of relief. He stayed by her bedside, still holding her hand, for a very long time. Eventually he stood up, bent over the bed and kissed her still warm lips. Then he straightened the sheet, pulled it up and tucked it under her chin.

He went into the dining room and poured himself a very large brandy, which he tossed down quickly. 'Heavens above,' he murmured as he shuddered. 'No going back now.'

Half an hour later, he left the house and drove to Epping Forest, where he parked the car. He opened the boot and removed the box that held his gun.

He walked briskly until he came to a dense ring of trees. There he settled himself, his back resting against a sturdy tree trunk, his legs outstretched, the gun held against his head.

Finally he pulled the trigger.

## Chapter 9

Three days Chloe had come to work knowing that Roger was not going to put in an appearance. There was, however, plenty for her to be getting on with. Roger, always meticulous down to the last detail, had left strict instructions as to how she should deal with any ongoing accounts. She knew her mind was not fully on her work; she still thought Roger might turn up or at the very least ring her. Every time the phone did ring, she half expected him to be on the other end of the line.

Chloe had gone into Roger's office to check on some details that she knew would be on his computer. She had left the door slightly open and the sound of several voices talking at once had her jerking her head up.

Lloyd Spencer came into the office and said very softly, 'I think you should come out to reception, Chloe. We have a detective sergeant and a WPC here.'

'What would the police want with me?' Chloe's voice was bewildered.

'Come along, Chloe, I'll go with you.'

Chloe stood up and together they made their way past several offices to the glass-walled office that served as reception. The two police officers were deep in conversation when Chloe entered, and Lloyd followed tentatively, closing the door quietly behind him. The police officers stopped talking as they entered and the DS asked Chloe to sit down.

'I'm sorry to be the bearer of sad news, Miss Collard.' The officer's voice was soft and sounded sincere. 'A body was found in Epping Forest yesterday and has since been identified as being that of Roger McKinnon. From a letter found in the deceased gentleman's pocket, we were able to contact his solicitor, who has made the identification. Regrettably I have to tell you that Mrs Thelma McKinnon has also been found dead at her home in Hove.'

Suddenly it was all too much for Chloe. She had a terrible feeling, as if her head was going to burst. She felt much too hot, she was having trouble breathing. She put her hand up to loosen her shirt away from her throat. The last thing she heard was Lloyd's voice, coming from somewhere in the distance, sad and full of sympathy.

'Poor Chloe, I truly believe they cared deeply for each other.'

Chloe woke up on the comfortable couch in the ladies' rest room. As she opened her eyes and took a deep breath, she vaguely wondered who had carried her up the steep flight of stairs to get her here.

'Oh Chloe, you gave us all such a fright. The blood drained out of your face and you were as white as a sheet.' Holly pointed to a cup of tea. 'Try drinking some of that, and when you feel a little better, someone will drive you home.'

Chloe pushed herself upright on the couch and picked up the cup of tea. It was hot and sweet, and before too long she felt much more like herself.

It was Holly who got Chloe through the next weeks. It had been agreed that she should stay with Chloe in her apartment, and she certainly earned her keep, shopping, cooking meals, insisting that Chloe should not leave the table until she had eaten what was on her plate.

A police investigation quickly determined that Roger McKinnon had killed his wife while his mind was disturbed and had then killed himself. However it was still several weeks before the bodies were released for burial.

On the day of the funeral, the weather took a turn for the worse. A fine rain had been falling all morning, and now dark clouds were gathering for the storm that would erupt this evening. Chloe was not crying; she had no tears left in her. Her eyes scanned the crowd of well-dressed people, the women in their smart outfits with their expertly made-up faces, the men all in dark suits and black ties, most of them looking genuinely sad. It pleased Chloe to see so many folk here, but she still wondered where had they been during those lonely years when Roger had been socially isolated because of Thelma's accident.

The bowl of earth was offered to her, and she took some in her gloved hand. She heard the thud as it hit the coffins lying side by side, and she allowed herself to remember that her alliance with Roger had brought a great deal of happiness to each of them. But oh, she was going to miss him.

Desperately.

Roger's death had sent shock waves through the whole company. Chloe had returned to work, and although every single member of the firm had gone out of their way to ensure that she was kept fully occupied, she knew that none of the directors would ever discuss with her the circumstances of the tragedy. To be honest, she didn't care. It was over, it had happened and now it had to be dealt with.

Holly had gone back to her own home.

Chloe was finding the apartment not only very large but extremely lonely. She had just got in from work and had been staring blankly out of the window. The marina, still a lively place where life carried on, was a long way down. This evening, her penthouse apartment gave her the feeling of being entirely cut off from the outside world. What was she going to do about it? That was only one of several questions that she would have to find answers to. She wasn't ready to face them, not yet anyway.

It wasn't until much later that evening that she remembered that the reading of Roger's will was to take place the next day, and she had received notice to attend.

Chloe sat in the solicitor's office with Lloyd Spencer, who had collected her and brought her here in his car. Seated opposite were four well-dressed gentlemen, two of whom she knew: Edward Kendrick and Stephen Goddard. Both of them were directors of the company, and she presumed the same was true of the other two. All four gentlemen were holding brandy goblets.

David Ferris was standing in the centre of the room. It was hard to believe that under his steely countenance the man was feeling deep sorrow. Chloe had met both Ferris and Dr Mansfold briefly during her time with Roger; she hadn't liked the solicitor at their first meeting, and she didn't like him much more now, yet she felt deeply sorry for him and more so for Percy Mansfold, who was approaching her with his hand outstretched.

'How are you, Chloe?' the doctor asked.

'Haven't really gathered my wits yet,' Chloe answered, doing her best to smile.

'Both of you come through to my inner office – and you, Mr Spencer – and have a drink before we start the proceedings. There are still several interested parties due to arrive,' David Ferris urged, placing his hand on Chloe's elbow.

Chloe settled for a glass of sherry while Dr Mansfold and Lloyd Spencer accepted brandies. There was no conversation between them and Chloe gave a sigh of relief when a tap came on the door and a young lady put her head round, saying, 'Mr Ferris, everyone listed has now arrived.'

'Thank you, Miss Barnsley.' Turning to his guests, he murmured, 'Shall we?'

Chloe sat between Dr Mansfold and Lloyd Spencer. Mr Ferris appeared to be more nervous than the people seated in front of him. He cleared his throat and began to speak.

'Businesswise, this will is very straightforward. Mr McKinnon was adamant that it be as short as possible, and in his own words. He hand-wrote the will himself and I drafted it for him.'

David Ferris glanced around. Only two

females were present, Miss Collard and Mrs Burton. The rest were businessmen, not the type to show emotion. They all remained blank-faced.

He started to read. 'I leave my holdings and my proportional part of Associated Securities to be equally divided amongst my five fellow directors. I leave twenty thousand pounds to my faithful housekeeper Mrs Amelia Burton. The house in Hove, in which my wife and I have lived for most of our married life, is to be sold and the money remaining after estate agents' and legal fees have been met is to be given to the Royal Society for the Blind. Other than these listed bequests, I leave everything I own to Miss Chloe Collard.'

He paused in surprise. Not a word had been uttered, and apart from Mrs Burton, who was smiling tearfully, no one's facial expression had altered.

He took a very deep breath and continued to read. 'I leave her my house at Ditchling, which has remained unoccupied since the day I bought it, and the money left in my bank accounts after the above bequests have been met. The bank is holding stocks and share certificates and the name on them will need to be altered, also several bonds which on reaching maturity should be paid to Miss Collard.' He relaxed and blew his nose before adding, 'Mr McKinnon also left a letter addressed to Miss Collard with instructions that I was to give it to her on this day. I have no knowledge whatsoever of its contents.'

He passed a buff-coloured envelope to Chloe, who sat for a long moment staring at the familiar handwriting. She was absolutely stunned, but at last she felt able to murmur, 'Thank you, Mr Ferris.'

'Please, Miss Collard, don't leave just yet. There are some documents that I need you to sign.'

Chloe was unable to form any more words, so she merely smiled.

David Ferris made sure that Chloe was seated at his desk before he spread the legal documents out. Leaning over her shoulder, he indicated where she should write her signature. When she had finished, he said tactfully, 'I have to put these papers into the main safe; while I'm gone, you might like to open your letter and read it.'

That was exactly what she had been longing to do, and yet she felt concerned as to what the contents might divulge. Hands trembling, she opened the envelope and slid out the single sheet of paper inside. Her eyes quickly scanned the few lines written there.

*My darling Chloe,*
*Words cannot convey what my feelings are. Saying 'I love you' just does not make known the depth of that love. I hate having to leave you but am truly grateful for the time we have spent*

*together. All the good times we shared, put the memories away in a special box and get on with your life. In truth, what we had was a good alliance.*

*God bless you,*
*Roger*

Half an hour later, she came out of the inner office to find that with the exception of Lloyd Spencer, everyone had left.

'Are you all right, Chloe? I thought you might like a spot of lunch.'

Lloyd certainly knew his way around. He took her to a very upmarket restaurant within walking distance, and after a few quick words with the head waiter, they were led to a secluded alcove.

Chloe felt she wasn't dressed for this establishment; there were many fashionable women there. Before she'd left the solicitor's office, she had bathed her eyes, made sure her hair was securely fixed in its bun and repaired her make-up. She was wearing a black trouser suit with a white polo-necked jumper underneath, and was relieved that she had her long black cashmere coat with her. It was one of the very first gifts that Roger had bought for her, and that thought brought tears to her eyes again.

Before they sat down, Lloyd helped her off with the coat and gave her a warm hug. 'Just try to relax and eat something,' he said quietly. 'You have not come up against a disaster; quite the reverse. Roger has made you a very wealthy young lady and he would want you to use the money wisely. Most of all, though, he'd want you to be happy.'

Chloe made no answer. She was grateful that Lloyd was taking care of her, but she couldn't help wondering what he and the other directors would make of Roger's will. Lloyd was a nice guy, and like all the directors he had class, the kind that only a great deal of money could sustain. Today he wore a charcoal-grey suit, white shirt and black tie and an expensive black overcoat. He was a striking figure and heads had turned as the pair of them entered the restaurant.

Now he handed her a menu, adding, 'I'm starving, what do you fancy?'

'I'd love a coffee but I don't think I want anything to eat.'

'You don't eat enough,' he complained as he studied the list, 'No wonder you are so slim. I am going to have a thick rump steak and fries; if that doesn't suit you, how about an omelette and salad?'

'That would be nice, thank you.'

It was at that precise moment that Chloe decided things were going to have to change. It was so sad that Roger had no living relatives, but to leave almost his entire estate to her was incredible. Lloyd had spoken the truth when he said it was not a disaster. This was a heaven-sent opportunity for her to have an entirely different life. She must take her time and give the matter a great deal of thought.

She watched as the waiter poured them each a glass of wine from the bottle that Lloyd had ordered. As they waited for their food to be brought to them, Chloe sipped her wine slowly then suddenly burst out, 'Lloyd, what do you know about this house at Ditchling?'

Lloyd's face lit up, his smile spread across his face. 'Lucky old you, have you ever been to Ditchling?'

'Obviously I have passed through there; it's quite near to Brighton, isn't it? I have heard the place referred to as a millionaire's paradise.'

'Quite right too. All I know is that most of the houses are really expensive. The story I've been told is that Roger bought the property with the idea of him and Thelma moving there. However, before the move could take place, Thelma had her accident, and so instead he had the house in Hove adapted to her needs. I've often wondered why he didn't sell the house at Ditchling; who knows what state it is in today.'

'Are you saying the property has been unoccupied all this time?'

'Apparently.'

'Do you know if it is furnished?' Chloe's

curiosity was getting the better of her.

'I rather think it is, or at least partly. I remember Thelma dragging Roger around numerous shops at the time, but it was some years ago.'

'I really can't believe this is happening to me,' Chloe murmured, sounding despondent. 'No one has cared for the place?'

'Only one way to find out. Did David Ferris give you the keys?'

'No, but I have a few questions to ask him. I'll phone him tomorrow.'

'Well give yourself time before you make any decisions and you'll be fine. Now here comes our meal. Eat up and we'll raise our glasses to Roger.'

That evening was a long, lonely one for Chloe. At ten thirty, when the news had finished, she switched off the TV and made herself ready for bed. 'Dear Jesus, what am I going to do?' she asked herself as she tied her dressing gown, knowing full well she was the only one who could answer that question.

She tried to sleep that night but couldn't. So much was running through her mind. Was she going to sell this apartment? If so, where was she going to live? She now owned the house out at Ditchling as well, she reminded herself. Good Lord, all of this was more than she could cope with.

So much to think about. So many decisions

to make. And the most awful thought, the one she couldn't rid herself of, was the fact that everything was down to her. 'Just me,' she said aloud as she punched her pillow. 'Me on my own.' She felt totally overwhelmed.

Soon after she woke up the next morning, there was a delivery from a local florist at her front door. Beautiful carnations and roses. The attached card read, 'Congratulations from the entire board of directors. We will always be here if and when you need any help.' She cried when she read it. Her emotions were up and down. She was thrilled to have learnt that Roger had thought so much of her, but she was scared half out of her wits about the contents of his will.

She had come to love Roger dearly and all she wanted was to have him back. She would give everything he had left her just to have him here with her, feel his arms tightly around her and his sweet lips pressing on hers.

It wasn't going to happen, though. He was gone for ever.

She collapsed on to her couch, agonising sobs racking her body, but there was no one to hold her in their arms. No one to give words of comfort.

She was on her own.

Eventually she calmed down and scrubbed at her eyes with a handkerchief. She had been reminded with great clarity that all the riches in the world didn't compensate for loneliness.

As the day wore on, the silence in her apartment became deafening. All she could think of now was those two wonderful years she had shared with Roger, how completely she had come to love him. She twisted the ring on her finger, the ring Roger had had made for her. She didn't wear it when she went out – she thought it conspicuous and tempting for a thief – but every night before she got into bed, she made sure she had it on her finger.

Now suddenly the dream was over. The good, kind man she had fallen in love with was gone. True, he had left her a fortune, but exactly how she was going to use it was another matter. She would have to think long and hard and more than likely take the offer of help from the board of directors at Associated Securities.

But she wasn't ready yet; she wanted a few more days on her own to sort out her thoughts, to remember all that he had been, and all that he was, and to thank the Lord that she had been allowed to share at least a small part of his life.

# Chapter 10

Chloe was standing in the lounge, gazing out of the huge front window of this fine detached house in Ditchling, and because these expensive houses had been built high on the hilltop, she had a glorious view of the sea.

She watched the sunbeams filtering through the leafy branches of the two great oak trees that stood one each side of the huge iron gates that fronted her property. It was a radiant scene, a day that offered so much. The problem was, she had nowhere specific to go and no one to spend the day with.

Turning away from the window, she walked over to an armchair and sat down heavily, thinking how drastically her life had changed since Roger McKinnon had died. Unexpectedly she felt tears burning the backs of her eyes as sadness mingled with disappointment flooded through her. But after only a few minutes she blinked and cleared her throat, telling herself to get a grip. How dare she wallow in self-pity!

She had landed on her feet and now lived a life such as she had never dreamed of. She possessed good taste and used it well. She had also learnt that good manners and graciousness said more about a person than their bank balance did. She could hold herself well in command when in sophisticated company. Roger had been good for her ego. He'd taken her everywhere and always told her how proud he was of her.

Now, seeing this beautiful room so clearly illuminated in the bright sunshine, she too felt proud of what she had achieved. She felt sad that Roger and Thelma had never got to live in this charming house. It wasn't often that she allowed herself to think back, but when she did, she always told herself that Roger had acted with Thelma's well-being at heart. Her poor body had been broken all those years, while he himself had been suffering from cancer and living on borrowed time. Supposing he had let nature take its course. When death had taken him, who would have cared for his wife? The only answer would have been a care home. Unable to live with that thought, he had made his decision.

To this day, Chloe firmly believed that he had acted out of kindness.

The first time she had entered this house, she had pulled back heavy curtains, opened windows and taken down dusty blinds, and by that afternoon, the house was full of light. Next day she had phoned the local staff agency and had acquired two cleaning ladies to start work the next morning.

Everywhere there was dust, and both women had been coughing by the time the remaining blinds and curtains were lying on the floor. What pieces of furniture there were had originally been expensive, but some of the upholstery needed to be restored and the carpets needed cleaning. Chloe had made a list of what needed to be done. The dining room proved to be the worst. The wood panelling needed expert care. However, in Brighton she found a small firm that really cared about what they were restoring.

Chloe herself was a hard worker and was often to be found with her two cleaning ladies, getting rid of all the dust and cobwebs. Her favourite task was waxing and polishing. She would rub away at a stretch of balustrade until she could see her face in it.

'You are amazing,' Holly had said in admiration when she dropped in, which she did frequently since the results had started to show.

Chloe's greatest find was a husband and wife team who had set up their own business. Their advertisement in the local newspaper stated that Jean Conway tailor-made loose covers for armchairs and sofas, as well as replacement seat pads, cushions, curtains and blinds. David Conway put up curtain tracks and rods, making sure that everything was hung to perfection. Chloe had put plenty of work their way and had been very pleased with every result.

The kitchen hadn't changed since the house had been built, however many years ago that was. Everything in it still worked, though, and Chloe was pondering on what to do about that. She didn't want an ultra-modern kitchen, yet she felt she would like some modern appliances. Could she combine the two and end up with a good working kitchen that was still a warm, welcoming place to sit and be cosy with a cup of coffee?

The decoration of the large rooms she was going to leave until she had got settled in. The wood panelling in the dining room now looked fabulous, and there was a huge table and eight chairs that Roger and Thelma must have chosen.

'When are you going to have your first dinner party?' Holly had asked. 'There must be some interesting people round here, living in all these big houses.'

Several times Chloe had to side-step Holly's questions. She didn't feel she was ready to socialise with her neighbours yet. In fact her thoughts had gone the other way. She had so enjoyed travelling with Roger – their holidays had been perfect – and because of that, she had been thinking about going to Europe.

'Wouldn't be the same on one's own, though,' she said aloud, and getting up out of the armchair, she shook herself. She was just thinking about taking herself out to town for the afternoon when she heard the shrill sound of what she thought was an ambulance siren.

Walking quickly to the window, she saw a paramedic on a motorbike, blue lights flashing as he came to a stop on the other side of the road only a few yards further down. Within seconds he had parked the bike and with a medical bag slung over his shoulder was already disappearing up the drive.

It wasn't long before the sound of more sirens could be heard, and very soon an ambulance was parked alongside the motorbike. Both doors had been hooked back and left wide open as the two ambulance men walked up the long drive and entered the house.

Chloe sighed heavily. Folk who lived in this area were vastly different. Their disposition and their approach to life was not what she would call friendly. As so often, she found herself wandering down memory lane, to the days when she and her two brothers had shared a bedroom in the damp basement flat a stone's throw from the docks. Peter and Matthew had slept in one bed, while she herself had made do with an old velvet armchair, the front of which pulled out to make a foot rest.

Had they been happy times? Of course they had. Londoners were the salt of the earth; hurt one member of a family and the whole lot would retaliate. As her dad had been fond of saying, 'Search the earth and you may find our equals but never will you find our betters.' Not one family she had known had ever had more than two pound coins to rub together, but they would never let anyone starve. Help was always readily given to any neighbour who needed it.

This morning, the minute she'd heard the sirens, she'd felt that she should go along to the house to see if there was anything she might be able to help with. She had suppressed that notion very quickly. Moneyed business folk hadn't time for other people's problems; they kept themselves strictly to what concerned them.

After the reading of Roger's will, Chloe hadn't gone near the office for two months. The amount of money and property he had left to her was truly astounding, and she couldn't help but worry what her colleagues would make of it all. Nevertheless, she couldn't spend very much more time on her own, often talking to herself, always feeling desperately lonely.

She knew that she would be made welcome back at Associated Securities. She had come a long way since first she had joined the firm, and everyone knew that she was an absolute wizard when it came to computers. She had always made certain she kept herself up to date with all the office equipment.

Now that Roger was gone, she didn't want to be seen as a hanger-on. She had to feel that she was still needed within the firm. She wanted the directors to trust her and when necessary to be able to rely on her. Sometimes she felt she knew almost as much about the business as they did.

She needed a job that was demanding and important, so she had gone to the top brass and told them exactly what her thoughts were.

'If I'm working, I shall recover much quicker. I have been made to realise that life has to go on. Here with all of you I shall pull myself together and not only do a very good job, but do it with a smile on my face.'

'We will welcome you back with open arms. Your office door still has your name on it,' Lloyd Spencer had hastened to assure her. 'You mustn't think that because Roger is no longer with you, this is the end of laughter and loving for you. Life is so extraordinary. Be patient. Wonderful surprises are just around the most unexpected corners. From where you are standing at the moment it may seem a bit bleak and empty, but yes, I think it would be a wise decision for you to return to us here at the office. However, I am going to suggest that you wait another month, decide where you want to live. Your apartment is so much nearer to the office than that house out in Ditchling. Also spend a few days with your girlfriends, spend money on yourself. Remember, Roger left you a substantial legacy.'

Chloe was not to know that fate would decide what she did with this coming month. Or what the outcome of meeting a lot of strangers would be. However, she was just about to find out.


## Chapter 11

After all the excitement of the ambulance arriving in the road, Chloe had changed her mind about going to town. Where better to spend the rest of the day than in her own beautiful garden?

She walked through the house, slid open the glass doors of the dining room and stepped out, thinking how wise she had been to keep the two gardeners that Roger had always employed. Although the interior of the house had been left unattended for years, he had made sure that the grounds were well maintained. Keeping up with the neighbours? More than likely, she smiled to herself. Now she let her eyes wander and was pleased at how well kept everything looked. The lawns so neat and green, the borders bright with geraniums and cottage pinks and further back rose bushes neatly organised according to colour. Everything was splendid, and so it should be, the amount of money she was paying the gardeners.

Arriving at what she called her hideaway, Chloe opened the double doors of the wooden summer house and brought a small table and a deckchair out on to the long veranda, quickly setting them up facing the tall oak trees that marked the end of her property. With two colourful cushions at her back, she was soon seated very comfortably. Within the summer house there was a good selection of books, but today she was content to just gaze over this pleasant spot and the surrounding landscape. She didn't want to ponder on why she was spending so much time alone, because the comparison with days long gone was too hard to bear. After only a few minutes, she knew exactly where her thoughts were leading her. She tried to stop reminiscing – she was exposing herself to more heartache – yet still her mind seemed to press on, letting the memories flood in, drawing her towards the East End of London like a powerful magnet. She was unable to resist the call.

Less than an hour later, she parked her car in Brighton's Railway Yard and bought a ticket to London. On arrival at Victoria, she walked out into Buckingham Palace Road and straight away was plunged into a differ-

124

ent world to the one she remembered so fondly. She had been planning to use the underground to get to the East End, but everywhere was so crowded, she was feeling anxious. She had been mollycoddled by Roger: chauffeur-driven cars or taxis wherever they went. As she looked around in bewilderment, she heard a woman's voice calling her name.

'Chloe, Chloe Collard, is it really you? We heard you'd gone up in the world. It's certainly a helluva long time since anyone from these parts has heard from you.'

Chloe stopped dead in her tracks. The voice belonged to Jane Wilson, an old school mate and a neighbour for years. She was lost for words.

'You've no idea how posh you look, love.'

Chloe was wearing a simple linen dress in a very pale shade of green and a beige jacket. The outfit looked wonderful and very expensive.

'It was your hair that made me certain it was you. Still a proper copper-nob, aren't you?' Jane said. Then, pointing across the road to the open doorway of a café, she suggested, 'Why don't we go and have a cuppa? It's not much to look at from the outside, but it's clean and there's a fair amount of room inside.'

Chloe didn't feel she had a choice, but on the other hand, a chance to catch up on all that had happened since she had moved to Brighton was tempting.

'If I'm not holding you up, Jane, I would love a cup of tea.'

Jane smiled and took hold of Chloe's arm. 'Let's cross now; quick, the taxi drivers aren't fussy who they toss up into the air.'

Chloe was astounded as she sat down at one of the tables. The inside of this café was marvellous compared to the outside, and a neatly dressed waitress came to take their order. Jane ordered tea and sandwiches for both of them, then leant towards Chloe and asked, 'Would you like to see some photographs of my babies?'

Chloe raised her eyebrows. 'You've got babies?'

'Two,' Jane laughed, 'only twelve months between them.' She took out several photographs and laid them out on the table. 'That's our Ann Jamison and that's her big brother Peter,' she proudly told Chloe.

Chloe was spellbound. 'They are beautiful, so bonny-looking. So you married Terry Jamison? That's no surprise. Even when we were at school you always had your eye on him.'

'You're dead right, Chloe, how about you? Must be a man somewhere in your life, but you're not wearing a ring.'

Chloe was almost tempted to tell her all about Roger, but she decided it was too soon.

Instead she smiled and said, 'No, I've never yet met the man who wants to marry me.'

Just then the waitress came back with their order. Chloe was pleased that the cups and saucers were bone china, and no one could fault the sandwiches, cut into four triangles with a delicious side salad and a bowl of salted titbits. The linen serviettes also impressed her.

'What kind of work does Terry do?' she asked, to keep the conversation going.

'He's at the smelting works at the moment, but he's trying hard to join the army. He wants us to see a bit of the world and we would be given accommodation wherever he was posted.'

'What do you do about housing now?'

'We rent a flat near the Elephant and Castle; it's a fair size, has two bedrooms, but it is five floors up.'

Chloe was feeling uncomfortable, and as soon as they had finished the sandwiches, she signalled to the waitress to bring their bill. A quick glance at the total and she slipped notes on to the tray and quietly said, 'Please keep the change.'

As they left the café, Chloe said, 'I'm so glad that we bumped into each other.' She hoped she sounded sincere.

'Me too. As I said, it was the colour of your hair, couldn't miss seeing you again after all this time.'

Neither of them knew what more to say. They kissed each other and had a final hug, and Chloe slipped some folded notes into Jane's coat pocket. When Jane started to protest, Chloe very quickly said, 'Please, Jane, put half each into Ann and Peter's money boxes.'

'Well if you insist, thank you, Chloe.'

As Chloe walked away, she was thinking about how much Jane and Terry must love each other, but then she herself knew that loving a man didn't necessarily make for happiness. Was she pleased that she'd met up with her old friend? Not really, she admitted. She was learning the hard way that you couldn't keep looking backwards. Talking to Jane had made her feel despondent, and she realised she had already had more than enough of London.

Before she had time to change her mind, she was back inside Victoria station and handing her ticket to the man on the gate. She was going back to her new world; she obviously didn't fit into life in London any more.

For the first part of the journey Chloe gazed appalled at the blocks of flats with lines of washing hanging from almost every balcony. It wasn't until the train stopped at Lewes and she could see the green fields, the beginning of East Sussex, that she realised just how fortunate she had been. The best thing you ever did was accept that job with Associated Securities, she reminded herself, and it wouldn't do you any harm to start counting your many blessings.

As Chloe turned into her road in Ditchling, she was mystified to see a cluster of people gathered near her gates. She pulled in to her drive, then switched off the engine and got out of the car.

'Can you spare a minute, please?' called a young woman dressed in a dark outfit.

Chloe took a few steps towards her, noting that the gathering outside had not moved.

'My name is Beryl Taylor and I work for Social Services,' the young woman said, showing Chloe an identity card with a small photograph of herself attached to it.

Chloe nodded. 'How may I help?' she asked.

'A neighbour of yours, Mrs Whitlocke, has been taken to hospital with a suspected heart attack, and there doesn't seem to be anyone in the house to take charge of her little daughter. Do you know the family?'

'I can't say that I do, actually. I have only recently become a resident. I have seen the mother walking with the little girl and a small dog, but more than that I can't tell you.'

'What about the husband, or the child's father?' The young woman looked as if she was about to cry; she seemed flustered, as if she was out of her depth.

'As I have just said, I can't help you.'

'Could you just come along to the house and talk to the child while I contact my office again?' Beryl Taylor's eyes were pleading with Chloe.

'What about those people out there? Don't they know the child?'

'Only one of them lives nearby, the elderly gentleman; the rest are just nosy parkers.'

Slowly Chloe nodded. 'All right,' she said, but she wasn't happy about it. As they walked, she said to Miss Taylor, 'I had better introduce myself. I'm Chloe Collard.'

Within minutes they were at Mrs Whitlocke's house. Miss Taylor took a bunch of keys from her pocket, selected one and unlocked the front door. 'The ambulance men told me to take charge of the keys as soon as I arrived; they also suggested I contacted the neighbours. I have tried but nobody seems to be at home, and I couldn't leave the little girl in the house on her own for very much longer.'

As they stepped into the entrance hall, Chloe ventured to ask, 'How come Social Services have become involved?'

'The ambulance men had no option but to take the mother straight to the hospital and were prevented by rules and regulations from letting an unescorted child travel with them. They notified Social Services, who rang me as I was already in the vicinity. Shall we go in?' Miss Taylor opened a closed door that Chloe presumed must be the lounge.

The spectacle that met Chloe's eyes she felt would be imprinted on her mind for ever. A tiny little blonde-haired girl with a tear-stained face was kneeling on the carpet patting and stroking a small white dog, which had rolled over on to its back and was holding all four legs up in the air. It was enough to melt the hardest heart. Chloe turned to face Miss Taylor, raising her eyebrows in question.

'Her name is Amberley, the ambulance men told me that much, but I haven't managed to get a word out of her and she's hardly moved from that spot since I arrived.'

Chloe laid down her handbag and removed her jacket, then went down on her knees beside the child. 'I know *your* name,' she murmured as she leaned towards the little girl, 'so shall I tell you mine?'

There was no response.

'It's Chloe, can you pronounce that?'

The child brushed at her eyes with a small clenched fist but still made no reply. Chloe looked at the dog, which had rolled over and stood up, then she bent her head and in a stage whisper began to speak to the animal. 'Can you tell me your name and whether you have had any dinner yet?' There was a pause. 'Shall I take you into the kitchen, find you

131

something to eat and fill your bowl with a nice drink of water, would you like that?'

'Fergus can't talk.' The words were shot out in little more than a whisper.

'Oh, that is a pity. Perhaps if I try to find where your mummy's kitchen is, I could make us all a nice drink and see if there are any biscuits for Fergus.'

'I'll show you, and Fergus does what I tell him.'

'Well that is good, and you must be clever to be able to make Fergus understand.'

'I'm not clever, not yet, but I'm nearly four, and when I am, I shall be allowed to go to school.'

Miss Taylor breathed a sigh of relief as she watched Amberley stand up and put her hand into Chloe's, and the two of them, with the dog trotting alongside, left the room.

'I'll be in the hall. I'm going to have to make a couple of phone calls,' she called after them.

In the kitchen, Amberley's eyes were glued on Chloe as she filled the dog's bowl with water before switching the kettle on to boil.

'The men who came to take Mummy to the hospital said I was brave to dial nine nine nine and they said Fergus was very well house-trained.' Amberley offered this gem of information, leaving Chloe to wonder how this delightful, pretty little girl came to have such an old head on her young shoulders.

By the time Miss Taylor came back from having made her phone calls, the dog was happy in his basket, Amberley was sitting on Chloe's lap and all three had had something to eat and drink.

Shuffling a sheaf of papers into order, Miss Taylor signalled for Chloe to put the child down and come outside into the hall.

'Well, the office has done good work. Apparently Amberley's parents were divorced nearly three years ago and no one knows where Mr Whitlocke is. Social Services have located a brother, who has been informed that a relative is needed to take charge of his niece. Unfortunately he is working in Scotland and the earliest he can arrive will be tomorrow morning. Mrs Whitlocke's mother, the child's grandmother, has also been notified, but she lives in north Devon.'

Chloe had listened to these facts with a growing sense of alarm.

'So who is taking care of Amberley tonight?' she queried cautiously.

'Who knows?' Miss Taylor shrugged her shoulders. 'We'll just have to wait and see. Mrs Whitlocke may not be kept in hospital for any length of time. We may be worrying for nothing.'

Maybe, maybe not, Chloe thought to herself. 'So what immediate arrangements have you been told to make?' She was losing her patience.

'I am waiting for the office to ring me back. If all else fails, I will be told to take her either to a fostering couple, although foster parents don't usually want to accept responsibility for a child for just one night, or–'

She was interrupted by the telephone ringing. Chloe waited in the hall, listening to the one-sided conversation. When Miss Taylor hung up and turned back towards the kitchen, she protested loudly, 'Hang on a minute, you're going to take this child to an orphanage for tonight?'

'Miss Collard, it is not an orphanage, it is a halfway house, and it is the best we can do at such short notice.'

'Is there someone on the end of that line who is able to make decisions, because if there is, I'd like a word with that person.'

Amberley had come out into the hall and was once again sitting on the floor with Fergus by her side.

Miss Taylor was speaking into the phone again. Suddenly her face went red and she held the receiver out to Chloe, saying, 'One of our senior staff would like a word with you.'

Chloe listened intently to what was being said, then it was her turn.

'Yes, my surname is Collard, Chloe Collard. I own Albany House, which is a few properties further along in Brentwood Avenue. I am also PA to a director of Associated Securities. You can check my credentials. Meanwhile I am quite prepared to take charge of Mrs Whitlocke's small daughter for tonight, as I understand her uncle will be arriving tomorrow morning.'

There was still quite a bit of verbal toing and froing, but at last Chloe breathed out, put the phone down and let a great smile spread across her face. Then she bent down towards Amberley and spoke gently. 'Your Mummy is going to have to stay in hospital for a while so that the doctors can make her better. How would you like to come to my house, help me cook dinner and stay the night with me? Your Uncle Laurence is travelling down from Scotland, and when he arrives in the morning he will take you to see your mummy. Does that sound all right?'

For a whole minute Amberley looked very thoughtful, then she asked, 'Please may Fergus come too?'

'Do you really believe we would leave him here on his own? Of course we shall take Fergus with us.'

'Thank you, Chloe,' the child said, adding, 'And he's called Uncle Laurie.'

'Well that's fine, I shall get to meet him in the morning. Maybe he'll arrive in time to have breakfast with us.'

'How will he know where we are?'

'We'll write a note and leave it on the kitchen table, where he's sure to find it.'

'You will like my Uncle Laurie, everybody does.'

'That's good to hear. Now, can you find your nightclothes and we'll pack you an overnight bag. Those pretty slippers you're wearing can go in the bag if you can find your outdoor shoes and put them on. And while you're doing that, I'll pack a bag for Fergus and look for his lead.'

Quite suddenly Amberley's face lit up and she gave a tinkling laugh. 'Fergus doesn't wear nightclothes, but he has got a nice basket with a lovely blanket inside.'

'Silly me.' Chloe laughed with her. 'Tell you what, Amberley, we'll take Fergus's basket with us, shall we?'

While all this was going on, Miss Taylor had just stood there looking utterly bewildered. With all her training, she hadn't been able to get the child to utter a single word.

'Maybe you should apply for a job in child care,' she said, smiling at Chloe, but there was just a hint of irony in her tone, which Chloe chose to ignore.

At exactly eight o'clock that evening Chloe stood just inside her spare bedroom staring at the long blonde hair that was spread out over the pillow. The little girl was sleeping peacefully, tucked up in the bed. Turning her gaze downwards, Chloe grinned broadly at the little white dog asleep in its own basket at the side of the bed.

What a wonderful evening she had just spent. One of the best since Roger had died.

She had cooked sausages, scrambled eggs and chips; Fergus had been given the same meal because of course her larder did not contain any dog food. All three of them had eaten ice cream for their sweet. After dinner they had let Fergus out into the garden to do his business, and they had both laughed when he had barked at the glass doors when he was ready to come back in.

She had helped Amberley to have a lovely warm bath using any of her bath products that she chose. Fergus had been allowed in the bathroom to watch.

After the bath, she had told a made-up story to Amberley, and they had both rolled round on the carpet playing with Fergus. Now she had to sit down and give some serious thought as to what the next day might bring.

## Chapter 12

Chloe was staring out of her front window, engrossed in her thoughts, when she realised that the driver of the big estate car parked outside was signalling for someone to open the gates. She also noticed that the back seat of the vehicle was piled high with luggage. It was only just ten o'clock; she hadn't been expecting Amberley's uncle until later in the day, but obviously he had managed to arrive earlier. More than likely he had flown down from Scotland and had hired the car at the airport. Having him take charge of Amberley would be a great relief, but the impression the Social Services had given her was that Laurence Walmsley was a man who travelled the world, and if that were true, how on earth was he going to take care of a little girl who was not yet four years old?

She pressed the button to open the gates and was halfway down the drive when a shout stopped her in her tracks. Next minute Amberley was running past her to leap into the arms of the man who had just arrived. He swept the child up and was hugging her and swinging her round and round when he caught sight of Chloe. He stopped abruptly and stared at her, a pair of clear blue eyes moving over her from head to toe and back again, openly appraising her slender body and provocative features.

'Are you Miss Collard?' he asked

Something in his tone made her bristle. 'Yes,' she said sharply. 'There didn't seem to be any other volunteer to take charge of your niece.' Then, realising she had assumed too much, she added, 'I am presuming you are Amberley's Uncle Laurence.' As she questioned him, she also studied the man, taking in the broad shoulders, the casual way he was dressed – tight trousers, polo-neck jersey and an expensive leather jacket that emphasised the general hardness of his tall, lean body – the well-tanned features and the thick mass of dark blond hair. She was trying to work out how old he was. Thirty-five? Thirty-six? She suddenly realised that he was looking right back at her with a glint of amusement in his eyes, and she felt the colour rush to her cheeks.

Laurence Walmsley was as astounded as Chloe was as he introduced himself. From what little information Social Services had given him, he had been expecting the woman who had taken charge of his niece to be a middle-aged matron. Instead he was standing face to face with a young lady dressed in beautifully tailored beige trousers and dark brown silk shirt, and in anyone's book she was a stunner, tall and slim, with long, shapely legs. But it was her hair that set her apart from other young women. It was a deep natural auburn, hanging thick and glossy down her back.

'This is all so unexpected,' he said. 'I never thought I would find myself in sole charge of a four-year-old child. My sister and I will be forever grateful to you for having taken Amberley under your wing.'

'Why don't we all go into the house?' Chloe suggested brightly, determined to let him know that the arrangement was purely a temporary one. 'You must be ready for a drink, and perhaps you'd like to phone the hospital for news of your sister. I'm not allowed to enquire, only members of the family.'

'Amberley, you run on and tell Fergus I have arrived.' As Amberley went to do her uncle's bidding, Laurence Walmsley turned to face Chloe and spoke seriously. 'I called into the hospital before coming on down here. The prognosis is not good. The doctor in charge assured me they are doing all they can, but at the moment Dorothy is scarcely holding her own. Your offer of a drink is the best suggestion I've heard this morning. If you're sure we won't be too much trouble, lead on.'

Over the following half an hour, while they sat side by side drinking coffee, Chloe came to the conclusion that Laurence Walmsley could charm the birds out of the trees, especially where his small niece was concerned. The little girl obviously adored the man.

Suddenly Chloe felt the need to ask a question. 'What about your sister's ex-husband? Amberley tells me that her daddy works abroad. Has anyone bothered to inform him that his wife is in hospital?'

The humour that up to now had been lurking in Laurence's eyes, more so as he

140

played with Amberley and her little dog, was banished. 'That damn man should be hung, drawn and quartered. Dorothy divorced him only weeks after Amberley was born. As far as I am aware, my niece has never set eyes on her father.'

Although he had kept his voice low so that Amberley would not hear, his anger was unmistakable.

'Aren't you curious as to why I hate Michael Whitlocke?' he asked when Chloe remained silent.

She shrugged. Feelings were running too deep for her liking.

'He made his floozy pregnant at the same time as his wife, my sister. That wasn't enough, he had to rub salt into her wounds. He booked his slut into a private nursing home for the birth and actually taunted my sister with the fact that his lover had given him a son. My sister had to have her baby in a National Health hospital.'

Chloe felt uncomfortable at the amount of anger this man was feeling. She reached for the coffee pot, and at that same moment the front doorbell rang. She refilled Laurence's cup and excused herself.

On opening the front door, Chloe was faced with a well-dressed man who looked every inch what his identity card said he was: a civil servant from the department for children's welfare. His companion was a middle-aged lady, slim and smartly dressed in a two-piece suit. Her identity card stated that she was attached to Brighton's Social Services. They wanted to know if Amberley Whitlocke's guardian had arrived.

'Yes, the gentleman has arrived, he is here with Amberley. Would you both like to come in?'

'This is Mr Bolton and Mrs Mitchell,' Chloe began as Laurence got to his feet. 'They are both connected with Child Welfare.'

Laurence, who was at least three inches taller than Mr Bolton, shook hands with both visitors. Then he picked Amberley up, whistled to Fergus, who came eagerly, and in a whisper asked Chloe, 'Would you mind if I put these two in another room while we talk?'

'No, you stay, I'll see to them,' Chloe quickly offered, taking Amberley from him and making sure that the dog was following as she left the room.

'Miss Collard, we need you to hear what we have to say,' Mrs Mitchell called after her.

'All right, I shall only be a few minutes settling Amberley,' Chloe called back.

When she re-entered the room, Chloe was horrified to hear Laurence ranting loudly. 'Nothing for it, then, my niece will have to be placed in a private boarding school.'

What on earth was the man talking about?

Chloe wondered.

'Mr Walmsley, will you please try to stay calm. Amberley is far too young for us to consider a boarding school.' Mrs Mitchell was trying to reason with him.

'There is nothing for you or anyone else to consider; the child is my blood relative and what happens to her is my responsibility.'

'I beg to differ, Mr Walmsley,' Mr Bolton said in a very firm tone of voice. 'The welfare of your niece for the foreseeable future will be under the jurisdiction of Social Services. In the circumstances, the only solution is temporary foster parents. We understand that the child's grandmother is elderly and infirm, and that within the next week or two you will be going abroad again on business.'

'Never.'

Laurence spoke sharply, and Chloe gasped but stayed silent.

'I should imagine that foster parents mainly come from working-class areas; well, that is not going to happen to my niece,' Laurence was declaring emphatically. 'Amberley will end up speaking with a cockney accent and more than likely she'll only be given a bath once a week.'

Chloe listened to this ludicrous exchange with a heavy heart. The man must know that he sounded ridiculous. She was sure he had the little girl's wellbeing at heart, but whether she was going to be happy didn't seem to concern him. His ideas might be sensible, but they certainly weren't kind.

Chloe sighed heavily. She didn't want it to look as if she were trying to muscle in. After all, she was only a neighbour, not even one of long standing.

'May I ask if you have already got foster parents in mind?' she asked hesitantly.

'The short answer to that is unfortunately no,' Mr Bolton replied.

'I could keep Amberley here with me for a few days, if that would be of any help.' Chloe had spoken without thinking, and immediately she felt her cheeks redden up.

Laurence Walmsley slid off his chair and bounded across to where she was standing just inside the door. Throwing his arm around her shoulders, he declared loudly, 'You are an absolute angel.'

Chloe forced herself to laugh. 'Hardly an angel, Mr Walmsley. I've led far too–' She broke off. 'Well we won't go into my previous life.' She turned and addressed Mr Bolton. 'Mr Walmsley has the keys to his sister's house, I presume, so he can sleep there for the short time he intends to be around, and I shall willingly do my best to care for Amberley until such time as her mother's health shows signs of improvement. That is if the authorities will allow me to do so.'

'While Amberley has a suitable blood relative around, that person has the ruling control over the child,' Mr Bolton informed her. 'Taking her into care will only become obligatory when Mr Walmsley leaves the country. He has made it known that he approves of your intentions, but myself and Mrs Mitchell will now have to check on your credentials. I understand that you gave your full details to a senior officer over the phone yesterday, is that correct?'

'Yes, it is.' Chloe breathed out. She was already heartily wishing that she had never made the offer to take care of the child in the first place.

Turning to Laurence, Mr Bolton said, 'Sir, if you wouldn't mind signing a couple of papers confirming that a temporary agreement has been reached in the best interests of the child...'

Laurence did as he was asked, and then shook hands with both of the officials.

'We shall be in touch, Mr Walmsley, and in the meantime we sincerely hope that you will soon receive better news from the hospital regarding your sister.'

'Thank you.'

Mrs Mitchell took a small card from her purse and held it out to Chloe. 'The number on there will reach me at any time. If you need any help or just feel like having a chat, please ring me.'

'I will,' Chloe promised, thinking that she might well be glad of a lifeline.

The rest of the day passed off much better than Chloe had anticipated. Laurence Walmsley took himself off to his sister's house to have a wash and brush-up and to contact his office.

Chloe looked at the dear little dog and decided to take her two charges to a nearby park, Amberley prettily dressed in a dark blue velvet coat with a head-hugging hat to match, from which her long blonde hair hung down over her shoulders. Fergus sat quietly and allowed Chloe to attach his lead. She had remembered to put some stale bread into a bag and was greatly amused to watch Amberley feed the ducks. Fergus was a problem. If she let him off his lead, he would probably jump straight into the water and start chasing the ducks. Better safe than sorry, she murmured to herself.

On the way home, she made a detour to a popular farm shop. Here she was able to purchase a chicken and plenty of fresh vegetables. Noting that Amberley was looking at the confectionery counter, she bent down and whispered, 'You may choose something to eat, it has been a long time since breakfast.'

The child's beaming smile lightened Chloe's heart as she watched Amberley choose a bag of Maltesers.

Back home, the first thing they did was set

a bowl of water down for Fergus. Chloe poured a glass of milk for Amberley and left her with some paper and pencils and a few magazines, promising herself that tomorrow she would buy some suitable children's books.

She lit the oven and started to prepare what she hoped might turn out to be a grand roast dinner. She did cook for herself, but not on a regular basis. Tonight she was making an exception.

It was six o'clock when her doorbell rang and Laurence presented himself. Just one look and Chloe's heart came up into her mouth. He looked immaculate in a sharp dark grey suit, pale blue shirt and darker tie, his thick blond hair smoothed down. Even though she was wearing heels, he was still so tall that she had to tilt her head backwards to meet his gaze.

'I've come to take you two girls out to dinner,' he said as Amberley threw her arms around his legs.

'We are eating here. I've laid a table in the lounge; it is so much more cosy in there. The dining room is far too big,' Chloe told him brushing the perspiration from her forehead and letting him know she wouldn't stand for any arguments.

'I helped Chloe to fold the serviettes,' Amberley piped up.

'Well in that case, just tell me what I can

do to help,' suggested Laurence as he took his jacket off and hung it over the back of one of the breakfast stools.

'Everything is ready to serve; in a moment you may help to carry in the vegetable dishes. In the meantime, would you go and choose a bottle of wine from the cabinet and also find a drink suitable for Amberley.'

'Sure,' he grinned, giving Chloe a mock salute.

Why was she getting so flustered? It'd been her own idea to cook dinner, and she still felt it was better than taking a little girl out to eat at this time of night. But what was she supposed to do about this flutter in her stomach that had started the minute she'd set eyes on Laurence Walmsley again? He did have that drop-dead-gorgeous look about him, and the tan he was sporting didn't do him any harm. By now she was in overdrive; knowing that he spent a lot of time abroad, she found herself imagining him on a sandy beach wearing only a pair of swimming trunks...

Stop it! she told herself, trying desperately to keep her mind on getting the food out of the oven and on to the table.

The dinner passed off even better than she had hoped it would. Strange but true, it was a happy threesome that sat around her table. Chloe was pleased to just watch Amberley. Her manners were impeccable, and although she ate little, she ate it well. A piece of chicken that she had left on the side of her plate was cut up into small pieces and added to Fergus's bowl. Both adults were moved as they watched the little girl sit on the floor beside the dog while he ate his dinner.

After Amberley had been bathed and settled down in bed, she said her prayers asking God to make her mummy better. Chloe told her the story of the three little pigs, with Laurence standing in the doorway looking on, until Amberley nodded off.

Life was so bloody unfair at times, thought Chloe as she straightened the bedclothes over the child and dimmed the light. 'Sleep well, Amberley,' she murmured.

Laurence Walmsley could not help but notice that her voice was thick with emotion.

Back downstairs, Laurence looked at his watch and told Chloe he was going to the hospital to sit with his sister for a while. As they walked together towards the front door, she had to fight to control the overwhelming panic that was threatening to engulf her. It would be an absolute disaster if Mrs Whitlocke were to die. What in God's name would she be called upon to do then?

There was another question that she couldn't banish from her mind.

This Laurence Walmsley had dropped on her from out of the blue and had sent the blood racing through her veins. She'd lay money that he had this effect on most women, because there was no getting away from the fact that he was a very attractive man. There had been a couple of times when she'd felt sure he was sizing her up, but then he'd made the mistake of catching her eye and they had both been embarrassed. Flinching from the memory, she felt sure it was due to the circumstances that had thrown them together. Had the situation been different, who knows? Stop right there, she told herself as she drew in a sharp breath and tried to dismiss such thoughts, but for the rest of the evening she felt restless.

Twice she had been upstairs to check on Amberley, and both times she had been tempted to pick up Fergus and bring him downstairs as company for her. But the little dog had looked so snug curled up on the foot of Amberley's bed that she'd resisted the temptation.

All evening the same thoughts nagged at her.

So much had happened in such a short space of time.

She was now sharing her home with a three-year-old girl and a small dog. Her neighbour, whom she hardly knew, might be dying. To top it all, a man she had never set eyes on before had flown down from Scotland and she had cooked dinner for him. It was so utterly different from her quiet, orderly life. It was all a bit bewildering.

Suddenly Chloe did a little dance; better a headache than a heartache, she told herself. She was never likely to come across another Roger, and thinking of him was a timely reminder not to let Laurence Walmsley get too close, and certainly not to let herself fall in love with him.

These thoughts pulled her up sharply. Indeed, she couldn't remember the last time such an idea had even crossed her mind.

Was that because she didn't think of any of the available men as suitable escorts?

No, if she was truthful with herself, it was because Roger had been the ultimate. Supreme lover, friend, companion, escort and attendant to her every need at any hour of the day or night. And most of all, he had loved her dearly.

How could any man follow that?

The very question filled her with a bleak sadness, and she blinked against the tears that were brimming from her eyes.

It was at that moment that she heard a child's laughter and a dog's bark.

Smiling weakly to herself, she straightened up. It was about time she remembered that she had volunteered to take charge of Amberley; nobody had used thumb screws on her. This beautiful house was for the time being Amberley's home too, and she needed to make sure that the child was happy and secure.

As Chloe walked into Amberley's room, she burst out laughing. The little girl was wide awake, kneeling up in bed holding one end of a long rubber bone. The other end of the bone was in Fergus's mouth.

'Chloe, come and see,' Amberley implored, smiling. 'Fergus found this bone under his blanket. I shake it ever so hard and he is trying to get it away from me. You watch.'

Amberley began to vigorously shake the toy from side to side while Fergus kept hold of the other end, his head eagerly keeping time.

'Come on, Chloe, see if Fergus can get it away from you.'

Sitting on the bed next to Amberley, Chloe had been about to scold the little girl and insist that she lie back down and go to sleep. One look at that sweet face, blonde hair hanging free, and she was lost. She was also thrilled that even Fergus had made this house his home for the time being.

She decided that the time had come for her to act as a child.

'Move over a bit,' she grinned, nudging Amberley in the ribs and taking the rubber bone in her own hands.

Later, alone in bed, Chloe chuckled as she plumped up her pillows before settling down to read a few chapters of her book. The game that she and Amberley had played with Fergus had had the house ringing with the sound of laughter, something that hadn't happened in a very long time.

When she had first learnt that Roger had left her this house, she had been in two minds as to whether or not she was pleased. Once she'd opened it up and put her own mark on every room, she knew she loved the place. In her daydreams, she had convinced herself that when the right man came along, they'd fill the rooms with brilliant, adorable children. The beautiful large garden would have a sandpit, maybe a swimming pool, at least two swings and loads of garden furniture.

She had almost given up on those hopes, but now that Amberley and Fergus had breathed new life into the place, she was again feeling convinced that given time this house could truly become a home.

'Time will tell,' she muttered to herself as she turned over and made ready to go to sleep.

## Chapter 13

Laurence arrived in time to join them for breakfast, and the smile on his face told Chloe that he was the bearer of good news.

'Uncle Laurie, have you been to see Mummy?'

'Yes, Amberley, I have.' Turning his face to include Chloe, he went on, 'Last night when I left Dorothy she wasn't breathing too well and so I got up early this morning and was in the hospital by eight o'clock. I'm so glad that I did. The doctor still has her attached to machines and drip lines, but he said the report is very encouraging. Your mummy certainly has roses back in her cheeks today and she asked that I give you a big cuddle from her and a big kiss. And Chloe, she asked me to convey her thanks to you for having taken Amberley under your wing.'

Chloe let out a sigh of relief, and as Laurie bent to hug his niece, Fergus set up a noisy few minutes of excited barking. The whole atmosphere in the kitchen had been greatly lifted. And even more so when Laurie said:

'How about I take my two favourite girls swimming this morning, and when we've had enough exercise we shall find a nice restaurant and have lunch.'

Amberley found the whole idea very exciting and couldn't wait to go home to fetch her bathing costume. Her uncle offered to take her, and as they were setting off, he said to Chloe, 'Might be better if we leave Fergus in his own house, what do you think?'

'Fine, make sure he has a bowl of water and some biscuits.' Then, looking at Amberley, she asked, 'Shouldn't you be taking his basket back with you?'

'Course not, silly, Fergus has a basket in almost every room in our house.' Looking thoughtful, Amberley added, 'Mummy lets him lie on the wide windowsill in the lounge, he gets up there by jumping off the arm of the big armchair. He will be able to see us through the window when we come home.'

'That's all right then.' Chloe beamed, wondering how this sweet little girl had managed to get such an old head on her young shoulders.

Later, when Laurence's car drew up outside her house, Chloe noticed that the luggage had been removed from the back. There was room for all three of them to sit together. Seat belts safely locked, bags holding towels and swimwear stacked away, Laurie was about to turn the key in the ignition when he paused and turned to Chloe.

'Any preference as to which swimming baths we should go to?'

'None at all,' she promptly told him.

'Good. I have some business papers to deliver to a place called Little Common, near Cooden. I suggest that we have our swim at Eastbourne swimming baths and then go on to Cooden for our lunch, and I can deliver my papers on the way back. All right by you?'

'Yes thank you,' Chloe said, then asked thoughtfully, 'Do you know if Amberley can swim?'

'Definitely, she's amazing actually.'

'That's good, we should all have a great time.'

Laurie hired armbands for Amberley even though she was a good swimmer. They joined in a ball game with two or three other families who were already in the water, and Chloe thought how great it was to be part of a family for once. She really was enjoying herself.

When the time came, Laurie let Chloe get out of the water first then lifted Amberley to the safety of the poolside before saying, 'I am going to do a few quick lengths.'

Chloe fetched their towels and wrapped Amberley and then herself up well so that they were able to keep warm and watch Laurie. He had swum six lengths when he surfaced a few feet away from where they were standing. He paused and trod water before hauling himself out of the pool.

Chloe found herself having to smother a gasp. His body above his white trunks was bronzed and superbly fit, with not an ounce of spare flesh in sight.

She had to sit down for a minute to pull herself together. Her heart was thudding against her ribcage and her imagination was running wild!

They didn't make it to Cooden for lunch; instead they found a table in the corner of the cafeteria adjoining the swimming baths. Amberley chatted away nineteen to the dozen and kept bursting into splutters of laughter over the fun they had had playing ball in the water. Chloe and Laurie had settled for plaice and chips and Amberley chose fish fingers. She was trying to stop her uncle from sneaking some of her chips and a mock fight broke out, forks clashing like swords as they battled over the food.

For Chloe, it was gratifying to see the child so happy. It was amazing just how well Amberley had settled down with a complete stranger after having seen her mother taken away to hospital. She was still reflecting on how this strange state of affairs had come about when Laurie told her it was time to make a move.

Laurence delivered his papers, then drove them back to Eastbourne, where he took them to Treasure Island. Every piece of equipment one could imagine had been installed at this pleasure park situated on the seafront. Laurie lifted his niece on and off any ride that took her fancy while Chloe drank a cup of coffee and watched.

When they eventually pulled up outside Chloe's house that evening, Laurie lifted a sleepy little girl up into his arms and carried her into the house.

It had been a perfect day.

'Are you going to stay for one last coffee?' Chloe asked.

'Thank you, but I won't. You have to get Amberley ready for bed and I'm going to the hospital to spend a little time with Dorothy. I'll fetch Fergus before I go.'

It was well after eight o'clock by the time Chloe had bathed and fed Amberley and also seen that Fergus had been fed, watered and let out into the garden. Now she stood next to the bed and watched as Amberley slept with one arm resting on Fergus, who was lying by her side. Just before she crept out of the room, she felt an enormous sadness overwhelm her. Never had the thought crossed her mind that being responsible for this small child would evoke such painful memories.

Downstairs, she sank down on to her large sofa. It wasn't long before recriminations took over. Peter had been twelve years old and Matthew only nine when she had agreed that it would be best for them both to be sent to Australia, everything arranged and paid for by the Catholic Church. She herself had only been fourteen years old, left alone with no one to turn to.

Could she truthfully say that what she had agreed to had been in the best interests of her brothers?

At that point in time she would have readily said yes. So much had been on offer – a family life, a good education – and from the letters that had arrived so regularly for the first year, she felt that she had done the right thing. But then communication had slowed down and after four years her letters had been returned marked Address Unknown.

Just recently she had asked David Ferris if he would try and contact her brothers, because she intended to send each of them a large sum of money. His eventual reply had been devastating. Both young men were fit and well, but at this point in time they preferred not to enter into any further correspondence with their sister.

What choice did she have in this matter? she had asked David Ferris.

'None,' had been his soft reply.

Now Amberley had appeared on the scene and awoken her memories of having a family.

Seven days had passed and still Chloe was in charge of Mrs Whitlocke's small daughter. Laurence had turned out to be a law unto himself. He had come in for breakfast the first three mornings, and spent most of the day with Amberley and herself. On the morning of the fourth day she had taken a phone call in which he had gaily declared that his sister's condition had greatly improved and he was going to be busy making arrangements so would probably be away for the next two days. He would ring as soon as he got back to Ditchling.

Chloe had been flabbergasted when she'd heard the click of the receiver being replaced. Where the hell was he phoning from and why hadn't he given her the chance to speak? Later that day she had found the keys to Mrs Whitlocke's house lying on her own front doormat. As she bent to pick them up, she rolled her eyes and sighed. What the hell was this man playing at? She didn't even have a mobile number for him.

That had been Wednesday, three days ago. She linked hands with Amberley and took hold of the dog's lead, and together they set off for their walk. Amberley was talkative and happy, and when they reached the park she was off running, throwing the ball for Fergus to fetch. Chloe was racking her brains still trying to figure out just what Laurence Walmsley was up to. She hadn't got a clue as to what he did for a living, or where he lived when he was in this country. Most important of all, did he have a wife tucked away some-where? She finally came to the conclusion that he was using her.

The park was Amberley's favourite destination. It was Saturday morning and there were plenty of children in the playground and lots of other dogs being taken for walks. There was also a dear little café where Chloe could sit outside with a cup of tea and a slice of home-made fruit cake and still keep her eyes glued on Amberley. She was

160

making for the café, keeping Fergus on his lead, when her mobile rang.

'Hello?'

'Where are you? I'm parked outside your house and can't get in to Dorothy's. I left you the only set of keys.'

'We're in the park if you want to join us. If not, we shall be home in about half an hour.' Chloe knew she was being rude, but she suddenly didn't care. The man only seemed to think of himself.

Her good temper was restored as Amberley came running to her. 'Please, Chloe, may I have a drink? The water fountain is out of order.' Chloe looked down at that sweet up-turned face and wondered how anyone could go off and leave the little girl with strangers.

Aloud she said, 'You sit at one of the tables out here and hold on tightly to Fergus's lead. I'll go into the café and get us both a drink.'

She came back carrying a tray holding tea for one, a glass of milk and three packets of shortbread biscuits. Amberley looked at the biscuits, raised her eyes to Chloe and giggled. 'May I open one packet for Fergus?'

'Of course. We couldn't leave him out, he's been such a good boy. And he can have a drink from the bowl of water the café owners put down for the dogs.'

'Shall I take him over there now or wait until he's eaten his biscuits?'

'Drink your milk, darling. Fergus can have

his water later.'

Amberley had her glass raised to her lips when suddenly she spluttered, spilling some of the milk on to the table. 'Look, look over there, it's Uncle Laurie, he's come looking for us. Shall I run after him?'

'No, Amberley, you eat your biscuits and drink your milk. Your uncle will soon see us and come over.'

Laurence was walking around the children's play area searching for them. Finally he spotted them at the café.

'You look great, the pair of you,' he said ruffling the top of Amberley's head and quickly bending down to pat Fergus to stop him from barking.

'I do not look great,' Chloe said, blushing ever so slightly.

'Okay, you don't look great with your lovely hair all shoved up under that woolly hat, but it is still good to see you.'

'I can't believe that you walked off for three days without so much as a word or a phone call.'

'Amberley, would you like to go and play while I have a coffee, and then we can all go home together?' Laurie lifted his niece down from her chair.

Looking first at Chloe, who smiled and nodded her head, Amberley said, 'I shall only be over there where those girls are playing netball. Shall I leave Fergus here?'

'Yes, he'll be fine and I shall keep my eye on you,' Chloe assured the child.

The minute they were alone, Laurence dived straight in. 'You have every right to be upset. I can't believe I lost touch. Trying to do my best for my sister. I suppose life just got in the way.'

'I think you've got a blasted cheek. I know I offered to care for your niece for two or three days, and that was fine. But to just drop off the face of the earth! I had no means of contacting you whatsoever. What kept you? Was it work, or maybe a wife and children?'

Laurie smirked. 'I can assure you I am not the settling-down type, or as my mother would say, I just haven't met anyone I've wanted to commit to.'

'So how old are you now. Thirty-three? Thirty-four?'

'Thanks for the compliment. I'm thirty-eight.'

Chloe shrugged.

'So.' Laurie studied her face for a minute, 'have you ever been married?'

'No, and before you put the question, nobody ever asked me. I am a good business-woman and I have ample funds to finance any type of lifestyle I choose. But that's enough about me. What type of work do you do? Are you hugely successful at something? A multimillionaire with gorgeous fashion models hanging off your arm?'

Laurie laughed. 'Hardly. Well, I have had a few glamorous models declare that they were in love with me, and I am relatively good at what I do, when I do it–'

He was interrupted by Fergus barking loudly. Both adults turned to look towards where Amberley had been playing, and like a shot Laurie was on his feet and running across the grass. She had fallen over.

Laurie picked her up and cradled her in his arms. She had badly grazed her knee and had a long dirty smear down her cheek. 'Come on, sweetheart, time for us all to go home. Say goodbye to your playmates.' Amberley sniffed away her tears, waved her hand and snuggled into her uncle's chest.

Chloe was ready and waiting, a pack of wet wipes taken from her handbag. As Laurie sat down with Amberley on his knees, Chloe knelt in front to administer first aid. When a big white clean handkerchief had been tied around Amberley's leg, Laurie stood up, still keeping the little girl in his arms, Chloe took hold of Fergus's lead and the little procession moved off to where Laurie had parked his car.

Back at Chloe's house, first priority was to settle Amberley on the big settee, and of course Fergus decided to stretch himself along the foot of it. He might be small but he certainly acted as a good guard dog for Amberley. Chloe fetched a soapy flannel and a bowl of warm water and soon had the wound on Amberley's knee nicely cleaned up.

'Try and have a little sleep, pet. I'm going to make some lunch for all of us. I'll wake you up when it's ready,' she murmured as she tucked a duvet around the tearful little girl.

'So, we have established that you are relatively good at what you do when you can be persuaded to do it.' Chloe threw the ball into Laurence's court as she took the remains of a cooked joint of ham out from her fridge.

'And you have never been married because nobody has ever asked you,' he said, grinning widely.

'Are you going to tell me what you do, or at least why you just cleared off for days on end without so much as a phone call?'

'First will you let me apologise? I had no right to disappear and leave my niece with you.'

'Never mind the apology, too late for that, let's hear the reason.'

Why was it that this guy always managed to rub her up the wrong way? Chloe felt she would dearly love to wipe that grin off his handsome face.

'My absence was mainly down to me trying to do my best for my sister. The doctors at the hospital are saying that Dorothy should be taken to a care home until she is fit enough to fend for herself. Where would that leave Amberley? Our mother lives in north Devon, on her own since our father died some years ago. Her house is beautiful, with lovely grounds, and she is financially very secure. She is sixty-five years old, though she doesn't look it, and leads an active life from a wheelchair due to a car accident many years ago. She has plenty of paid help and wants for nothing, but cannot travel as much as she would wish. However she has impressed on me that nothing would give her greater pleasure than to have her daughter and granddaughter come and stay with her. The delay that has kept me away was largely down to arranging transport. I have found a private company that will take Dorothy to Devon by private ambulance, but the arrangement cannot include Amberley. So...' Laurie paused as Chloe digested what he had told her.

'Obviously I shall drive down to Devon, see my sister is comfortably installed and that my mother is truly happy about having her there; the question is, what am I going to do about Amberley?

Chloe was busy chopping salad but those last few words set alarm bells ringing in her head and quickly she pressed her lips together.

Laurence was disappointed. He had firmly believed that Chloe would offer her assistance straight away. He tried again.

'I can hardly be expected to drive all the

way to Devon with a three-year-old strapped into the back of the car.'

'Amberley is almost four years old,' was Chloe's only response.

'Three, four, what difference does it make? She'll need to use the toilet at some time, it is quite a long way.'

Chloe would not be drawn. Instead she returned to their original conversation.

'Why did you suddenly change the subject? I thought you were about to enlighten me as to what this very special job of yours entails. The one that you apparently do only when it suits you.'

Laurence gave a small grin, then changed it to a sigh before saying, 'I am a commodities broker.'

'That could cover a good many acres of ground,' she challenged, knowing she was being contrary.

'A broker is a person employed to buy commodities, articles of trade, and sell them to others. In lay terms I am a go-between. A negotiator or intermediary. In the short term I get paid commission for transacting business for others. Some would simply regard me as a stockbroker. I love the life because it takes me to so many parts of the world.'

'Wow!' Chloe raised her eyebrows. 'You really are a dark horse.'

'Oh don't you start.' He laughed.

'Well, doesn't it mean that you have opted

out of real life?'

'Depends on what your view of real life is. If you mean I haven't settled down with a wife and three kids, a large mortgage and a monthly saving plan for a pension, then you're dead right.'

Chloe remained silent.

Laurie laughed. 'I'm living a life that makes me happy; wouldn't you say that's the most important thing of all? I can honestly say I love doing what I do and I enjoy my life. How many people do you know who can say that?' When he got no reply, he grinned again and asked, 'Can you?'

'Can anyone?' Chloe tried to shrug it off. 'As a concept it's great, but honestly, I think most of the time I'm just getting on with life. Sure, at times I'm happy, but happy all of the time? I think that is unrealistic.'

Laurie nodded his head. 'That's the point. While I can't say I'm happy all the time, I can say I'm happy most of the time. I wake up in the morning and I love my life. I enjoy all of it and I get to see the world. That's why I do it. If I wake up one morning and decide that now's the time to settle down, I'll find myself the right woman, buy a house, have children and do everything else that comes with that life. But right now my job not only keeps me happy, it pays very well, and that makes me feel good.'

Chloe shook her head with a resigned

smile. 'If it works for you, that's great, lucky old you,' she said, thinking at the same time that this guy was way too sure of himself. For all that, she had to admit he was devastatingly handsome, and life with him could be very exciting. She shook her head in amazement at her thoughts, yet couldn't help remembering all the gorgeous glamorous clothes she had worn when Roger had taken her on business trips. And where were all those beautiful clothes now? Packed away, out of sight. Oh why had Roger had to die? It wasn't fair. But then who the hell ever said life was going to be fair?

'I have to finish getting our meal ready,' she said.

'I'll help you, but tonight, after Amberley is in bed, you can tell me how you come to own this house plus an apartment in Brighton Marina, and apparently have unlimited funds, without doing a full-time job.'

Chloe shook her head with a resigned smile. 'Tit for tat. You have done your homework.' She threw him a pair of oven gloves. 'I put some jacket potatoes in the microwave to soften; would you take them out and put them in the oven, please. It will be hot enough by now to nicely crisp them up and they'll go well with cold chicken and salad. All I have to do is chop up this fresh fruit, and we can have that for sweet with some ice cream.'

Chloe knew she was talking to keep Laurie from asking questions. However, she was aware that when the time came, she would have to tell him the truth. When he finally learnt that her monetary situation and life-style were down to the alliance she had made with Roger, would he still want her to travel to Devon with him and meet his mother?

Did she care one way or the other?

At this point in time she was not going to even try to answer that question.

Their evening meal was eaten, the dishes were washed and the kitchen was tidy. Amberley was in bed, Laurie had taken Fergus for a walk, and the little dog was now happily settled at the foot of Amberley's bed.

Chloe wandered around her lounge, switching side lamps on, setting out two glasses and a bottle of white wine. God, how she wished she could get out of this. Repeatedly she had tried to convince herself that her previous life had nothing whatsoever to do with Laurence bloody Walmsley, or any other living person come to that.

She forced herself to sit down and look at this stranger, and suddenly it came to her that she had no man in her life. But this was no ordinary man; if she were truthful, she thought he was drop-dead gorgeous. Tension built up within her as their eyes met and held. Her breathing quickened. She had to force herself to look away. This shouldn't be happening; she knew nothing about this guy, except that he was well dressed, stood about six foot two inches, and had a good head of hair and what looked like a permanent tan. According to him, he had a fantastic job that took him to all corners of the world, but only if and when he chose to take on a particular contract.

It all sounded far too good to be true.

Now he was waiting for some answers to his questions. If she told about the agreement between herself and Roger, wouldn't this man be in a position to say exactly the same thing about her?

'Shall I open the wine and pour us each a glass?' Laurence asked, getting up from his chair.

'Yes please, and I have done a cheese tray, it's there on the sideboard. Please help yourself.'

Having handed a glass to Chloe, Laurie sipped his own drink and walked to the sideboard. 'Hmm, Stilton. You certainly know how to please a man.' He grinned.

For a moment Chloe's temper rose. How dare he act so presumptuous? However, she felt it gave her a starting point.

'I take it you are aware that I worked as PA to Roger McKinnon at Associated Securities because I had worked hard and had all the necessary qualifications. It didn't take

171

Roger long to appreciate my worth. Later, he put a proposition to me.'

Chloe paused, took a deep breath, and then a few sips from her glass of wine. One glance at Laurence's face told her nothing except that he would make a good poker player. And so she continued.

'Roger became a dear friend, generous to a fault. He chose the Marina apartment, bought it and presented me with the deeds. He also increased my monthly salary and became lavish with my expense account. I accompanied him on every business trip. Roger was very proud of me. Always made sure that I knew he felt honoured to be seen with me, and that alone meant a great deal to me. I would be the first to admit that our arrangement changed my whole lifestyle from one extreme to the other, but for now I think I've told you more than enough and I am going to leave it there.'

'Thank you, Chloe, I appreciate your frankness, but I am aware that you have only told me half the story. The rest can wait,' he told her, rising and picking up the bottle. 'Refill?' he asked, holding it over her glass.

'Yes please, and as we are being so frank, why don't you tell me your plans for taking Amberley to Devon?'

Laurie had the grace to look ashamed. 'I will admit I was counting on your support, but I am aware I have taken advantage of your good nature too much already.'

'Well at least you have admitted that fact, so carry on and tell me what you have in mind.'

'I was thinking that if I could persuade you to travel down to Devon with us, you could turn it into a short holiday. I know my sister and my mother would be pleased to meet you; it would give them both the opportunity to thank you for caring for Amberley. If you should decide you don't want to stay with us, there are plenty of good hotels nearby, and I will bring you back home whenever you decide you have had enough. It goes without saying that you being in the car to see to Amberley will make the journey that much easier for me.'

'Why the hell couldn't you have said all that in the first place?'

He gave her a sheepish grin.

'Hmmm, I like the sound of that plan, plus the fact that I have never been to Devon. Long journey, though. So maybe it *would* be a good thing to have someone else in the car to help with Amberley.'

'There's no maybe about it, and if you're telling me that you will come along with us, then I once more have to say how grateful I am to you.'

'You're more than welcome. If you tell me when you are thinking of setting off, I shall go along to your sister's house and pack some clothes for Amberley.'

Laurie grinned. 'And better bring a basket for Fergus; we can put it in the back of the car.'

'That's a good idea,' Chloe told him. She herself would fish out some of the beautiful underwear she owned and take it with her. Maybe some of the naughty pieces that Roger had thought were great.

That might be a very good idea indeed.

'Well I am away to my bed,' Chloe told him when they had finished the bottle of wine.

'You'd better come to the door with me and shoot the bolts after I've gone,' Laurie told her sensibly.

There was an uneasy moment, before the force of mutual attraction pulled them together into a tight hug.

It was their first serious physical contact. Chloe hadn't planned a hug; now she was far too busy attempting to calm her nerves to worry whether he was going to kiss her. Her arms automatically wound themselves around his back; his were around her as they held each other close and he rested his head on top of hers.

After what felt like ages, he pulled away to lean down and plant a kiss on her cheek, all the while grinning like a schoolboy.

Chloe was shaking. She hadn't realised the effect it would have on her to be in such close proximity to him. Her head was spinning and her heart was hammering away nineteen to the dozen.

She hadn't realised until this moment how much she had missed this.

Real affection. That was what was absent from her life.

Laurie was the first to step away, and as he opened the front door, he turned and grinned down at her. 'I'll see you first thing in the morning. Don't forget to lock up.'

Later, Chloe lay in bed, smiling. True, she might not know what the future would hold, but right now, for the first time in many months, she felt genuinely happy.

## Chapter 14

Chloe was not the only one reflecting on the past week. Laurence was in bed in his sister's house, but there was far too much going on in his mind for him to think about sleeping.

Chloe Collard was turning out to be a big surprise. He was beginning to see beyond the quiet, competent, self-contained facade that she chose to display to strangers.

He knew much more about her than he had let on. Stephen Goddard, one of the directors at Associated Securities, was a close friend of Laurence's, and had filled him in on Chloe's early life, as well as her relationship with Roger McKinnon and the tragic circumstances of his death.

Laurence was glad that they had sorted out the travel arrangements. He got out of bed and went to stand at the window. He didn't need to pull the curtains open to know that the rain was coming down in torrents. If the weather kept up like this, God knows what they would do when they got to Devon. For his mother and sister's sake, he felt he should stay at least a couple of weeks, but Chloe might want to leave earlier than that.

He admitted to himself that he was drawn to Chloe. He generally preferred a more sophisticated type of woman, but over these past few days, he had come to the conclusion that there was no predicting sexual chemistry. When all was said and done, Chloe was a looker: slim, a gorgeous body, with all the right bits in the right places, and that hair of hers! Several times he had imagined waking up to see that silky mass of red hair spread out over the pillow next to his own. It cost nothing to dream!

And she was attracted to him, he was sure of that. He'd seen it in those big green eyes of hers, felt it in the way her body had softened and melted when he had held her in his arms tonight.

'Ah well,' he sighed, 'life is for living. We'll just have to see what happens when we get to Devon.'

Chloe woke up smiling, and when Amberley climbed into bed with her for a snuggle, she stroked the little girl's face and gazed into her big blue eyes. At that moment, she felt it was no bad thing she had done in offering to care for the child. Who couldn't feel love for such a sweet little thing? She had certainly worked her way into Chloe's heart.

'This won't do, young lady, we have to wash and dress ourselves very quickly this morning because your Uncle Laurie will be here soon and we are all going to Devon.'

'Yes, and Mummy will be there, and Grandma will be pleased to see us all. You'll like Grandma, she gets about ever so quickly in her wheelchair.'

The first half of the journey passed with a lot of laughter and singing of songs, mainly instigated by Amberley. They had travelled a good distance when Laurie decided to stop at a motorway service station. Amberley needed to go to the toilet and it would be a good chance to have some refreshments. Fergus was given a quick walk on the grass verge first.

Once they were fed and watered, Chloe could see that Amberley was tired. So far she had been riding in the back of the car with the little girl; now she swiftly cleared the back seat, found a soft cushion to put behind the child's head and tenderly covered her with the car rug.

'There we are, sweetheart, you stretch out and have a nice doze, and when you wake up we should be at your grandma's.'

'Chloe, where are you going to sit?' Amberley raised her head and cried out as Chloe got out of the back of the car.

'It's all right darling, I'm getting into the front seat beside Uncle Laurie.' She put her head round the back of the seat so that Amberley could get a glimpse of her before they set off again.

Amberley must have been reassured, because when Chloe looked again, the little girl was a picture of loveliness, her eyes closed, her long silky blonde hair spread out over the cushion.

The emotion that seized Chloe at that moment was unbearable. She had always thought she didn't mind not being married, because she didn't want to have children anyway. Roger had felt he was too old to be a father, and so she had religiously taken the pill. Yet while she told herself that she was still of the same mind, something stirred deep within her heart and she remained very quiet for the rest of the journey.

Some time had passed since the road signs had told them they were now in Devon. Laurie slowed his speed as he approached the village of Parracombe and drove up an extremely steep hill. Chloe felt they must be nearing their destination. They were now in real countryside, passing a school surrounded by low stone walls and a very old church around which lay a cemetery with a great many old headstones marking the graves.

About two miles beyond the village, Laurie turned the car into a wide lane and brought his speed down to ten miles per hour. Ten minutes later, he stopped the car and switched off the engine.

'Every time I return home, the sight of this place brings a lump to my throat and I thank my great-great-grandfather who had the sense to buy this property many, many years ago.' Laurence's voice as he said these words was full of pride.

Chloe was having a job to catch her breath. The house, the setting in which it stood, surrounded by what looked like parkland, was amazingly beautiful. It was obviously very old, and she thought it looked like a castle or a stately home.

Laurie switched the engine back on and drove through the open gates and up the very long drive.

Scarcely had he brought the car to a halt and opened the rear door than Amberley and Fergus were out of the vehicle and running towards the stone steps leading to the massive front door that by now was standing wide open.

An elegantly dressed lady was seated in a wheelchair holding her arms outstretched. Her white hair was set in waves that framed her lovely face, and her smile was wide and warm as she leaned forward and gathered her granddaughter up into her arms. 'Oh Amberley, I could eat you,' she murmured as she tenderly kissed the child.

'Grandma, we've brought Fergus to see you.'

Laurence had reached his mother by now. 'Fergus, sit and be quiet,' he ordered. Fergus knew when he was beaten.

'How are you, Mother,' Laurence asked softly as he placed his arm across her shoulders and kissed her on each cheek.

Chloe was standing way back watching this tender coming together of dearly loved family relatives. Laurence turned, held out a hand and drew her forward

'Chloe, this is Odette, my mother.' He paused for just a second. 'Mother, this is Chloe Collard who has made herself responsible for Amberley from the day Dorothy was taken into hospital.'

Mrs Walmsley held out her hand and, still smiling warmly, said, 'I am so pleased you have agreed to visit us, we owe you such a great deal. My daughter arrived quite early this morning and the ambulance men saw her safely settled into her own bedroom.' Turning her chair a little, she looked at a gentleman who had been hovering nearby. 'This is my nearest neighbour, Charles Bradford. You will meet his wife Anne later on; she is coming over to join us for dinner this evening.'

Charles held out his hand and Chloe smiled as she shook it. This man had a warmth about him that was very appealing.

Introductions over and their luggage fetched out of the car, Laurie was about to take Chloe to her room when Charles spoke. 'Laurie, you go with your mother. There's a good fire burning in the lounge. I'll see Miss Collard to her room and then I'll bring tea for all of you.'

He picked up Chloe's bags and led her upstairs to a really lovely guest bedroom decorated mainly in white with touches of pale blue, and with views over the vast grounds beyond.

'I think everything has been laid out for you, but if there is anything missing, just say.'

Charles was about to leave the room when Chloe called out, 'Mr Bradford, would you mind if I ask you a few questions?'

He looked startled, and thought for a moment before answering. 'Depends. Ask away, but I can't promise I'll be able to answer.'

'Laurence has suggested I stay here, but if it doesn't work out I should maybe book into a hotel. I don't want to add to the burden. What do you think?'

Charles smiled. 'This house runs on very well-oiled wheels, believe me. A carer comes in every day, helps Odette to shower and dress, and as well as that, she has a daily cleaner, a capable woman twice a week to do the laundering and ironing, and two men to take care of the grounds. Oh, and I almost forgot, a cook comes three days a week, Mrs Walker, a very obliging woman who will always come in for special occasions like tonight. Truly, Chloe, take it slowly, form your own judgements and I am sure you will enjoy your stay here in Parracombe.'

Charles had gone from the room when suddenly he popped his head around the door again. 'I forgot to say I'm the chauffeur, both for my wife and for Odette. The pair of them do a lot of good work for the church and its congregation. I also forgot to ask permission to call you Chloe.'

He was gone again in a flash, but not before Chloe was sure he had winked at her. She was laughing to herself as she unpacked her cases. Suddenly she wasn't sorry that she had come on this holiday.

Not sorry at all.

Five days had flown by since Chloe had ar-

182

rived to stay with Laurie's mother, and she was having a fabulous time.

Meeting Dorothy had been quite an experience. With all the problems that Laurie had outlined regarding his sister, Chloe had been expecting a downtrodden woman who had been dragged through a messy divorce. Dorothy Whitlocke might have been distressed by her husband's disgusting behaviour, but oppressed she certainly was not. She had found the courage to divorce her husband, and even though she had never met Chloe before, she had been very open about the fact that her legal advisers had done extremely well for her, 'taking high-and-mighty Mr Whitlocke to the cleaners', as she put it.

Chloe had sealed the budding friendship by telling Dorothy how much she had enjoyed taking care of Amberley. 'She is a beautiful little girl, so well-mannered and very intelligent, and I do hope that when you are fully recovered and return to your own home, you will allow me to continue to see her sometimes.'

Dorothy had been quick with her answer. 'I think I might have trouble keeping her away from your house.' She had paused before adding, 'I'm hoping that you and I will do more than just pass the time of day when we meet.'

'Then we are both of the same mind. When you are well enough to come downstairs, we shall have a drink, and our first toast will be to friendship.' Chloe's reply had been sincere.

Chloe was being pampered, spoilt and extremely well fed. She was also having a lot of male company, which was awfully good for her ego. Odette Walmsley might be confined to a wheelchair, but by God she enjoyed life. Yesterday afternoon they had all gone to a tea dance in the village. Odette had played the piano for a sing-song while the band had taken a break, and Chloe hadn't lacked for a partner all afternoon. She had had two dances straight off with Laurie, and the feel of his body as he held her close had set her blood racing and her imagination running riot.

True, more than half the folk present were old enough to be drawing their pension, but they were up and on the dance floor just as much as the younger people. What struck Chloe was that nobody was left out of the activity. No one was left sitting alone.

The afternoon had set Chloe thinking; in fact it had totally altered her outlook on a good many things to do with her own life.

The people at the tea dance were good, kind, caring folk who had had full lives but now were living mostly on memories. They had money and beautiful homes; what they did not still have was their youth.

Chloe told herself she was too young to settle for a life such as this. She had realised that if she were to remain living in her big, comfortable house in Ditchling, she would be setting herself up for a very dull, lonely future.

There was a whole big world out there, and in the short time she had had with Roger, he had opened up new horizons. What was she waiting for? She had the means to travel in comfort; now all she had to do was to stop feeling sorry for herself and start to be a whole lot more courageous.

It was fine for Laurence. When his duty to his mother and sister had been fulfilled, he would be off again, seeing the world. Money was no obstacle and he had openly admitted that women of all ages threw themselves at him.

Yes, Laurence Walmsley certainly had the best of both worlds.

All the while these confusing thoughts had been running through her head, Chloe had been standing staring out of the lounge window, unaware that there was anybody else in this part of the house.

She shivered as a wave of familiar loneliness came over her.

It was then that she felt his strong arms wrap around her from behind, and she was pulled backwards to rest against the length of his body. She let herself slump against him before saying, 'I thought you had gone out. You said you had some business to attend to.'

His closeness was sending her blood pounding and she wriggled round to face him. Tension built up as their eyes met. This was the only time they had been alone since they had arrived in Devon.

She forced herself to look away.

Despite the resolution she had just made to herself, she didn't want this. Not now. Not in this house, not with Laurence.

Eventually he released his hold on her and stepped away before saying, 'Chloe, tomorrow morning I am going to Barnstaple on business. It is only a few miles away but I will need to stay there at least one night and maybe two. Would you like to come with me?'

He could see that Chloe was contemplating just what this offer would entail, and so he added, 'We could return here when I've finalised all the details of what I have to do, or we could say our goodbyes before we leave tomorrow morning and go straight home from Barnstaple. The choice is yours.'

This ... this proposition. Wasn't it a heaven-sent gift? Hadn't she just made a promise to herself to start living again? To visit new pastures, whether they be dangerous or not? If only she could be sure that there were no hidden complications in his offer.

She closed her eyes, counted to ten, then slowly opened them again and said, 'I would very much like to come to Barnstaple with you. I feel I have probably imposed on your

186

mother's hospitality long enough. If it fits in well with your business arrangements, I think it would be a good idea for us to travel home from there.'

In two strides Laurie was beside her again, cradling her face between both his hands and kissing her with incredible gentleness. It seemed ages before he released her, and as his eyes looked into her own, they were overflowing with emotion. 'Until tomorrow, then,' he whispered.

At dinner that night it was just the four of them, Odette, Dorothy, Laurence and Chloe. They ate a little later than usual because Chloe had been allowed to bath Amberley, then she'd read her a story and said goodbye to her and Fergus. Of course she had to give firm promises that when Dorothy was well and truly fit and she and Amberley returned to their home in Ditchling, they would all be seeing a lot more of each other. She had also agreed that she would take both Amberley and Fergus to the park some Saturday mornings.

Dorothy was the first to go upstairs, then Laurie left saying that he was going to put some petrol in the car ready for their journey in the morning. Chloe found herself alone with Odette. After a somewhat strained silence the older woman spoke.

'Chloe, be careful.' Her voice was soft.

Chloe's cheeks flushed bright red.

'Careful? In what way?' she asked quietly.

'You are a very lovely young lady and we owe you a great deal for what you have done for my granddaughter. I mean with Laurence.'

Chloe attempted a laugh. 'Odette, there is nothing going on between Laurence and myself. It is simply that circumstances have thrown us together.'

'Dear Chloe. Please, I am not aiming to judge, and if I am wrong then I do apologise.' Odette took a deep breath. 'Just don't assume that Laurence will ever settle down with you.'

Chloe was mortified. Rendered speechless. Wishing she had stuck to her guns and never come to Devon. There was a long silence as she drank from her glass of wine and Odette sipped at her Horlicks.

'What if...' Chloe began, standing up and setting her glass down quietly on the table, 'what if Laurence were ever to really fall in love?'

She didn't receive an answer; hadn't expected one. When she reached the door, she said as calmly as she could, 'Good night, Odette, thank you for having me to stay in your lovely home.'

# Chapter 15

There had been quite a party of Odette's friends there to see them off, for which Chloe had been grateful. Otherwise their leaving might have been a bit frosty. Dorothy, together with Amberley and Fergus, had walked with them to the car, and Chloe had to renew her promises to Amberley before she was allowed to kiss her.

Laurence couldn't have driven more than a couple of miles when he pulled the car into a lane and parked beneath a huge leafy tree. Their feelings didn't have to be hidden any more. Now they were able to touch each other, kiss each other properly, no holds barred. Chloe couldn't stop smiling as she took Laurie's face in her hands and began to plant soft kisses all over it, on his forehead, his cheeks, even his nose.

Laurie was loving every minute of it. Over the years he had got himself involved with many women, but they had always been of the same mind as himself. No small talk and no promises, and when it was time to part, they were as eager to be gone as he was. Never once had marriage come into the picture. Single and fancy-free had been his status, and he wasn't aiming to alter that.

Yet here he was with Chloe. She was definitely different. She had him dreaming fantasies, though he was fully aware that the reality rarely measured up.

He threw caution to the wind and covered her mouth with his. Her lips parted to receive him, and their tongues met. She tasted so good. He tried to hold back; he would force himself to, because they were headed for a hotel where he had already booked a double room, and Chloe deserved better than a romp in the back seat of a car.

'Darling, straighten your clothing. I have booked us a room at the hotel, and the drive will give you time to contemplate how you feel about that before we arrive.' He turned the key in the ignition.

Chloe pulled herself together. Had she ever been kissed like that before? The meeting of tongues had vibrated through her whole body. She had been thrilled by Laurie's tender whispered words as much as by that single dazzling kiss. She needed him.

How the tables had been turned on her. She had thought to play hard to get, to tease him, but to keep it light and simple. Now she was thrilled to learn that he had booked just one bedroom for their stay in Barnstaple.

He had still barely touched her, and yet she knew their lovemaking was not going to be on her terms; she was not the one in control.

Laurie took his eyes from the road and smiled at her, and at that moment she was lost. She didn't care what he did to her.

It was still very early in the day when they arrived at the Imperial Hotel. Chloe held Laurie's briefcase and his laptop while he signed the register. A smartly dressed young man came from behind the desk, picked up their bags and took them up in the lift to the second floor, where they were shown to a very large double bedroom.

Laurie slipped him a note; the young man thanked him and said, 'Being Friday, the town is very busy and our restaurant too will be crowded. Shall I book you in for lunch?'

'No thank you, a tray of sandwiches and a pot of coffee will do for now, but we shall be dining here this evening.'

'I'll have a selection sent up right away and reserve you a table for this evening.' He nodded his head at Chloe. 'Enjoy your stay with us, madam, and you, sir,' he murmured as he laid the room key down on top of a chest of drawers.

When he had gone, silence hung heavily for a moment before Laurie took hold of Chloe's hand and brought it to his lips. 'It feels as if I have spent my whole life searching for you.'

Chloe reached up to undo his tie and the top button of his shirt, then said, 'You have just ordered a light lunch and a pot of coffee, which will be here at any moment. I suggest

191

that we take out the clothes we are going to need from our suitcases and hang them up in the wardrobe while we're waiting.'

'My God, the woman will try anything to dampen my passion,' remarked Laurie, trying not to smile.

Chloe hung up her long emerald-green evening dress to wear to dinner, put her saucy underwear and night attire into a drawer, and had just sat down to take her high-heeled court shoes off when there was a tap on the door.

Laurie opened it to admit a middle-aged woman in a black dress and crisp white bibbed apron.

Chloe quickly removed a vase of flowers from the coffee table and the waitress laid the tray down. 'Thank you, madam – oh, and thank you, sir,' she added as Laurie slipped her some money.

The sandwiches were very attractively set out, garnished with salad and crisps. Chloe was pouring the coffee when Laurie said, 'Good idea for us to eat first.'

She was tempted to ask why, but merely grinned to herself and poured Devonshire cream into her cup.

When she had finished eating, Chloe went into the bathroom and washed her hands. Coming back into the bedroom, she stripped her clothes off and stood before Laurie in her flimsy panties and see-through lacy bra.

He came to her and stroked her cheek, then ran both hands down her back and over her bottom as he drew her to him before sweeping her up into his arms and carrying her over to the big double bed.

He had barely touched her and already her whole body was tingling.

'Are you cold?' he asked when he saw her tremble.

'No.'

He smiled and nudged the straps of her bra down from her shoulders. 'Very naughty,' he murmured, skimming his hands over the fine lacy cups and then on round to the back, where he easily unhooked the fastener. He gasped as he flung the bra aside and stared at her taut, firm breasts, her nipples already erect and hard. No man could have resisted such a sight. His lips closed over her right breast and he drew on the nipple as if he were a starving child, nipping the point with his teeth before letting go and starting work on the left.

Her heart was hammering. She was lying beneath him naked, wanting him, needing him. She could feel his longing, his hardness. She arched against him and shuddered.

Sheer pleasure, he was telling himself. This was not just fulfilment of a need. If he weren't careful, he would find himself telling Chloe that he loved her. He wanted to please her, leave her with a sensation the like of which she had never known. His slow, skilled hands moved over every part of her body.

When at last he stretched her legs even wider apart and placed his hands beneath her buttocks to raise her up before he slipped into her, she arched her back still further and rose to take all of him, and they moaned together.

'Chloe, oh Chloe my darling, you are unique,' he whispered later, as he let his body slump down into her outstretched arms.

Completely satisfied, they lay entwined until Laurie said, 'Come on, sleepy-head, let's take a shower, then I will run you into Woolacombe, which is a most beautiful place right on the coast. There is also a decent café where you can sit and wonder at the beauty of north Devon, because I have to leave you for a while.'

'Must you?'

'Yes, I did tell you that I have some business to deal with.'

It wasn't far to Woolacombe, and Laurie was soon opening the car door for her and telling her that he was pushed for time. At that moment his mobile rang and he stepped a good few paces away from her before attempting to answer it.

After a while he suddenly shouted, 'I have to go.' He waved a hand and climbed back into the car, calling, 'Back as soon as I can.'

The engine started up and Chloe watched him drive away.

She was utterly dumbfounded. How dare he leave her stranded like this? She looked around to get her bearings. True, it was a beautiful place – soft green hills rolling down to the most fabulous sandy beach she had ever seen, small waves gently lapping the shore – but what the hell was she supposed to do with herself?

She could see a restaurant and a few shops but the place wasn't exactly what she would call busy. At that moment a black car with TAXI and a telephone number printed on its side drew into the car park and the driver got out.

Without any hesitation, Chloe hurried towards him. 'Please, are you for hire? I need to go to Barnstaple.'

'Well, me beauty, I was about to be off for me lunch break, but no matter, that'll still be 'ere when I gets back.' He had that lovely Devonshire accent and was smiling as he held the car door open for her. 'Sit you up in front with me, midear. 'Tis nice to 'ave company.'

Chloe had been in a blazing temper as she watched Laurie shoot off, but having been spoken to so nicely by this Devonian, she was beginning to calm down.

'Where would 'ee like me to drop you off?'

he asked, grinning broadly.

Her knowledge of Barnstaple was vague, but she thought there must be shops.

'Anywhere that sells good clothes – oh, and shoes,' she said.

He gave her the name of a store and she smiled her thanks. Once there, he got out of the cab and helped her on to the crowded pavement. He touched his cap and grinned when she paid him; she had added a very large tip to the fare.

She went up the steps, under the shade of the deep awning, and in through the doorway. Her temper was rising again. What the bloody hell was she doing here? What on earth did that man think he was playing at? Again!

Last week he'd cleared off leaving his niece for her to take care of. At least then she had been in her own home. Today he'd left her stranded in an unfamiliar town in the middle of nowhere.

Chloe shook herself and took a few deep breaths. Then, telling herself that this department store was not very different from John Lewis or Harrods, she looked around, got her bearings and made for the dress department. It was a long time since she had spent any real money, she thought, reminding herself of her intention to get out and start living again.

She couldn't think where she should start, and was standing dithering in the middle of the floor when she was rescued by a friendly sales person of about her own age, very smartly dressed in a silver-grey suit with a charcoal-coloured shirt. 'Would you like some help?' she asked.

'I really don't know what I'm looking for. I just felt like going on a shopping spree,' Chloe told her as she shrugged her shoulders.

The assistant laughed. 'What were you thinking of buying?' she asked.

Anything that would make me feel I hadn't been used, Chloe almost said. She was still smarting from the fact that Laurie had found time to have sex with her and then had abandoned her without so much as a goodbye.

She pulled herself together and tried to think. Finally she smiled and said, 'Long evening dresses, a suit perhaps – oh, and a pair of black slacks, and of course shirts that will go with them.'

'Right, let's get started.' The sales assistant was more than happy.

Garments were scooped from racks; some Chloe approved of, others she rejected. Most were piled on to the sales girl's arm. 'You must try them on,' she urged.

Curtained cubicles were bypassed and Chloe was taken into a private dressing room with full-length mirrors on two walls, carpet on the floor and two gilt armchairs. She removed her jacket, then stripped off her shirt and slacks. She tried the evening dresses first; three in all were admired, considered and then removed. One was a glowing red with a chiffon overlay, which clashed with her auburn hair. The second was a vivid multi-coloured number, not at all her choice. Finally the stark simplicity of slinky black, with silver threads framing the deep neckline. It was a perfect fit.

As well as the black dress, she bought two pairs of slacks, one white and one black, and a black suit that the sales girl told her was perfection personified. For once Chloe knew it was not just sales talk. It was a suit to die for, and it would be good for her image, especially when she was called upon to accompany Stephen Goddard or one of the other directors on a business trip. She wasn't taken with any of the blouses or shirts; they could wait until another day.

By now her bad temper had gone and she had the bit between her teeth. New clothes necessitated new accessories.

'Do you only work on this floor, or are you allowed to stay with me?' she asked her delighted helper.

'If I notify my floor manager that you have requested me to accompany you...' She paused. 'Which department have you in mind?'

'Shoe department, please.'

'I will just speak to my manager. Would

you like a glass of wine or a coffee before we carry on?'

'A glass of white wine would be very nice, if you are able to join me.'

A uniformed young lad came to carry away the articles that Chloe intended to purchase. They would be packed ready for her when she had finished shopping. Meanwhile the two young women sat back in the private dressing room and enjoyed a glass of chilled wine.

Afterwards they made their way to the shoe department, where Chloe bought brightly coloured sandals and two pairs of evening shoes with wicked four-inch heels, one pair with gold buckles and the other with silver straps, to wear with the black dress. Moving on, she bought two cashmere scarves, and two wide leather belts, each of which had an enormous fancy buckle. She loved wearing a wide belt; it served to emphasise her very small waist.

Back on the ground floor, the cosmetic counters filling the air with delightful scents, she bought perfume – Chanel No. 5 – eyeshadow and mascara, and three different shades of nail varnish. Finished at last, she thanked her assistant while the store manager hovered nearby, waiting to dance further attendance on her.

'Are you staying locally?' he enquired politely.

'Yes, I am, at the Imperial Hotel. May I ask you to call me a taxi, please.'

'I will most certainly do that for you, madam, but there is no need for you to wait whilst your goods are being packed. We shall send everything round to the hotel. Your packages will be there almost as soon as you are.'

She had been back in the bedroom of the hotel for less than twenty minutes when there was a knock on the door. Her parcels, all packed neatly into one huge posh box, had arrived.

'Would you please bring it in and stand it against that wall,' Chloe asked, picking up her purse and removing some cash, which she gave to the delivery man.

Alone again, she realised two things. One was that she had a great deal of talking to do with Laurence. The other was that, although she had been in a raging temper when she had entered that department store, she now felt both stimulated and sleek. Yes, that's right, she told herself, there is no other word. Every item she had tried on had fitted her like a glove. I do have a good body and I have just had a great time. A lot of that had to do with the fact that she didn't have to think about the cost of anything. Money had not come into it.

For the first time in her life, she understood

the compulsion that drove women to shop. To buy and spend money and accumulate about them an excess of unnecessary material possessions. It seemed that shopping could provide consolation if one was unhappy, self-indulgence if one had been rejected. Extravagant and frivolous maybe, but better surely than self-pity, allowing one's temper to take hold, taking to the bottle or turning for comfort to casual lovers.

She found herself smiling. The black dress was fabulous and the suit was to die for. She must go shopping more often.

But – and it was a big but – that in no way excused Laurence for dumping her. She glanced again at her watch. It was a quarter to five and still there had been no word from him.

She had a shower and wrapped herself in the towelling robe the hotel provided. She'd longed to wash her hair, but it would never dry in time. It was getting dark outside. I don't care whether Laurence is back or not, I am going down to the dining room to have my dinner, she vowed to herself.

She sat at the dressing table and fixed her silver earrings in place, then opened her make-up case and slowly and carefully applied foundation. She touched up her eyebrows and eyelashes, chose a lipstick and painted her lips. Last but by no means least, she sprayed her hair with a tonic, then bent over from the waist and began to run a comb through it from the roots to the ends.

Perfume next; she wouldn't open today's buy, but took the stopper from the bottle she'd brought with her and touched it to the base of her neck and the inside of her wrists.

Laid out on the bed was the black dress and the shoes with the silver straps that she had bought today. It had been a last-minute decision to wear her new purchases, but whether or not Laurie was back by the time she was dressed she no longer cared. She was hungry, she was going down to dinner at seven thirty even if she had to go alone, and she was going to make sure that heads would turn as she made her entrance.

She dropped the towelling robe from her shoulders and let it fall to the floor, pulled on panties and a tiny front-fastening lacy bra, slid her feet into the high-heeled sandals and then, having taken a quick glance at the mirror, went to pick up the dress. She let the silky material slip over her head, settled the skirt and made sure that the long side-slit reached high enough to give a glimpse of the sheer black stockings she was wearing. Then she reached to the back for the zip.

Oh dear... She wriggled, trying to reach the zip first from one side and then the other... This was a real predicament.

The zip ran all the way up the back from the waist to the top of the dress, and it was utterly impossible for the person wearing it to manoeuvre it into position. A real quandary. The sales girl had zipped her in and out of the dress at the shop, and Chloe had not foreseen a problem. But this was clearly a garment that required the assistance of another person.

At that very moment, a loud rapping began on the door. Using both hands, she picked up the hem of the dress and walked across the room, the soft, silky material slipping off her shoulders.

Laurence could not believe the sight that met his eyes. He threw back his head and roared with laughter.

Chloe let go of the hem and the whole dress slithered slowly down to lie around her feet. She was left wearing nothing but flimsy panties, bra, and black stockings held up by support bands with a ring of embroidered red roses.

'I just can't believe my luck,' Laurie was declaring as he entered the room, kicking the door closed behind him.

If Chloe had had a knife to hand, she would have slashed out at him. Instead she stepped out of the dress, gathered it up and walked over to lay it on the bed.

'There is not a man on this earth that has ever come home to a welcome such as this. You look so damn tantalising, I could cheerfully forgo my dinner and stay here and make love to you all night,' he told her, still laughing uproariously.

'In your dreams, Laurence Walmsley. I am telling you now, if we aren't ready, both of us, to go to dinner within half an hour, I shall open that door and cry rape.'

'You wouldn't dare,' he protested, but her words had wiped the grin from his face.

'You drive off, leave me stranded with no transport, and I don't hear a word from you all day – and don't say that my phone isn't working, because I've had two texts from Holly. It's just a repeat of last week. I suppose this time I should be grateful that you haven't stayed away for three days.'

Her outburst had brought him to his senses.

'Okay, I owe you a thousand apologies, but now is not the time to go into the whys and wherefores. It won't take me long to shower and get dressed, and you are more than halfway there, but what's the matter with your dress?'

Chloe saw sense. She could wait and bide her time, she told herself. 'I need you to do the zip up … please,' she added quietly.

She slipped the dress back on and went to stand with her back to him, and he zipped her up with all the expertise of a man well used to the task. Then she turned to face him. She felt suddenly very self-conscious.

'Do you like it?'

'Fabulous, you look sensational altogether. By the look of the box and all the wrappings, you must have taken yourself on a shopping spree.'

'You didn't leave me with much choice. I had to do something to while away the time.'

'Truly, Chloe, my absence was unavoidable. When the time is right, I'll explain why it was so important for me to go off like that.'

She felt herself begin to soften, and when he said admiringly, 'You look a million dollars,' she was almost on the point of forgiving him.

'Okay, we'll call a truce for now, but will you please hurry up and get ready. I am very hungry.'

'You go on down and have a drink at the bar and I will be as quick as I can.'

She didn't answer; merely picked up her evening bag and left the room.

When she entered the bar, she knew she was causing a stir and she smiled as a waiter approached. 'Would you care to be shown to your table straight away?'

'Yes, I think I would, thank you,' she said.

The dining room was a delight and went a long way to smoothing Chloe's ruffled feathers. The attention from the waiter who seated her also helped her to remain calm.

'I'll fetch you a menu, and while you're waiting, would you like a drink?'

'Yes please, we'll have a bottle of Dom

Perignon. We're celebrating.'

The waiter laughed but did not ask the cause for the celebration; he merely said, 'The wine waiter will bring the champagne straight away.'

Minutes later, Laurence was standing at her side. He leant down to place a gentle kiss on her cheek, and as he straightened up he said, 'You really do look stunning.'

'And you look well turned out and very handsome,' she replied seriously.

The champagne arrived, and the menus. Chloe sat back, saying, 'I ordered the drink, you order the food.'

'Seafood salad as a starter, steaks to follow, and you may choose your own dessert – the sweet trolley looks gorgeous,' he declared.

The wine waiter had opened the bottle and poured the champagne. Laurence picked up his glass. 'What shall we drink to?'

'How about the truth?' Chloe ventured.

'Too much to tell, and now is not the time or the place.'

'To life, then.'

'I'll drink to that,' he said, grinning, 'and I'll add, to the pursuit of happiness.'

They clinked glasses. It was a while before either of them spoke again, then Chloe asked, 'Are you taking me home tomorrow?'

Laurie had the grace to look guilty. 'Actually I need to get to London as quickly as I can. I would like to leave here at the crack of dawn. You can stay on if you like. I'll get you a hire car or you can use a travel firm to drive you back. Really, Chloe, I do feel bad about this.'

Out of the blue it came to Chloe that Laurie might just be genuine. At least she should give him a chance. She took a sip of her champagne and said quietly, 'Let's finish our meal, then go upstairs and pack our cases. Whatever time you leave, I am going with you. I've had a great time, thank you, but I won't be sorry to get back to my own home.'

He stretched across the table and took her hand; she didn't resist. 'Thank you, Chloe, I shall feel a whole lot better if I see you safely home.'

Back in the bedroom, Chloe changed into her black trouser suit, white shirt and a cashmere cardigan, and was busily repacking the articles she had bought in Barnstaple when Laurie came back from settling the bill at reception.

'You look ready for travelling,' he said, surprise showing in his voice.

'As you said time was important, I thought why wait until the early hours to set off?'

'Aren't you tired?'

'No, well not yet anyway. If you like, I'll drive for a while and then you can take over.'

'That will not be necessary. I am used to

driving hundreds of miles when I'm abroad. If you're sure, it would help a lot if we set off whenever you're ready.'

Chloe went to the bathroom to pack her washing and cosmetic bags. Her mind was in a whirl as she wondered about the future of this strange relationship. One thing she did know was that no matter what happened, she couldn't walk away from Laurence Walmsley. She was caught up with him and needed him more than she cared to admit.

She was also well aware that he would probably break her heart.

## Chapter 16

The dark morning was so cold and now the windows of the car were frosty. Chloe pulled her hands out from the warm car rug that Laurie had wrapped around her. The clock on the dashboard told her it was five fifteen.

She put her hands quickly back under the blanket and rubbed them together between her knees. Laurie took his eyes off the road for a moment to turn and smile at her. He didn't look tired, even though they had been on the road for five hours. They had made two stops at motorway services and the coffee had been hot and strong. They hadn't even started to talk; Laurie said there would be enough time once they had arrived home.

She would believe that once it became a reality. Laurie was just as likely to do another of his disappearing acts, leaving her none the wiser as to what he was up to or where he had gone. She settled her head against the back of her seat. It was getting lighter now and she was seeing familiar sights. When the car finally turned into Brentwood Avenue, she was aware of a strange feeling, and turning to Laurie she said, 'You're never going to believe this, but I am suddenly missing Amberley and Fergus. My house won't feel the same without them.'

'I don't imagine that it will be too long before Dorothy returns home,' he said. 'She and my mother won't be able to live together for much longer; they never have seen eye to eye.'

Chloe had to stop herself from commenting that there was no room in Odette's heart for anyone other than her blue-eyed boy.

Within half an hour of Laurie parking the car in her drive, he had been out into her garden and fetched in a huge box full of logs.

'What on earth do we need them for? I have turned the central heating way up; the house will soon be nice and warm,' Chloe told him.

'Nothing in this world beats sitting in a decent armchair in front of a roaring log fire,' he told her laughingly as he got to work.

'I've granary rolls in the deep freeze, they won't take long to defrost, and plenty of butter in the fridge, but only cans of soup,' she said, eying the shelves of the larder. 'Will Stilton and broccoli soup be all right? And would you like a drink while you're waiting?'

'Yes please, to everything on offer.' He sat back on his heels and surveyed the already crackling fire with satisfaction.

Chloe put the food out on the table, then went to the sideboard and poured herself a Baileys. She handed Laurie the whisky bottle, saying, 'I think you have earned yourself a double; that was a long drive.'

They ate their scrappy meal in silence, both of them feeling suddenly exhausted. When he'd finished, Laurie said, 'I'm going along to Dorothy's house to get a few hours' sleep. Can I take you out for dinner tonight?'

'I'm still wondering when you are going to spare the time for the explanations you owe me,' Chloe told him, sounding tired.

'Well, now is not the time–'

She cut him off. 'It never is with you. Your disappearing acts have gone beyond the limit for me, so unless you intend to enlighten me as to what I have got myself mixed up in, I'd rather you just left now and never came back.'

'All right, we'll clear the air right now,' he said. 'Do you object if I smoke?'

'Not at all,' she replied, then quickly added, 'That's another thing I've learnt: you smoke. You never have before, at least not when I've been around.'

From his jacket pocket he took out a leather wallet and removed a thin cigar. He took his time lighting it, and only when the tip of the cigar was glowing did he look at Chloe and ask, 'Just where do you want me to begin?'

'Well, to begin with, just from casual conversations while we've been in Devon, I get the feeling that you know a damn sight more about me than I've told you. How come?'

'Well that's an easy one. In the past I have negotiated deals on behalf of Associated Securities, and because of that Stephen Goddard and I have become good friends. He has always spoken very highly of you.'

'That certainly does explain a lot,' she agreed. She raised her head and looked directly at him. 'But it doesn't come anywhere near to explaining your disappearing acts.'

'No, it doesn't, and I am sorry. As a commodities broker, I spend my life on the lookout for deals. In every case, being able to move quickly gives me an advantage; speed is always of the essence. Also having ample funds that I can afford to lose if things go wrong helps, because every deal I do is a gamble.'

'Okay, so you've to be in the right place at

the right time and be able to lay your hands on plenty of money, but that still doesn't explain why you can't keep in contact.'

'Knowing that a certain party has a large amount of a useful commodity is one thing; the art is finding another person who hopefully will have need of that commodity, and that is where expediency comes into the equation. Even if I manage to do a deal between two parties, I still have to make the exchange, and that could well mean transferring goods from one side of the world to the other. In plain English, I am a negotiator, I get paid commission for transacting business for others.'

'Thank you for that explanation, which I do understand must involve you having a lot of your own money tied up in a deal, but I am still in the dark as to why you disappear so suddenly.'

Laurence took a deep breath. 'If I hadn't had you with me in Devon, I would have been on my way to Johannesburg by now.'

For once Chloe was lost for words.

Laurie grinned. 'When I raced off and left you in Woolacombe, I'd been offered a deal too good to miss. I needed to be able to prove that I was good for a substantial amount of money to close a deal.'

Chloe felt incapable of forming an answer. Eventually she asked, 'You lost the deal because of me?'

'No, I managed to delay proceedings.'

'Why did you do that?'

'You never wanted to come to Devon with me in the first place, and it wouldn't say much for me if I had just gone off and left you stranded.'

He got to his feet, took an ashtray from the sideboard and stubbed out his cigar before going out into the hall, coming back a few moments later carrying his laptop. He opened it up and began tapping away. Eventually he gave a sigh of satisfaction as the screen disclosed what he wanted.

'Here we are. My flight to Johannesburg takes off at two a.m. I will have time to take you out for a meal, but it will have to be fairly early. I need to be at Heathrow by midnight. Meanwhile, do you mind if I go and get some sleep?'

'Of course not,' Chloe managed to mutter, then she cleared her throat before adding, 'You are the most incredible man I have ever come across.'

'I agree with you,' Laurence laughed. 'Take my advice and get your head down. I'll pick you up about six o'clock.'

And with that he closed his laptop and was gone.

'Like a bloody whirlwind,' Chloe muttered as she looked at the dirty plates that were still lying on the kitchen table. 'They can stay there. I'm going to bed.'

It was exactly six o'clock when he rang her front doorbell. He was dressed in the same clothes as when she had first set eyes on him. Casual gear for travelling, she guessed.

'Chloe, I really am sorry that I have to eat and run. Would you mind if we go to the local steak house?'

'Not at all, whatever suits you,' she told him smiling, but her thoughts were all of the previous morning at the hotel in Barnstaple. Oh how vividly she remembered the thrill of him.

Little did she know that the same kind of thoughts were worrying Laurence. Why had the timing been so bad? he continually asked himself. Chloe Collard was unique, a wonderful person. He regretted the fact that he had acted with too much haste after they had left his mother's house, and then, talk about Sod's Law, this diamond deal had been sprung on him, and if he had refused to negotiate, his reputation would have been on the line. There was a craving in him now, a hunger that bordered on pain.

He was left with no choice: weeks of separation, of denial.

He sighed heavily, holding out Chloe's coat for her. 'Bear with me if you feel that you can, and I promise I will make it up to you. Why don't you begin to plan a holiday, anywhere in the world, and I will take you there once I have put this deal through.'

Promises, promises: did she believe him?

Did she have any choice?

They ate their meal in silence. There was so much to discuss, and so little time.

Back at her house, he took her in his arms. He wanted to stay to prove his feelings to her. God above knew he wanted so much more for them both.

Their kisses were bittersweet. Eventually he let her go.

'I really must get going,' he said reluctantly.

'That's all right.' She wanted him to leave. This lingering was breaking her heart. Had she found a man she could think about sharing the future with? Well one thing was for sure, she was going to have plenty of spare time to sort things out in her head. Laurence was about to put a good few miles between them, and God alone knew when, or even if, he would turn up again.

She waited until she heard her front door close behind him.

Then she wept.

The next morning, she was back behind her desk at Associated Securities. She needed to work and to meet people. This was another step.

'You want coffee?' Holly asked her.

'Yes please, may as well get back into the old routine.'

By the time Holly came back with two coffees, she was no longer able to keep her curiosity under control. 'Where the hell have you been?' she blurted out as she handed Chloe the sugar bowl. 'Going off without a word to anyone, you had us all worried.'

Knowing she was in the wrong as she usually kept her up-to-date, Chloe murmured, 'Sorry, it started off with me being a good neighbour, but I ended up going off to Devon with a handsome guy and a three-year-old girl.'

'Your first day back at the office and you're telling me that you've been away with some guy? Have I got that right?' Holly was trying to sound shocked but wasn't succeeding. In fact she was having a hard job to smother her laughter.

'Yes, but I can't talk now, I need to get settled in. I'll treat you to dinner tonight if you've nothing better to do.'

'Just you and me, that will be great. Can't wait to hear the lowdown on this new man in your life.'

Holly's high spirits were infectious and Chloe felt the sudden lift of her own heart. The dark days of Roger's death, with all the anxieties, anguish and loneliness that had followed, receded, and all at once she was filled with hope, glad to be back at work. To feel wanted and hopefully needed. She had every right to feel that way, as the next half-hour was to prove. Every member of staff came in to tell her that she had been missed and that they were glad to have her back.

Chloe and Holly sat at a table in the window of the Waterfront Restaurant, looking out over the harbour, being attended to by a charming waiter.

They had gone to Chloe's apartment after work to freshen up their make-up and brush their hair, though they didn't change out of their work clothes. They knew they looked good in their slick black suits, Chloe in trim white shirt, Holly a flirtatious red one with the two top buttons left undone.

They didn't pause for an aperitif but went straight into the restaurant, where a bottle of champagne stood chilling in a silver bucket of ice in the centre of their prestigious table.

It was a splendid meal; the food was delicious and the wine flowed. Holly was on great form, bringing Chloe up to date with the office gossip and news of her latest boyfriend, who had lasted for all of three months, a record for Holly.

Other diners, friends of Roger and Chloe, spied them and paused to chat on the way to their tables. Others waved and blew kisses from where they sat.

Holly talked excitedly about Chloe being back, and was already planning outings together.

'What are you going to do about your apartment and that great big house?' she wanted to know.

'Haven't decided yet, but it's not a problem,' Chloe assured her. 'You haven't told me much about what's been going on at the office, only gossip. Anything else I should know?'

'Well, Kevin Bennet and his PA, Anthony Moore, left the firm quite suddenly, nobody seems to know why, which means we are even more short of attractive men.'

'Pity,' Chloe muttered, 'I rather liked Anthony. I wonder why Kevin always chooses a male to work closely with.'

'Your guess is as good as mine.'

At that point they both burst out laughing and their light-hearted mood lasted the rest of the evening.

With dinner over, Chloe said, 'Why don't you stay the night at the apartment with me?'

'I'd like nothing better, but I'd have to get up early to go home and change my clothes. Can't work two days running in the same suit.'

'We are practically the same size, you and I. I'm sure you can pick something out from my wardrobe.'

'You mean you've still got loads of clothes here? I thought you'd moved everything over to Ditchling.'

'Well it seemed sensible to keep my work

stuff here. Come and stay with me for a while, you'd be doing me a favour. When you were here after Roger died, I was a wet blanket, no company at all. Now I'm beginning to think it's about time I sowed a wild oat or two. Do you agree?'

'Wholeheartedly. Just lead on.'

It was well past midnight when they kissed each other good night and went off to their bedrooms. Holly grinned as she entered her room.

A grey suit, an immaculate pale blue shirt and a striped dark blue scarf were hanging outside the wardrobe ready for her to wear to work next day. It was one of many outfits that Chloe had urged her to try on. The top drawer of the chest held a great assortment of lacy underwear and a couple of pairs of nylons, and laid out on the dressing table was an array of cosmetics. Chloe was indeed a very generous friend.

On Tuesdays, Mrs Bolton came to clean the apartment. She was one of the cleaning ladies that Chloe had first taken on to help set the Ditchling house in order. She arrived at eight thirty on the dot while Chloe and Holly were still drinking the last of their breakfast coffee, her arrival heralded by the slam of the front door as she let herself in. Then a pause while she took off her outdoor clothes and donned a large white apron and a trendy pair of trainers. Chloe and Holly waited. The dining room door was flung open and Mrs Bolton appeared.

'Morning, my loves, knew there were two of you 'cos two bedroom doors are open and both beds have been slept in. Nice to see you again, Holly.'

'You too, Mrs Bolton, how are you?'

'Freezing,' came the answer as the woman rubbed her hands together to get her circulation going. 'There's a terrific wind, goes right through yer like a knife.' Chloe put down her coffee cup. 'Make yourself a cup of tea before you start work, I know you don't like coffee.'

'All right, I will. Kettle's boiled, has it?'

Chloe laughed. 'You'll need to switch it back on again. Holly and I will be leaving shortly so we'll be out of your way.'

'All right for some, not 'aving to start until ten. Still, I was glad to hear you'd gone back to work. You've been spending too much time on your own. Mind you, what's this I've been hearing about you having a little girl to stay?'

They both stared at her. Then Chloe said, 'News travels fast. Have you been talking to Mrs Wilson?'

'Yeah, we met up in Brighton yesterday, we always do on a Monday. We've stayed friends ever since you took the pair of us on. Molly still does twice a week for you out at Ditchling, doesn't she?'

'Since you seem to know everything, I

wonder that you haven't come across Mrs Whitlocke and her daughter Amberley; their house is just down the road from mine.'

'Oh now I know who you're talking about; they've got a little dog. Molly also said there was a man who was supposed to be looking after the child while the mother was in hospital.'

Chloe looked at Holly, who was grinning smugly. 'I think we'd better gather up our things and be on our way, don't you?' she said.

'I don't know,' Holly laughed. 'I've enjoyed listening to Mrs Bolton, a real mine of information. I'd love to know a whole lot more about this mysterious guy that you spent so much time with.'

For a ridiculous moment, Chloe felt a bit weepy. She shook herself, put her jacket on and picked up her car keys. 'Right, let's go and prove to the men that they can't run the business without the help of us women.'

## Chapter 17

Holly's overnight stay had been extended; it was now a month since she had come to stay with Chloe in her Brighton Marina apartment. She had told her boyfriend that she wasn't ready to have a steady relationship, while Chloe's only contact with Laurence Walmsley had been a postcard from Tunisia. Both girls had decided that it was time just to enjoy themselves.

'You know,' Holly had urged, 'we should try being frivolous, go to some nightclubs, buy loads of clothes and find ourselves some dashing men who will take us to lunch at the Ritz, or cruising on their yachts, where we would lie on deck and sip cool drinks.'

Chloe laughed loudly. 'You're letting your imagination run away with you. Just where are you proposing we look for these men?'

'I don't know. Sometimes I can't help thinking that you were so happy with Roger that it has rather spoilt the future for you.'

Chloe was so quiet that for a moment Holly was afraid she had put her foot in it and immediately made an attempt to apologise.

'Don't worry, please, Holly, I am not in the least upset. Not a day goes by I don't think about Roger, but I promised him that I wouldn't spend the rest of my life feeling frustrated or cheated in any way. So if and when the right man should come along, I know that on the day I get married, it will be with Roger's blessing.'

'Did you mean what you just said?'

'Which part are you referring to?'

'The day you get married.'

'Of course. All I've got to do is find the

right man.'

'You've never heard a word from the chap you went off to Devon with, have you?'

'Only the one postcard, but out of sight, out of mind.'

'I know that's not true. But not to worry, there are plenty more fish in the sea, we'll just have to use a more attractive bait.'

Suddenly they were both laughing. Eventually Chloe said, 'Shall we pull ourselves together for a minute and try to decide what we are going to do this coming weekend?'

'Good idea. We could write down some suggestions, put them in a bowl and pick one each.'

Chloe scrunched up a piece of newspaper and threw it at Holly. 'Why don't you go and put the kettle on?' she said.

Holly heaved herself to her feet and went to do as she had been told, but she was laughing all the way to the kitchen.

For the next two weekends, Chloe and Holly did their best to live their lives to the full, but eventually they admitted to one another that visits to the theatre and nightclubs were not the same unless one was accompanied by a male. It came as a relief when Holly said she was going home to visit her parents, and Chloe went back to Ditchling for the weekend.

It was ten o'clock on the Saturday morning and Chloe was still lingering over a cup of coffee when the front doorbell rang. She hardly ever had visitors in Ditchling and so she opened the door slowly.

'Am I interrupting something?' Dorothy Whitlocke asked, smiling.

'Dorothy, how lovely to see you. How are you, and how is Amberley?'

'Am I going to have to answer your questions standing on your doorstep?'

Chloe found herself dumbfounded, her emotions all mixed up. Quickly she stepped back and opened the door wider. 'Come in. I'd no idea you were home, when did you arrive back?'

'Early yesterday evening, and I've had one hell of a job keeping Amberley from coming with me today and bringing Fergus.'

By now they had reached the kitchen. Chloe made sure Dorothy was seated comfortably and set about making a fresh pot of coffee.

'I had no idea you were back,' she said again.

'Never mind, you know now. I must ask, am I intruding, were you going out?'

'No, no plans. I was just thinking it was going to be a lonely weekend.'

Dorothy took the cup of coffee that Chloe was holding out. She had been looking about her, and suddenly she said, 'My goodness, what a transformation. This place used to be so gloomy. Of course I couldn't help but notice you had various people working here; you must have had a great time choosing just what you were going to do to a house that had stood empty for so many years.' She stretched her legs out, her neatly booted feet crossed at the ankles. 'I do think it's great to have a couple of comfortable chairs in the kitchen; after all, the kitchen is the heart of any house.'

'Are you back home for good?' Chloe asked.

'Definitely. My mother is best taken in small doses. Would you believe me if I said that even Amberley had had enough? It came to the point when neither of us could do anything right. Elderly people and young children don't mix, not for any length of time, and more so if the child has a dog.'

Chloe grinned. 'Poor old Fergus.'

'Exactly. How's everything with you?'

Chloe shrugged. 'All right. I have gone back to work, was bored to tears once I had the house in good order.'

Dorothy drained the last drop of her coffee. 'I should go, mustn't overstay my welcome on the first visit...' She paused. 'I hesitate to say this...' Another pause.

'Dorothy, I really am hoping that we shall become good friends, so whatever it is you want to say, stop dilly-dangling and say it.'

They both grinned, and Dorothy said,

'Amberley remembered that you said you would take her to the park some Saturdays, and–'

'Stop right there,' Chloe interrupted forcefully. 'Nothing would give me greater pleasure. We'll go this morning if that's all right by you.'

'Are you absolutely sure? It means taking Fergus along as well – oh, and me too if that's all right.'

They looked at each other, then Dorothy stood up and held her arms wide, and Chloe went into them to be held close in a loving hug. Not a word was said, but the very feel of that embrace meant such a lot to both women.

Half an hour later, Chloe was waiting at her gate when Dorothy came out of her house holding fast to Fergus's lead. As she stopped to lock her front door, Amberley spied Chloe and began to run.

Chloe's eyes misted over with ridiculous tears and she felt her face begin to crumple like a baby's. 'Oh Amberley,' she murmured as she opened her arms and caught the little girl. Mercifully, before they could fall, the stupid tears receded and in a moment she was able to find a handkerchief and blow her nose.

Dorothy caught up with them and of course Fergus had no intention of being left out of all these affectionate demonstrations.

Chloe scratched him beneath his chin and rubbed her hands along his soft furry back.

'Right.' Dorothy took charge. 'If we are going to the park, I suggest that we make a start rather than standing around here in the road.' She led the way still keeping a firm hold on Fergus's lead.

Amberley slipped her hand into Chloe's and looked up into her face. 'I have missed you, Chloe, and Mummy and me are so happy to be home.'

'And Fergus?' Chloe said, teasing her. 'Wouldn't he rather have stayed in Devon?'

'Well,' the little girl looked up at Chloe again and gave her a wry smile, 'some days he wasn't in Granma's good books.'

'Well I am jolly glad to have all of you back home. Come on, let's get going. I haven't been to the park since we last went together,' Chloe told her.

'That was when Uncle Laurie came and found us and the next day he took us swimming.'

'My goodness, you have got a good memory.' Chloe smiled at her.

As soon as they reached the park, Dorothy let Fergus off his lead and Amberley made a beeline for the play area. The two women took to the cinder paths and had a good walk, all the time keeping a watchful eye on Amberley. After a while Dorothy put two fingers in her mouth and let out a very unladylike whistle to bring Fergus scampering across the field.

'You need a drink, don't you, old fellow,' Dorothy said, patting the dog. 'We might as well make our way to the café. Do you prefer a big meal in the evening and a snack at lunchtime, or vice versa?' she asked Chloe.

'The first option mainly. Being back at work again now, dinner in the evening is a much better idea.'

By the time they had collected Amberley and watched as she washed her hands under the water fountain, it was almost one o'clock. It wasn't warm enough to sit outside, but there was an unoccupied table in the bay window to which Chloe led Amberley while Dorothy took Fergus to the water bowl then tied him up nearby.

'Do you fancy a baguette?' Chloe asked.

'Umm, not sure. I could do with something warm. Wonder what the soup is today.'

Chloe nodded her head. 'It's up there, written on the blackboard. Asparagus.'

'Oh, well that will do me fine.'

'Me too,' Chloe agreed.

Amberley leant nearer to her mother and whispered, and Dorothy laughed. 'Of course you may have scrambled egg on toast, and what would you like to drink? As it's so cold, how about a mug of Bovril?'

'Yes please, Mummy, that would be nice.'

Both women had finished their soup and

were waiting for the toast and pâté they had ordered when Dorothy suddenly said, 'Have you heard anything from my brother lately?'

'No, I haven't.' Chloe's answer was sharp. The question had brought back the warning that Odette had slyly delivered.

Dorothy was well aware of her mother's disapproval, and she quickly said, 'My mother warned you off, right?'

Chloe nodded. 'I could have done without her advice. I never wanted to go to Devon with Laurence in the first place. I agreed for Amberley's sake.'

'I'm aware of that and am very grateful. Laurence has always been the apple of my mother's eye. It comes from him being so handsome. He was such a beautiful child, he was indulged by everybody, wherever he went. I used to hate him for it when we were children. He was the object of adoration; people were dazzled by him. Then they'd look at me and wonder how such an adorable boy could have an ugly duckling for a sister.'

Chloe smiled, but she felt sad for Dorothy. She was a truly lovely person and her husband must have been a right bastard. Going off with another woman was bad enough, but to get her pregnant at the same time as his wife was disgusting.

Just then their food was brought to the table and they began to eat in silence, Chloe watching just how well Amberley was coping with her scrambled egg on toast.

After a while Dorothy said, 'I know my daughter is a beautiful child but I won't let anyone make a big issue out of it. I want her to have confidence, but not the sense of entitlement that I sometimes think ruins my brother's life. Having said that, Laurence is not a bad man. Self-centred a lot of the time, but never malicious, and he is great at his job. You know he has no need to work; our father left our mother well provided for, but the greater part of his wealth went to Laurence and myself, and my mother's share is held in trust for us both.'

'Why do you think Laurence carries on with his job when there is no need for him to work at all? It doesn't make sense.' Chloe couldn't hide her curiosity.

'You'll get no argument from me on that,' Dorothy told her firmly.

Leaning towards Amberley, her mother said, 'Darling, you've cleared your plate, good girl. Now go outside and make sure that Fergus is all right, and if you want to go over to the play area, Chloe and I will come and join you. We're just going to have a cup of coffee.' As Amberley stood up, her mother drew her close and kissed the top of her head.

With her daughter gone, Dorothy sighed. 'Laurence loves a challenge, and every deal he pulls off is another notch on his bedpost. By the way, I don't know how much you know about what he does, but it certainly is not all for personal gain.'

'I know very little, just that he is a commodities broker.'

'Well, if he admitted that much to you, you've got a whole lot further than most people do. What I'm going to reveal to you now stays between us, is that understood?'

'Absolutely.'

'Well, some of the deals that Laurie gets himself involved with he does purely and simply for charity. He travels all over the world and he sees sights that rip at his heart-strings. On television there are always numerous appeals for help – when children are starving, a depressed country that needs medical aid, even education comes into it when there are no schools or books available. My brother does not belong to any organisation, nor is he affiliated with any well-known charities. He just sees where help is needed, and if he can, he contributes, all under the banner of silence. I doubt even my mother knows. When I was on my own and pregnant, Laurie came and stayed with me and threw me a lifeline. I was in such a desperate state, I truly considered killing myself. Without him, neither myself or Amberley would be alive today. Out of bad often comes good. It was during that time that I got to know my brother so very much better.'

You could have heard a pin drop as the

two women sat and stared into space, each busy with her own thoughts. Chloe had shuddered when Dorothy had said she had considered killing herself. That thought had struck far too close to home.

It was Dorothy who spoke first. 'Shall we make a move. I can show you a different route home.'

'Is it a better way to walk?'

'It's much shorter, and it is getting very cold outside.'

'Come on then,' Chloe said, getting to her feet. 'I'll untie Fergus while you fetch Amberley.'

'There's a path from here down through those trees to a huge pond and then a track that leads up to our road. They sell bags of food here to feed the ducks with. I'll go to the counter and buy one. Amberley will be thrilled.'

They set off, their footsteps scrunching on a few frozen patches. On reaching the pond and seeing the ducks, Amberley cried out, 'Oh I wish we had brought some bread.'

'Here, try this,' Dorothy said as she held out the bag of food. 'I'd better go down to the edge of the water with her, don't want any accidents. Will you keep a hold on Fergus, please, or else he'll be in that pond before we know it.'

It was a happy little party that finally arrived back home, but Dorothy had the feeling that she had upset Chloe, and so as they were parting she said, 'I'm sorry.'

'What for?'

'Because I hadn't planned to tell you about my brother, or about that unhappy period of my life. I didn't mean to upset you. This was supposed to be an outing for Amberley's benefit. We just got on to the wrong subject.'

'Dorothy, I am not upset; indeed, I am grateful to you. I understand Laurence a whole lot better now. I promise I will keep everything you told me to myself. We won't let it affect our friendship, will we?'

'Most certainly not. I rather think Amberley would have something to say on that matter.'

At that moment Amberley caught hold of Chloe's hand and said, 'Aren't you going to come into our house?'

It was Dorothy who answered. 'Chloe knows she will be welcome any time to come and visit us, but we have monopolised her enough for one day.'

Chloe bent down and said her goodbyes to Fergus, then looked at Amberley, uncertain as to what she should do. The little girl had no such doubts, however. She linked her arms around Chloe's neck, and as Chloe straightened up, she had no option but to clasp the little girl to her and hold her tight. As she stood there with the soft skin of Amberley's cheek resting against her own, she realised what was missing from her life.

'It's Sunday tomorrow,' Dorothy suddenly stated.

'So?' Chloe queried.

'I have a leg of lamb in the freezer; why don't I let it thaw out overnight and we can have a roast dinner together tomorrow.'

'Please, please say yes, Chloe.' Amberley was imploring.

'Only if I'm allowed to come early and help with the vegetables.'

'Come as early as you like.' Dorothy was beaming at her.

'I can't wait.' Amberley had her arms tightly around Chloe's waist and Fergus was up on his hind legs.

That first outing, and the outcome, was to set the seal on what would prove to be a long-lasting and loving friendship.

## Chapter 18

Although Laurence had been gone for five weeks, the worrying about him, even the longing for him, had lessened. Chloe felt that in the month she'd been back at work, she had achieved so much, career-wise. Her days were full, and she had Holly and Dorothy to keep her company in the evening and at weekends.

This morning, however, from the moment she got out of bed and stepped into the shower, she had felt different. She had let her mind run back to the one and only time that she and Laurence had made love, at the hotel in Barnstaple. She wondered whether Laurence thought of her as an easy lay.

Why hadn't she stopped him? Why indeed.

Because the experience had been wonderful. Indescribable.

And since? Nothing. He'd upped and left for Africa.

So why was she pondering the memories this morning?

She had no answers to her own questions. But she did have a feeling that anything might happen, and soon.

Lloyd Spencer and Edward Kendrick came into her office together. Two directors; that in itself was unusual.

'A very special ball is to be held in London. Successful companies only are to be involved. Here is your invitation, Chloe.' Lloyd leant across her desk and handed her an envelope.

'I can't go, I have no male escort,' she answered softly, not bothering to open it.

'Don't be so ridiculous, you can't refuse. It is like being invited to Buckingham Palace, only this is being held at the Ritz.'

'Chloe,' Edward came nearer to her desk, 'would you consider me as your escort? It would be my pleasure and I would deem it an honour.'

Chloe felt bewildered. Edward Kendrick was among the top brass of this company and she knew he was happily married, had been for years. She was murmuring her thanks when Lloyd said, 'I must be off, glad we've settled that point.' Chloe was left alone with Edward.

'Life can change with such shocking abruptness,' he said sombrely.

'I know.' Chloe thought about Roger. She said again, 'I know.'

'And how are you coping, Chloe?'

'Me? I'm fine.'

'I don't think you are. For one thing, you look pale, and dreadfully thin. Why did you suddenly come back to work?'

'In one word, loneliness, I guess.'

'I thought it might be. I wish I could help.'

'You are helping by offering to be my escort for this ball.'

'In that case, I will say no more. Except to reiterate how much I am looking forward to it.'

Chloe came round her desk and gave him a hug.

'Thank you, Edward, for coming to my rescue.'

He leaned down and kissed her forehead.

'It will be my pleasure. Every male in the room will be envious when I arrive with you on my arm.'

The evening was everything one could have hoped for, held in an incredible room, an orchestra playing at one end. The world and his wife seemed to be there: handsome men, lots of uniforms, beautiful women. Still Chloe managed to stand out among the crowd. Her chestnut hair was piled high on her head, with several tendrils left curling loosely. Two richly jewelled combs kept the French pleat in place. Her silk ballgown was a pale shade of jade green, which served to emphasise her big green eyes, and as always the dress fitted her slim body as if it were a liquid that had been poured over her.

Edward had departed to procure some more champagne, and Chloe was standing alone on the edge of the dance floor when she heard someone saying her name. She turned around to find Laurence standing there, looking immaculate in evening suit, white dress shirt and black tie.

'My God, you look fabulous, Chloe.' Her heart turned over as he took hold of her hands and added softly, 'You are truly beautiful.' He hesitated. 'I am sorry I haven't been in touch.'

She was saved from having to form an answer by Edward approaching with a tray holding two glasses of champagne. Smiling broadly he said, 'Take these, Laurence. I think I may safely leave the pair of you now and rejoin the party of friends my wife came with.'

Chloe was at a loss, realising how little she knew of the lives of the directors she worked with daily. Still, she smiled, they could just as easily say the same about her.

Laurence nodded at the nearest vacant table and said, 'Shall we?' Once he had put the glasses down, he waited until Chloe had seated herself and then looked down at her with enormous tenderness before he kissed her on both cheeks.

For a while they just gazed at each other. It was Laurence who broke the silence. 'I suppose the only way I can get you into my arms is to take you on to the dance floor.'

Hardly had he uttered the words than the announcement came that the band was leaving the rostrum and the presentation of the awards was about to take place.

Chloe took one look at Laurie's face and wanted to laugh. Frustration was written all over it.

Actually the proceedings were not too lengthy. Congratulations were in order for Associated Securities, and every member of staff was well pleased with the prestigious awards the company had won.

'At last.' Laurence smiled as the band

struck up once again.

He was a wonderful dancer, and Chloe was enjoying herself, but she was well aware of the heat that was rising between the pair of them. Suddenly Laurie was leading her off the dance floor. 'We've got to get out of here, and fast,' he murmured.

He gathered up Chloe's stole and clutch bag and began walking her rapidly along the corridors of the Ritz, speaking into his mobile phone as he went. As they came out of the lift on the ground floor, he looked toward the entrance and said, 'Good, our transport is here.'

He helped her into the rear of the waiting limousine, then got in himself and closed the glass partition separating them from the driver. It was only then that he took her in his arms and let out a great sigh of relief.

They had been driving for some time when he sat up straight and softly said, 'I asked the chauffeur to just keep driving, but now I think we should give him a destination. Where do you suggest?'

'Since I returned to work, I haven't been living in my house much; the apartment is so much more practical. It will be warm there; I always leave the central heating on.'

Laurie laughed, a real big belly laugh. 'Ever the practical one, that's my Chloe.' He leaned forward and partially opened the glass partition, 'John, how far are we from Brighton?'

'About twenty minutes, sir.'

'That's great, will you please make for the marina.'

'Certainly, sir.'

Gently closing the partition, Laurie leaned back until his shoulders were touching the leather upholstery. Chloe had been watching his every move and suddenly she murmured, 'I don't believe it.'

'What don't you believe?' He pulled himself upright.

'The fact that you turned up out of the blue tonight, all fitted out in evening dress. How long have you been back? When did you learn about tonight's event? Edward must have been in the know, but what I can't fathom out is why he offered to be my escort when he must have known you were back in the country.'

'Hey, slow down, one point at a time. Bit complicated, so don't interrupt.'

She didn't. He talked and she listened.

'I touched down at Heathrow two weeks ago, but I wasn't able to leave London. There were still some loose ends flying around with regards to the deal I was brokering. Had I come to you in Brighton, I could have been called away at any time, day or night. I had done that to you twice already and I wasn't prepared to upset you again. I did so want to be your escort at tonight's big event, and when Edward came up with his offer – which incidentally his wife was totally in agreement with – I grabbed at the chance. It wasn't ideal. Felt like I was waiting in the wings for a curtain call.'

There was a lengthy silence. Broken by Laurence.

'At this point in time I am footloose and fancy-free. Last deal safely and successfully put to bed. I will refuse all offers of deals or contracts for the time being, and so, my dearest Chloe, the ball is in your court.'

'Are there any rules to this game?' Chloe asked timidly, feeling as if she had just taken a punch to her stomach.

'Oh no, Chloe. You have got that completely wrong. I have never felt like this about any woman in my life before, and if it is only a game you are wanting, then I shall see you safely home and we'll call it a day.'

Chloe couldn't believe that he was being so straightforward. She was saved from having to form an answer by a tapping on the glass partition.

Laurence slid the glass back and John said, 'We are just entering the marina, sir. Can you give me directions, please.'

'First apartment block to the west of the harbour, please, John.'

Having held on to her elbow as she got out of the car, Laurence left her standing by the entrance while he spoke with the driver.

'I'll see you to your apartment,' he said,

taking hold of her hand. She didn't resist; simply returned the pressure and kept her eyes looking downwards.

They walked towards the lift.

'You are not a true romantic, are you, Chloe?' Laurence said.

'Try teaching me then.' She turned her face towards him in the shadows and he kissed her very gently, still keeping his arm around her shoulders.

'Oh Laurence Walmsley, your life sounds so complicated and yet you are a lovely man.'

When the lift came to a halt, she got the key to her apartment from her clutch bag and handed it to him without a word, standing there waiting as Laurence unlocked the door and opened it. He stood to one side, then followed her in.

She crossed the floor of the lounge to the glass doors, slid them open and stepped out on to her balcony, looking down at the busy harbour. Laurence came up behind her and slipped his arms around her waist.

'Are you quite sure about this?'

'Oh, yes,' she said. 'Never more sure of anything in my life.'

Back inside, he sat on the huge settee and she curled up in his lap. He could feel the warmth of her through her thin ballgown. She pressed herself against him, making slow, small circles, and she felt him respond. Very slowly she rose and slipped out of her dress.

Laurie watched her, marvelling at her slim, beautiful body. How could he have let business keep him away from her for so long?

She was undressing him now, and there was a sudden urgency in him. They were both naked, and their bodies were pressed together. He stroked her, lightly touching face and neck, down to the swell of her fantastic breasts. She was moaning, and his hands moved down until he felt the velvety softness between her legs. His fingers stroked her, but it was the words he was whispering that made her shudder with complete contentment.

Now they were lying on the deep soft-pile rug, and she felt the strength of his body on top of her. 'I love you, Chloe, so much. It has been unbearable at times. In future, I go nowhere I cannot take you with me.'

'Stop talking, Laurie, but don't stop showing me how much you truly love me, please.' He raised himself for a moment, then there was a long, sweet thrust and he was inside her, and in complete harmony she moved with his rhythm, because he was sweeping her higher than she had thought was possible. The sheer ecstasy was almost too much to bear.

Much later, they lay in bed together, Laurence propped up by three pillows while Chloe slept quietly beside him. It had been the most wonderful experience of his entire life. Again and again he vowed to himself,

'Never again will I go anywhere without my lovely Chloe. No land or sea will ever separate us again.'

When Chloe woke in the morning, feeling rather tired but extremely happy, she prayed to God that fortune would be kind and allow them to spend the rest of their lives together.

## Chapter 19

It was nearly midday, but already getting dark, and beyond the kitchen window the garden was turning white with the falling snow. Ever since the snow had started, drifting down from a darkened sky, Dorothy had been worrying about Amberley, blaming herself for being irresponsible and letting the child go off on her own, imagining every sort of horror. She had given permission for Amberley to take Fergus along the road to see Chloe, but when the snow had started to fall she had telephoned Chloe and got no answer. Her little girl was sensible, she had the dog with her, and Dorothy was always telling herself that she must not mollycoddle her only child.

She had finished peeling the potatoes and was putting the last one into the saucepan of cold water when she heard her front door open and voices in the hall. She abandoned the potatoes and rushed out, wiping her hands on her apron. To her enormous relief, Chloe and Amberley stood on the doormat, both with a light dusting of snow on their coats.

'Come into the warm kitchen,' Dorothy ordered.

Amberley shed her coat and hat, then sat down on the rug to pull off her boots. 'Mummy, there was this horrible dog, it wasn't on a lead and it went for Fergus, which wasn't fair because it was so much bigger than he is.'

'A council lorry came along and it was the driver that rang my bell.' Chloe took up the story. 'He was a decent bloke; apparently he had quite a slanging match with the woman who owned the other dog. Eventually she stumped off and Amberley told him which house she was going to. I'm sorry I wasn't outside, though I don't think I could have stopped that dog. It sounds as if it was huge, and poor Fergus has got bites and scratches. It must have been very frightening for Amberley. Thank God that lorry driver turned up.'

'While we were indoors it started to snow, and Chloe said we couldn't go for a walk, we had to come back home.' Amberley had to have her say.

'Quite right too,' her mother said. 'I'll fetch the bottle of Dettol from the bathroom and the tin bath out of the garden shed, and you can help me give Fergus a nice warm bath.'

When everything was ready, Dorothy lifted Fergus into the bath and used a jug to pour water over his back. He sat in stoical silence. She was relieved to discover no serious wounds, simply a mass of nips and small punctures that would in time heal themselves. By and large he seemed to have emerged from his battering with little lasting harm.

'So we won't have to take him to the vet?' Chloe asked.

'I don't think so. Just as well, looks like it is snowing quite hard now.'

Dorothy lifted Fergus out of the bath and carried him into the lounge, wrapped up in a thick, warm bath towel. With Amberley watching her every move, she patted him dry before settling him comfortably on the settee. She hugged Amberley tight. 'He'll be fine, and you were a clever girl to get that driver to ring Chloe's bell. Now you stay there with Fergus and Chloe and I will get some lunch ready for all of us.'

It was three o'clock before Chloe went back to her own house. The snow had stopped falling but the dark day was already turning into evening, and she had to turn on lights and draw curtains before she checked her messages. Laurence was in Scotland; a very quick overnight stay, he had promised, but with the severe Scottish climate, who could tell?

Three weeks had slipped by since the night of the company ball, and Chloe had begun to think she was living on cloud nine. Each evening after work, Laurence had met her at the office and taken her home. Not once had Chloe dithered; no matter what Laurence suggested they do or where he wanted to take her, she gladly went along with his suggestions. She still couldn't grasp the fact that her life was now on an even keel.

She was whispering silent prayers as she picked up her phone to listen to her messages. Life had become so good, too good! Her heart was pounding as she heard his voice: 'Hi sweetheart, I'm taking a flight back down to Gatwick tomorrow morning. I should be back by lunchtime.'

As she replaced the receiver, Chloe sighed. At times it seemed totally impossible to believe that she could have found two remarkable men. Sharing her life with Roger had been wonderful; to now have Laurence was truly remarkable.

Laurence had a window seat, no one beside him, and a new book in his lap that he couldn't find the concentration to read. The stewardess asked if he wanted something to drink and he declined, then changed his mind and asked for a whisky and soda, which he drank quickly before leaning his head back and falling asleep.

He did not wake until the stewardess tapped him on the shoulder, smiled like an angel and asked him to buckle up for landing.

He hated airports, couldn't get out of Gatwick quick enough, was relieved to see John waiting alongside the barrier.

'Lucky today, got a parking space on this level,' the chauffeur told him as they walked.

'Radio?' John asked, leaning forward to switch it on as soon as they were settled in the car.

'I'd rather we didn't,' Laurie said as he settled back in the passenger seat.

They drove in silence for a while. In his mind, Laurie was going over the events of the last three weeks, but he realised he was concentrating on anything he could find to take his mind off the mass of feelings that were swamping him.

During the time he and Chloe had spent getting to really know each other, everything had been great. He had promised that never again would he leave the country without her, but now he was going to have to break the news that first thing in the morning he was once again leaving for foreign parts.

Right now he was caught between the devil and the deep blue sea.

He had slept throughout the journey. Unbelievable. John was shaking his shoulder and telling him they had arrived outside Chloe's apartment block. It was just twelve midday.

'Thanks, John. I shall need picking up from my own apartment in Hove about six tomorrow morning to go to Dover. Will you be driving me?'

'I don't know until I get back to the car pool, but if you have notified the office, I will find out as soon as I get back.'

'Okay, thanks, John,' Laurie said, slipping him some folded notes.

Chloe had been on the lookout, and as the lift reached the top floor, she had her front door open and a wide smile on her face.

A rush of pleasure ran through Laurie's entire body as he stared at her.

For her part, Chloe was glad that he'd kept his word and had only been away for one night. He was back now. The very thought of what they might do for the rest of the day sent a delicious thrill through her body.

'Are we going to stand on this landing for much longer?' he laughingly asked.

Then they were in the lounge and she was in his arms. 'I'll make you some coffee,' she murmured.

'Bugger the coffee. I badly need to talk to

you, but maybe you feel the need of me as much I do you, in which case I suggest we move into your bedroom.'

No sooner the word than came the action.

Laurence swept her up into his arms, her long hair hanging loose and her face snuggled into the hollow of his shoulder. He placed his lips over hers. What started as a sweet, soft, lingering kiss very soon became an urgent, passionate need. He set her down on her feet so that she was standing directly in front of a full-length mirror. She began to get undressed, Laurence watching her every move, his eyes burning into her. Finally she stepped out of what was little more than a G-string, leaving herself wearing only a flimsy bra made of delicate lace.

His hands slowly caressed the swell of her breasts and he felt a thrill run through him as her nipples hardened and he removed her bra.

'Wait, let's get your clothes off,' she cried, at the same time undoing the buttons on his shirt. Two naked bodies now. Her fingers slid down his flat belly and his hands became entwined with hers as they both moved slowly downwards. Hands had reached thighs, they were between legs now, gently touching each other in turn, stroking, rubbing, harder now, faster and faster until they were both caught up in a frantic whirlpool of sensation that finally exploded as they gasped each other's name and fell on to the bed.

It was four o'clock when they finally came out into the lounge, both showered and dressed. They had made gentle love, taking their time and exploring one another's naked bodies. At least that was how it had started; the climax had still taken each of them to heights beyond description.

Now Laurence was aware that he could no longer put off telling Chloe his bad news.

'Chloe, I want you to listen to me, and when I've finished, you may ask questions. Some I may not be able to answer, but I will do my best.'

Fear grabbed her heart. 'All right,' was all she offered, sitting herself down facing him.

'I am going to take you down to the marina for a meal now. Then I am going to go to my apartment, pack a suitcase and make several phone calls, because I have to be in Dover by half past ten tomorrow morning.'

Here we go again, she thought. She spoke slowly. 'Dover... I presume you are going by sea. Am I allowed to know your destination and for how long you will be away this time?'

'Chloe, I know I said I would never take on a job that wouldn't allow you to travel with me, and I am sorry. This journey is going to be one of sheer desperation. It is not a new deal, it is an agreement that I brokered in good faith and it has sadly gone wrong. One party has failed to meet their agreed payment and the folk on the losing end can ill afford to be deprived of their money. I have already received my fee. I am in no way bound to interfere but I just cannot stand by and do nothing. I can't help feeling some responsibility.'

He paused, and there was a heavy silence between them.

When he spoke again, Chloe was aware of the determination in his voice.

'One well-known charity has come forward with offers of help. It really is a sad situation, with a lot of underprivileged children involved. More than that I cannot tell you.'

Chloe's mouth had turned down at the corners. She leaned forward to look him straight in the face. 'Are you going to be in any danger?'

'At some point, the honest answer would have to be yes. However, most deals I set up are to everyone's advantage and by and large we all come out of it with a good feeling. Sorry, Chloe, but I have to take the bad with the good. In any case, if I were to walk away from this one, my integrity would be lost; I would never again be trusted. I don't need to work, you are well aware of that fact, but I like what I do and I feel great when I can help the underdogs.'

'All right, Laurence, you have my blessing. But please try your best to come back safely, because these last few weeks I have kind of got used to having you around.'

Laurie laughed; whether it was from relief or not he wouldn't have been able to say.

'You can be quite a cheeky bitch when it suits you, Miss Collard, but just remember, I shall be back, probably sooner than you expect, so don't go letting my side of the bed. Oh, and by the way, my first appointment when I get back is already written in my diary.'

'And what is that then?'

'I'll tell you over dinner; all that lovemaking has made me hungry. Come on, let's go and show all the other ladies how lucky you are to have me as your escort.'

He managed to dodge the cushion she threw at him and they went down to the restaurant with happy smiles on their faces.

It would be true to say, though, that their lightheartedness in both cases was a covering for their apprehensive thoughts.

Settled in the harbourside restaurant, Laurie ordered steak and a salad for each of them and a bottle of whatever the wine waiter was recommending this week.

Quite suddenly Chloe remarked, 'Dorothy told me that when you left university and came out into the big wide world, you wanted to be a writer. What made you change your mind?'

'Well, as a great man once said, as the

times change, all men change with them.'

'You've got a point there, but a man like you would need a better reason than that.'

He looked thoughtful before forming an answer. 'I became aware that many countries were in need of certain commodities while other countries had more than they required and needed to find a market. Let's say it seemed a good idea to bring the two together.'

'Since then you've helped many charities, and I've been given to understand that your main indulgence is underprivileged children.'

'Ah yes, Dorothy has been talking. Let's say that for most deals I get very well paid. But it never hurts to do a freebie now and again. Ah, here comes our meal. Let's change the subject and enjoy our steaks.'

Later, while Laurie was eating cheese and biscuits and Chloe was smiling her way though a very creamy slice of coffee cake, she suddenly laid down her fork and said, 'This first appointment when you get back, does it involve me?'

He almost choked on a mouthful of cracker but swallowed deeply and tried hard not to laugh as he told her, 'Very much so, and you'd better start preparing, because we're going to a very important wedding.'

'Oh, thank you for telling me. Who's getting married?'

'We are.'

It was several minutes before Chloe could speak. Laurie was thoroughly enjoying watching the various expressions that were moving across her face.

'What about my job?'

'The directors will probably close the business down for the day. No one will want to miss our parade.'

'To be fair, I shall have to ask for leave.'

'Yes, you shouldn't waste any time. I have already been told that you are due two weeks' holiday, but I think you should add compassionate leave on to that. Which would give you a month.'

'A *month?*'

'Now don't come up with any more objections, because I have already set the ball rolling.'

At this moment in her life Chloe knew that there was no man in the world she would rather be married to. But...

Laurie saw the bleak look come to her face and he sighed. 'Now what?'

'You've never even proposed to me!'

It took a full minute, but when the penny did drop, they both fell about laughing.

Suddenly Chloe straightened her face, looked up into his eyes and said, 'Well?'

He got to his feet, came around to her side of the table and knelt down. 'My dearest Chloe, please will you do me the honour of becoming my wife. I swear before God I shall do my utmost to make you happy.'

She had to quickly brush away her silly tears before she was able to lean forward and allow him to kiss her.

Everyone in the restaurant, staff included, had got to their feet and was clapping and cheering, while the manager appeared carrying an ice bucket holding a bottle of champagne.

What a mixture of emotions she had gone through that day, Chloe was thinking as she lay in bed that night. Now she silently prayed that Laurence would be able to settle his business to everyone's satisfaction and come back home safe and sound.

## Chapter 20

The telephone was ringing as Chloe opened the door to her apartment.

'Chloe, it's me, Laurence.'

'Darling! Where are you?'

'You don't need to know that, but listen carefully. Make sure your passport is up to date, and when you receive the package I have already sent by Special Delivery, follow the instructions and I'll be there to meet you when you arrive.'

'Oh Laurie, it is such a relief to hear from you. It's been a helluva long time.'

'No it hasn't, only nineteen days, and I have to tell you, I have worked a miracle. All parties concerned are now friendly and completely satisfied.'

'Great, but what's this about meeting me?'

'No time to talk, wait till you receive the package. Darling, I have to go now, I love you to bits. Bye.'

'I love you too. Bye.'

Well that was short and sweet, Chloe thought as she walked through to her kitchen. She was shivering and so she turned the central heating up. Laurie had asked about her passport; was he thinking of taking her somewhere warm? God, that would be wonderful. She half filled the kettle and switched it on. She was badly in need of a cup of tea. Her mind was running rings inside her head. Why all the mystery? Why couldn't he have told her outright what he was planning? Never look a gift horse in the mouth, she chided herself.

She had tossed and turned for half the night, but all the anxiety was wiped away when at seven forty-five the postman rang her bell and asked her to sign for her package. Slow down, she repeatedly told herself as she tore at the wrappings.

'Jesus wept,' she cried out in delight; a

first-class ticket to Paris, and it was for a flight at four thirty today.

Within minutes she was following instructions and phoning the car pool.

By midday John was there with a very nice car. She had with her only one suitcase, which held her washing things and night clothes, plus some gorgeous underwear, one slinky evening dress and a pair of high-heeled silver sandals, an outfit for the first evening as per Laurie's instructions. He had added that Paris would supply all the other changes of clothes she would need. Her handbag held a good supply of cosmetics.

As it turned out, her mad dash to get to the airport and then the flight across the Channel proved to be fantastic. Laurence was waving furiously as she came through customs at Charles de Gaulle and she broke into a run. He caught her up in his arms and swung around. 'Put me down quickly before people think we are mad,' Chloe implored.

'My darling Chloe, hush, we are in Paris, a city where everybody loves a lover. Come on, let me take you to the beautiful hotel where we shall be staying for a few days.'

He got no objections from Chloe. The only thing that was worrying her was the fact that she might be dreaming, might wake up and find herself in her own bed.

When the taxi drew to a halt in the Place Vendôme, she looked around in amazement.

The Ritz hotel was only a few yards away.

'Your mouth is gaping, Chloe,' Laurence whispered as he took hold of her arm and led her up the steps and into the foyer of the Hôtel de Vendôme.

Chloe did not find her voice until Laurence had tipped the two smart young men who had brought in their luggage and closed the door of their suite behind them. Luxurious was an understatement. There seemed to be elegant mirrors everywhere, and so many chandeliers, each with gold fittings.

'Have I chosen well?' Laurence asked with a sneaky smile spreading over his face. Before Chloe could answer, he led her to the floor-length windows and told her to look down. 'The Place Vendôme gives on to Paris's most brilliant quarter, but I chose this area because it is known to be the temple of Parisian jewellery, and since you are in the trade, so to speak, you might see something that catches your eye.'

For once in her life Chloe could not find words to describe how she was feeling. There was a lump in her throat and her eyes were glistening with tears.

It was no different for Laurence. The very sight of his lovely Chloe here with him in Paris was almost unbelievable. Wait until I show her the bedroom! he thought.

The first night they dined well, danced dreamily for a couple of hours and then went up to their huge bedroom and slowly but surely made wonderful love.

Next morning promised a cloudy, cold day, but who cared, they were in Paris. Croissants and coffee for breakfast, and then Laurie insisted on taking her shopping. They cut a striking pair as they set out. Laurie's clothes were expensive; from the white silk shirt beneath his charcoal-grey suit to his hand-made leather shoes, he looked first-rate. Chloe herself was elegance personified. Laurie had no idea where her simple navy suit and crisp white blouse had come from, but it definitely wasn't a high-street store. Her glossy chestnut hair was today wound up into a French pleat and moistened with a light spray that gave it the kind of lustre most folk had only seen on television adverts.

As she walked, Chloe couldn't help remembering the hand-me-down clothes she'd worn as a child in the East End. Glancing down at her expensive high-heeled shoes, she couldn't help but feel grateful, not only for what she had now, but for what she had left behind.

The shops on the Champs-Elysées were incredible. The elegant assistants praised Chloe's slim figure and admired her taste in clothes, and all the while Laurie was persuading her to be not only rash but daring. Laurie wasn't feeling left out of the goings-on, not by a long chalk. The French young

260

ladies were dancing attendance on him and shooting him admiring glances.

Come lunchtime, they were loaded with smart carrier bags imprinted with famous names and were only too pleased to stroll back to their hotel, where they had lunch before retiring to bed for the afternoon.

On the morning of their second day, Laurence had a mischievous look on his face as he said, 'My turn to do some shopping this morning, and you have to come with me because I shall need your advice.'

Chloe assumed that he too was going to buy clothes and she grinned to herself. He was always immaculately turned out and was not the type of person who needed advice on how to dress. She was surprised then when he asked, 'Do you have any preference when it comes to a jeweller?'

She laughed. 'My personal dealings with such folk are very limited.'

'Well, my darling, you may choose. We have the magnificent Cartier, famous worldwide, and also Van Cleef and Arpels, who have been trading here in Paris since 1906 and are the creators of inspirational jewellery and jewellery watches.'

To say Chloe was amazed would have been putting it mildly, and her long silence forced Laurence to ask what was wrong. She only managed to shake her head.

'My darling, you surely don't need any

telling. I am asking you to come with me to pick your engagement ring.'

There, in the centre of the Place Vendôme, Chloe went towards Laurence, who immediately took her in his arms and held her close. No words were necessary, but minutes later Chloe had to borrow Laurie's handkerchief, not only to wipe away her tears but to dry the lapel of his jacket where her face had been nestling.

An hour spent in the opulent showrooms of Cartier had Chloe spellbound and Laurence pleading with her to try on yet another of the sparkling diamond rings that were being set out in front of her. She finally settled for a wide gold band with a solitary large diamond flanked by two smaller stones.

Laurence had several times suggested that Chloe should try on a ring with a coloured stone such as an emerald or an intensely blue sapphire.

There had been a shocked silence amongst the genteel male assistants when they had heard Chloe's reply: 'Clear diamonds sparkle brilliantly; one can tell they are the real thing. With those coloured stones one is never sure if they are real.' Laurie had almost choked as he coughed to cover up his laughter.

Having been toasted and congratulated by the entire staff, Chloe linked arms with Laurence, and as they walked from the premises suddenly there was no one else in the world that mattered. Just herself and her future husband.

That night as Laurie's hands roamed over her naked body, she relished every movement, and at one point when his mouth closed over her erect nipple, it felt all the more exquisite because very soon she was going to be his wife.

Back in the office after three unforgettable days in Paris, everyone admired her engagement ring and wanted to know the date of the wedding. Holly's questions were endless!

One thing Chloe herself could hardly believe was the fact that she was pregnant. Neither she nor Laurence had given the matter a single thought. Unbelievable but true! How would a man addicted to globe-trotting feel about being a father?

She and Holly were sitting in her lounge having a coffee together. She had told Holly her secret in a moment of panic, and already she was regretting it.

Holly threw caution to the wind and dived in. 'Well, you've had a great time, but that doesn't mean you *have* to marry him.'

Chloe was irritated by Holly's outspoken opinion and it showed in her quick answer. 'No have to about it. I want nothing more in this life than to become Laurie's wife.'

Holly had the sense to quickly change

track. 'Well I can't see the problem then. Women get pregnant every day. It's no big deal, especially where you two are concerned.'

'And what is that supposed to mean?' Chloe asked sharply.

'Well, face facts, the pair of you are rolling in money, the baby will never want for anything, and if you don't want to bring it up yourselves, you can always employ nannies and get on with your own lives.'

After that outburst, there was no going back.

'Thanks for putting it so delicately, Holly. I am happy to tell you that the minute I got over the shock, I have been over the moon. I shall have a family of my own once again.'

'How are you expecting Laurence to react?' Holly asked timidly.

It was a while before Chloe formed an answer.

'Astonished mainly, but once he gets over the shock, I know he will be delighted. He is absolutely marvellous with Amberley. I shall tell him tonight.'

Which meant there would be no point in any more discussion.

Chloe suggested that she and Holly wrap themselves up warmly and take a walk around the marina. The sea air blew away any remaining doubts, and she kissed Holly good night with a warm feeling of anticipation for the evening to come.

Laurence's arrival home was all Chloe could have hoped for.

He had let himself into the apartment using the key she had had cut for him since they had returned from France. She wasn't able to see his face because he was holding high a huge bunch of winter blooms.

She took the flowers from him and, smiling sweetly, held her face up to be kissed. He opened the conversation by saying, 'How about we spend Christmas in Spain?'

'Laurie, may we please put that decision to one side for the moment. I have put a bottle of wine in the fridge, I'll fetch the glasses if you will open the bottle.'

'Darling, you sound very serious, is anything wrong?'

'I don't happen to think so, but it depends. You will probably be astonished.' Chloe couldn't hold back any longer; she hadn't even given him time to take his coat off before she blurted out, 'Laurie, I am going to have a baby.' Suddenly she was smiling, despite the pricking of ridiculous tears behind her eyes. 'Oh Laurie, I'm sorry.'

'Well I'm not.' He came towards her and they met in the middle of the room, and they were both laughing and exchanging kisses. Finally he set her aside while he took his coat off, then she was back in his arms.

'I shouldn't be surprised, but I am.'

'I know, I kept telling myself that same thing, over and over again.'

'I'm just a bit taken aback, but thrilled to my very backbone. I am going to be a dad! I'll fetch that wine, but you must be careful, my darling: a small drink now, and then even at our wedding, fruit juice only for you.'

While Laurie went to the fridge, Chloe let out an enormous sigh of relief, because now she could stop being worried and fearful and start being pleased and excited instead.

Laurence poured some wine into each glass, and as they raised them he said, 'Here's to us being the best parents ever.'

'Please God,' Chloe murmured.

'First on the agenda is setting a date for our wedding, don't you agree?'

She grinned at him cheekily. 'I don't think we'll be able to have a big white wedding in church now. I'll never be able to get into a slinky wedding dress, and anyway I shouldn't be seen wearing white.'

Laurie couldn't help himself, he was doubled over with laughter. When finally he straightened up, he took out his handkerchief and wiped his eyes before saying, 'Have you stepped back into the Dark Ages, for Christ's sake? Worried about what folk will say? What are you thinking of wearing? Sackcloth and ashes?'

His high spirits were infectious and Chloe

felt her own heart lift. The dark days of loneliness, with all her anxieties and anguish, were over, and all at once she was filled with happiness. She was going to be a wife and a mother and together they'd be a real family.

For the rest of that evening they talked excitedly about the forthcoming wedding and the birth of their first baby as though they were the only couple in the world to whom this happy event had ever happened.

It was only as they were getting ready for bed that the thought of Laurie's mother came to Chloe's mind. She would have to be told, no two ways about that. Would she think Chloe had trapped her son into marriage by getting herself pregnant?

Two days later, they were no nearer to setting a date for their wedding. That morning Laurie suggested they go for a spin in his car. 'Think I have come up with the best answer for our immediate plans,' he told her.

It was a beautiful morning, a heavy white frost covering the grass and the bare trees glowing with a covering of icicles. The sun was shining as Laurie drove towards the South Downs to reach Eastbourne's famous landmark, Beachy Head, There he stopped the car and switched off the engine. The view was glorious. Chloe gazed out over the sparkling sea and waited to hear his plans, feeling slightly apprehensive.

'I want us to be married as soon as possible, but that is not going to happen if we're talking about a huge do. Sending out invitations, deciding which children are to be pageboys and bridesmaids and God knows what else. Finding a date that suits everyone is always a nightmare, then there's picking the church, ordering flowers ... the organisation alone will take days. Time is of the essence because of the baby, so I am suggesting that we go off somewhere on our own to get married and have a big celebration in the new year.'

There didn't seem to be anything else to say. Chloe sighed, but it was a happy sigh. 'I couldn't agree with you more,' she said at last. 'I don't have any family, and my friends will all be wanting to be with their families over the Christmas period.'

The whole idea was so wonderful that she felt quite winded. Finally she said, 'Whatever you decide, Laurence. As long as I come away from your chosen location as your wife, I shall be as happy as the day is long, and so will he.' She smiled broadly as she patted her tummy.

'Oh, so you have decided that you are carrying my son, have you?' Laurie laughed before leaning towards her and gently kissing her lips.

'I kind of hope so; it would please your mother so much.'

'Well you can stop that before it gets going.

Boy or girl, if my mother doesn't like it I shall see that we put an even greater distance between us.'

'I'm sure it will be all right. We must go to great lengths to explain to her and your sister why we are getting married quickly, and when we do have our celebration day we must make sure they are able to attend.'

'Amberley will feel cheated,' Laurence laughed.

'I shall buy her a new dress and we'll think of something special for her to do during the party.'

Chloe's high spirits were infectious and Laurie felt the sudden lifting of his own heart. The worries of organising a wedding, with all its anxieties and anguish, receded, and all at once he was filled with complete happiness, something he had not experienced for a long time. He smiled, sat up straight and switched the engine on.

'Are we going home already?' Chloe asked.

'No we most certainly are not. Look over that way,' he said, pointing a finger. 'That is the Beachy Head Hotel, and I am going to take you there for a slap-up lunch.'

What a wonderful welcoming sight met them as they entered the saloon bar: a huge open fireplace in which several large logs were burning.

They ordered lunch from the menu, and

while they waited, the waitress brought a pot of coffee and a jug of cream. Chloe poured them each a cup while Laurie waited patiently. After a long pause he said, 'Well?'

All Chloe could think of to say was, 'You make it sound so easy, but I am truly thrilled, honestly I am.'

'You won't feel cheated, losing your big day?'

'I shall have my special day, with you all to myself. Then when we do celebrate with friends, I shall be able to say to them, "Meet my husband."'

He laughed before saying, 'And you're quite happy to leave all the arrangements for a simple wedding down to me?'

'Yes, of course I am.'

They thoroughly enjoyed their lunch, but Laurie was inwardly smiling to himself. Chloe couldn't have even an inkling of what he was about to set up.


## Chapter 21

The second Saturday in December was a beautiful day. It was bitterly cold and the sky was promising snow, but a weak sun had broken through and Chloe felt she had never been happier in her whole life.

Laurence was unique! There was no other word to describe him. How in God's name he had managed to organise so much in such a short space of time was beyond her.

Here she was standing in the harbour at St Peter Port, looking at yachts, cruisers and seagoing vessels of all shapes and sizes. Here in the Channel Islands there was no shortage of money.

She was still having a job to get her head around everything that had taken place over the past few days. First off Laurie had told her that they would be getting married on a cruiser out at sea. He had a friend who owned a boat, and this friend was willing for Laurie to charter the vessel over the whole of the Christmas period.

Hardly had that information sunk in than four days later Laurie had them both at Gatwick boarding a plane for Guernsey. During the flight, almost as an afterthought, he had thrown in the fact that his friend was a master mariner and thus was by law allowed to officiate at weddings that took place on the high seas.

Now Laurie was holding her hand and hurrying her along, at the same time going to great lengths to point out which yacht was the one they were about to board.

Dear Jesus, Chloe thought, her imagination must be running away with her. She was finding it impossible to believe her own eyes. At the rail of this massive luxurious-looking vessel a woman was holding a little girl up in her arms. The girl was waving furiously to attract their attention.

It couldn't be!

But it was.

Dorothy Whitlocke, Laurence's sister, and the child she was holding was Amberley.

From a small motorboat a burly-looking man with a weather-beaten face was shouting something up at Laurie, who went down a few steps to enable himself to hear what the man was saying.

When he came back up, he took hold of Chloe's elbow. 'Tommy Goodwin has asked that man to take us out to the boat. He'll pick our luggage up later on. Be careful how you come down these stone steps, they are very wet and slippery.'

Chloe had not uttered one word since she had sighted Dorothy and Amberley. The lengths this man had gone to just to please her were unbelievable.

After a short ride in the motorboat, they were safely aboard *The White Star*. Laurie introduced Chloe to Tommy Goodwin, who was a tall man dressed in corduroy trousers and a thick white Aran jersey. He welcomed her aboard warmly as he shook her hand.

The next five minutes could only be described as uproar, until Tommy clapped his hands and said, 'Quiet, everyone, allow me to do the introductions.'

Chloe, who had Amberley in her arms, put her down. The little girl stood still but she was still clasping Chloe's hand very tightly.

'First off, me and my family. I am Thomas Goodwin, a fully fledged master mariner, this is my wife Audrey and our son John, who is five years old. Dorothy and her little girl I gather you already know. Last but by no means least is my first mate Pete, full name Peter Bolton, and as you will find out as we travel on the high seas, Pete is a very useful fellow to have on board. There are eight lifebelts on the vessel, and as you can see, both John and Amberley are wearing theirs. When below and we're battened down it is okay for them to take them off, but up on deck they must wear them at all times. I think that is about all for now: eight of us in all, a nice round number.'

'Go and play with John,' Dorothy quietly told Amberley. 'I have a few things to straighten out with Chloe.'

The little girl trotted off obediently.

'I am convinced that my brother has his own whirlwind installed in his body. I just can't keep up with him,' Dorothy confided when they were alone.

'That makes two of us,' Chloe assured her.

'Not that I'm not truly grateful to him for including me and Amberley on this trip,' Dorothy continued. 'Until he came up with this offer I had two choices: Christmas alone with Amberley and Fergus or pack up and go back to my mother's. What on earth persuaded him to come up with this idea?'

'Your guess is as good as mine, but I am truly so pleased to have you and Amberley along. What have you done with Fergus?'

Dorothy laughed. 'Your gardener offered to have him, and as Fergus knows him well, it was a godsend.'

'Would you mind if we talk later,' said Chloe. 'I am dying for a cup of tea, and more importantly I need a wash and the use of a toilet.'

At that point they heard Laurie calling. He was waiting to give Chloe a tour of the ship.

Below deck was a world of wonders. Spectacular and extremely impressive. She had got used to luxury living whilst travelling with Roger, but this was beyond anything she had seen before.

There were four large bedrooms, two on each side of the craft. Chloe was informed that the fourth bedroom, for the time being, was out of bounds. The Goodwins had one of the remaining rooms, Chloe was to share with Dorothy and Amberly, while Laurence and Peter were bunking together temporarily.

The galley was a real eye-opener. Audrey Goodwin took over the tour at this point. There was far more space than Chloe had imagined, and every piece of equipment that a fully qualified chef would need.

'The deep freeze is very well stocked and so are the dry cupboards. I imagine Tommy will be taking us into port some evenings to dine, but just in case we should decide to celebrate Christmas Day on board, everything is here down to the last detail and between us three women I am sure we shall not be found wanting. There is a goose and a crown of turkey, which we should take out early on Christmas Eve just to make sure they thaw out thoroughly. I do hope that all meets with your approval.' Audrey turned to face Chloe and was pleased to notice that she was smiling and showing her admiration by clapping her hands together.

Chloe couldn't believe her luck. An outstanding sea voyage and every single thing laid on for a fantastic Christmas. Behind her back she crossed her fingers, just in case it all turned out to be too good to be true.

Once *The White Star* had left Guernsey, they settled into a routine that suited everybody. The two children were shown how to make an ordinary paper sack into a Christmas one that Father Christmas would come and fill with presents if they were good. There were loads of questions and arguments as to how Father Christmas would know where they were. Peter Bolton was great; taking the children up front, he switched on several machines that lit up and explained that these were tracker lights that told people exactly where *The White Star* was at any time of the day or night. As to how Father Christmas would get on to the ship, he told them that once they were asleep on Christmas Eve, a helicopter would fly overhead and Father Christmas would lower down their presents for their parents to put into their sacks.

'How will you know which parcels are for me and which ones are for Amberley?' John badly needed to know.

Pete replied quickly. 'Everyone knows, even the reindeer, that pink parcels are for little girls and blue parcels are for boys.'

Congratulations all round. The children seemed well satisfied.

Christmas Eve. All three women had been busy, but now it was early afternoon and the preparations had been finalised. The huge oven had been set on to low and the smell from the slow-roasting birds was making everyone feel hungry. The ship hadn't travelled far; Tom Goodwin had chosen to keep close to the islands, and tonight they were all going ashore to have their evening meal on the isle of Sark. Meanwhile the men were amusing the children up on deck.

Chloe was intrigued by the presence of Peter Bolton on board. He was a nice enough man, tall, with a well honed figure, and he spoke with an educated accent, but what was a man in his late thirties doing working on board a ship over the Christmas period? Her curiosity got the better of her and she had to put the question to Laurence. He admitted that he had asked the same question and Tommy's answer had been short. Three years ago Peter's wife had died giving birth to their first child; the child had only lived for a few hours. Ever since, Peter had been a bit of a loner.

Chloe heard Dorothy calling her to come to the bedroom they had been sharing. On the bed she had laid out a large white box, and as she asked Chloe to open it, the expression on her face was a mixture of pride and delight.

'Chloe,' she said, her cheeks flushing, 'when my brother told me of his plans, I couldn't believe that Amberley and myself were to be included. This is my way of saying how happy I am for both of you.'

Chloe knew even before she lifted the lid that it was a wedding dress. When she glanced down, she gasped.

'It is so beautiful,' she exclaimed, carefully lifting the white silk from the box. 'I wonder if it will fit me?' she said, patting her tummy.

'I know it will,' Dorothy laughed. 'You're not showing yet, and I asked Laurie to sneak your emerald-green evening dress out and took it with me to Harrods to check your size.'

Chloe held the fabric up to her face. It felt creamy against her cheek. There were yards and yards of it, yet it felt light as air. The bodice had her staring in wonder: intricate metallic lacework with interwoven gold and silver threads. The result was stunning.

She turned, smiling. 'Dorothy, it was so thoughtful of you. I just don't know how I shall *ever* be able to thank you.'

Yesterday they had talked about the forth-coming wedding and Chloe had shown Dorothy a white linen suit that she had bought to wear for the ceremony.

Now she laughed. 'You certainly kept your intentions close to your chest.'

'I have another surprise. In that box over there is a dress for Amberley. It is of the very palest shade of pink and she hasn't seen it yet, doesn't even know about it.'

Chloe strove to keep back the tears, but she wasn't able to resist the temptation to once more hold the dress up to her body while she stared at her reflection in the full-length mirror fixed to the wall.

'You will look so beautiful,' Dorothy whis-pered.

Chloe let the dress fall back down on to the bed and the two women, soon to be-come related, hugged each other warmly.

It was a wonderful way to spend the evening of Christmas Eve.

The children had had a sleep in the afternoon, and during the meal they were both polite and well behaved. At nine o'clock they said good night to all the islanders they had become friendly with, and the party left the restaurant. For once the children were anxious to get to bed, to hang their sacks up and wait to see what Father Christmas would bring them.

Christmas morning. The fourth bedroom had been opened and Chloe couldn't believe her eyes as Dorothy ushered her into it. It'd been transformed into a wedding parlour.

'Close the door quickly,' Dorothy ordered. 'We don't want the groom to see his bride before the wedding.'

Chloe was rooted to the spot. She was having a hard job to keep her composure. Everyone had done so much for her; all she had to do now was get herself dressed in her wedding gown. This was the most important day of her life, the day she was going to get married.

Sitting on a stool facing a mirror, wearing pure white silk underwear, she started on her make-up, using only a little blusher and just a fine outline of lipstick. Dorothy helped her to slip her arms into the long sleeves of the dress and lifted it on to her shoulders, then she knelt down and began to do up the long line of satin-covered buttons that ran from the waist right up to the neck. She couldn't help smiling when she thought of her brother, later on tonight, having to help his bride get out of the dress!

Finally she fixed a headband into Chloe's hair. She had personally bought the band and had covered it early this morning with fresh white freesias. It looked truly wonderful set into Chloe's silky auburn hair.

Standing back, she gasped at the sight of this beautiful bride who would soon be her sister-in-law. 'Are you ready?' she asked.

'Thanks to you, yes, I am.'

'Okay, here we go.'

Music was playing in the dining room and sweet-smelling candles were burning as Chloe walked the length of the room on Dorothy's arm, Amberley and John making a lovely picture as they followed behind.

Tommy Goodwin had taken his duties very seriously. A well-polished table had been set up with a vase of fresh flowers at each end. He stood behind the table, a bible and several legal documents set out in front of him.

Laurence and Peter Bolton, who was acting as best man, stood to the left of Thomas.

As Chloe neared, Laurence took her hand. They gazed deeply into each other's eyes, and Chloe felt his love reaching to the depths of her soul.

Laurie was so overwhelmed, he had a job to find the right words. 'There has never been a more beautiful bride,' he murmured softly.

'Chloe?' Tommy asked. 'Laurence?'

Laurie nodded. 'We're ready.'

'Do you, Laurence, take Chloe to be your lawful wedded wife, to love, honour and cherish, in sickness and in health, forsaking all others, until death do you part?'

'I do,' Laurence said.

'And do you, Chloe, take Laurence to be your lawful wedded husband, to love, honour and cherish, in sickness and in health, forsaking all others, until death do you part?'

'I do,' Chloe murmured, tears burning behind her eyelids.

Tommy nodded at Peter. 'Do you have the ring?'

Peter hastily put his hand into his jacket pocket and produced a small leather box. He took out the plain gold band and placed it on the open page of the bible that Tommy was holding out to him.

'Please take the ring and place it on Chloe's finger,' Tommy instructed.

Laurence did so, repeating the words that Tommy read out: 'With this ring I thee wed, and with all my worldly goods I thee endow.'

There was a slight pause after that as Dorothy moved forward to place another gold band into Chloe's hand. This ring had belonged to her father, and it was a surprise to everyone except the two women, who had previously arranged it.

Sliding the ring on to Laurie's finger, Chloe kept hold of his hand, repeating after Tommy, 'With this ring I thee wed, and with all my worldly goods I thee endow.' As she spoke, she gazed into Laurie's eyes, and now they clasped hands and Chloe felt her heart would burst, so full of love was it.

Tommy gave a discreet cough.

'By the powers vested in me by the Church of England and the Maritime Board of Directors, I now pronounce you husband and wife. You may kiss the bride.'

Tilting her face upwards, Chloe received her first kiss as a married woman. Laurie's arms were around her, holding her so very tightly.

'Till death do us part, Laurie.' Chloe murmured the words.

'And beyond, my darling,' he confidently vowed.

'Chloe, please Chloe.' Amberley had been so good and so patient, but there were a couple of things she really needed to know.

Laurie had released his hold on his bride and was about to shake hands with Tommy and Peter when Chloe, who had knelt down to speak to Amberley, looked up at him with a cheeky smile on her face. 'It seems your niece would like to ask you a couple of questions.'

'Well Amberley, no one else ever had a more beautiful bridesmaid than we have had today, so ask away.' He bent down and lifted her high in his arms.

'Uncle Laurie, now you are married to Chloe, does that make her my real auntie?'

'It sure does, next question.'

'Does it also mean you are allowed to sleep with her?' Without waiting for Laurie's reply, Amberley rushed on. 'Because if you two are going to sleep in that wedding room where we got dressed, then tonight I won't have to sleep in Mummy's bed. I shall have a bed to myself and that's good because Mummy kicks sometimes when she is asleep.'

Laurence set Amberley down on her feet. He dared not glance at the other adults, who were plainly waiting to hear his reply.

'Sweetheart, I shall personally come and tuck you into your own bed tonight, and yes, it does mean that Chloe and I shall have our own room. Now, I think we have a great Christmas dinner waiting for all of us. Shall we troop in?'

Little John had stood by looking very serious as all this conversation took place. Now he decided to speak up. 'My mummy said we haven't got a Christmas dinner today, we're having a wedding feast instead.'

All eyes were turned to Audrey Goodwin and a chorus of thanks went round the room.

'No thanks are needed. What a memory we all shall have of today. It has been such a privilege to be part of it all.' There was great sincerity to be heard in her voice.

The meal really was a feast. No one was in a hurry, course after course was served and the two children being there to pull the crackers made it perfect.

Now and again Chloe found herself watching Peter and Dorothy deep in conversation, and she hoped and prayed that maybe when this trip was over they might want to see each other again. She felt so loved and wanted herself, knowing that her days of loneliness were gone, and she very much wanted Dorothy to feel the same.

Finally no more food could be eaten and the day was drawing to a close. Laurie bent his head and whispered in his wife's ear, 'What will be a decent time for us to retire?'

She grinned, knowing full well what he was aiming for.

Getting no reply, he again drew her close and in a low voice asked, 'Will sex seem any different now that it's legal?'

'Yes, I might have to tell you that I have a headache.'

'And then I shall throw you overboard.'

'You wouldn't dare treat a pregnant woman like that.'

'Bit early in the day for you to be using that excuse.'

Their happy laughter said it all.

It was a pleasant evening, with good music and excellent wine, and the children kept everyone on their toes, but at last Tommy opened a bottle of champagne and made one last toast to the bride and groom.

Dorothy and Audrey had been into what was now to be Chloe and Laurence's bedroom. Everything had been made tidy, the bedspread turned down, and the bed did look extremely inviting. Yet somehow Chloe felt different, and Laurie too seemed reluctant to make the first move. However, when she pointed out that there were a couple of dozen buttons on the back of her dress that needed undoing, he sat down on the floor and fell about laughing.

It took a minute or two before he could bring himself to explain.

'Do you make a habit of acquiring dresses that need a man's hand to get you in and out of them?'

Chloe hadn't the faintest idea what he was talking about.

Noting her bewilderment, he said, 'In Devon, when I came back to find you with that slinky dress around your ankles because you couldn't reach to do the zip up? Remember?'

The same day we first made love, she told herself, but aloud she said, 'If you don't hurry up and help me out of this dress, I might fall asleep the minute we do end up in bed.'

'I'll tear it off you before that happens,' he threatened, and began undoing the buttons, working from the bottom upwards. Finally the dress fell to the floor. Her arms were around him, and he felt her hands sliding down his body. Wearing only lacy silk panties and bra, she pressed her hips against him. She felt him respond, and she straightened up and stepped out of the dress, which was still lying around her ankles.

Laurie watched her, marvelling at her loveliness. She was undressing him now, and there was a sudden urgency in both of them. It was like a tidal wave sweeping them both along, but it felt so very different tonight. They weren't new with each other, yet it felt as if they were only just discovering each other for the very first time.

'Take me to bed, please, Laurie.'

He needed no second bidding. He quickly scooped her up into his arms and laid her on the soft mattress. She felt the strength of his body on top of her. She didn't think there was a particle of her flesh that he hadn't kissed. Then his movements became urgent. There was a long, sweet thrust and her husband was inside her, and as his wife she moved to his rhythm. It was different, magnificent, and she was saying over and over again, 'Oh Laurie, oh my darling.'

Their faces were close, although he remained still. Chloe leant forward and placed her lips on his. It was a gentle kiss, a promise, and as such he received it. And so warm and tender was the light in his eyes, so deep was his expression of love for her that she knew with a surge of certainty that married life with this man was going to be wonderful.

Much later that night, as she lay in Laurie's arms, she silently thanked God for having sent her this man, and for allowing her to have such a wonderful wedding day.

Her husband's thoughts were running along the same lines, though he was looking a whole lot further ahead than today's events. His sincere prayer was for a long and healthy life for them both.

## Chapter 22

Just seven months after their wedding day, Chloe gave birth to their son. She was certain that there had never been a prouder father, and no mother had given birth to a baby more beautiful than Bradley John Walmsley. Thick blond hair and deep blue eyes, weighing a healthy eight pounds. She heaved a happy sigh as Laurence brushed the damp hair away from her forehead before placing his lips to hers to deliver the sweetest and most gentle kiss.

It seemed to Chloe that the wheels of time were spinning faster than they used to and there were not enough hours in the day for her to do everything she wanted to.

Laurence still held a passionate conviction that wealthy folk should help underprivileged children, and with Chloe's memories of her own early life and her first-hand knowledge of poverty, she was a hundred per cent with him on that.

Every single day she was aware of how fortunate she had been. Since meeting Laurence, there had not been a single moment that she would have changed in any shape or form.

Best of all was the fact that her hopes for Dorothy and Peter Bolton had been realised. Four months after her own wedding day, Laurence, as promised, had arranged a celebration for all their friends and relatives. It was a really impressive affair held at the Grand Hotel in Brighton, where he had had the foresight to book several bedrooms for the night so that folk would not have to travel home in the early hours of the morning. By then Chloe had been showing signs of her pregnancy, and so many congratulations had been in order. It was also on that very night that Dorothy and Peter had made a point of telling Laurence and Chloe that they were an item and that they intended to be married in the near future.

Laurie had also arranged for a limousine to be sent to north Devon so that his mother and three of her friends could travel to the party in comfort. Mrs Walmsley had had to take on board the fact that her new daughter-in-law was already pregnant and that her only daughter had now met a man who had already proposed marriage to her, but she had done so without once letting slip the smile on her face.

As he'd asked for yet another bottle of champagne to be opened, Laurence felt more than pleased that everything had gone so smoothly.

Life took on a regular pattern, and when, eighteen months after Bradley was born, Chloe gave birth to their second son, Alistair Bruce Walmsley, both she and Laurence decided that their family was complete.

Chloe would often remind herself of just how well Laurence had settled down to married life. They still lived in Brentwood Avenue, in the house Roger had left her. Dorothy was still a few doors up the road, and was extremely happy with her new husband and pleased that Amberley had taken to Peter so quickly. The two families got on well together and social life was shared. Yet as the years went by, Chloe couldn't help noticing that Laurence was not as comfortable with this life as he led her to believe. Oh, he'd been a great dad to their two boys all the years they had been growing up, there was no doubt about that, but time had rolled by and very soon both their sons would be leaving home, hopefully to go on to university.

Laurie might not admit it, but there was something missing from his life. Within the last year he had only been abroad once, yet he couldn't abandon his past altogether. He kept himself abreast of the news, saw where help was needed, and if he could, he contributed help, all still under the banner of silence.

This morning, with breakfast over, she noticed that he was poring over a copy of the *Daily Telegraph*. That in itself was not enough to ring any alarm bells, but when he got up to fetch a pen and a notepad and began to copy down details from the paper, she dearly wanted to ask questions.

She knew him well enough to keep her thoughts to herself, however, and wait until Laurie raised his head. His first question threw her. It wasn't at all what she'd been expecting.

'Chloe love, do you know if Peter got any feedback from that interview he went to in London last week?'

'Dorothy hasn't mentioned it. She did talk to me about it during the two days he was away, but that was mainly airing her worries, that kind of thing.'

'Really? I know you can be a damn good listener, but what worries have Peter and Dorothy got that need airing?'

'Well I can only tell you what I think. For the first time in his life Peter hasn't got a full-time job. Dorothy didn't want him going back to sea, and I don't know what his money situation is. I know Dorothy is very well off, and maybe Peter thinks he should be earning a wage.'

'God, I never gave it a thought! You might well be right. On the other hand, he must have an income from somewhere. They've been married a good many years. Perhaps it isn't money; he might just feel the need to be doing something, which I understand only too well.'

'Don't tell me you'd rather be brokering deals halfway around the world than being at home with me and the boys.'

'Oh don't be ridiculous, of course not, but I do need to be up and doing something. If it will keep my mind active and help good causes along the way, all the better for everyone involved.'

'It sounds to me as if you already have something ticking away in that busy mind of yours.'

'If you had suggested that yesterday I would have denied it.' With a thoughtful look on his face, Laurie got to his feet and handed her the newspaper.

'Umm,' Chloe murmured as she finished reading the article. 'It doesn't bear thinking about.'

'That's just the point. It is about time that somebody did start making decisions. You've only read the headlines and you're obviously horrified. Since the Africans decided that white farmers should no longer be allowed to work their land, matters in Zimbabwe have gone from bad to worse. There has been so much killing and destruction that normal life has become impossible. Mainly it is the poorer section of the population that is suffering the most. It began with local workers being shot if they dared to put a foot on a white man's farm. Families who have lived and farmed in Zimbabwe for years have been ordered to leave, and if they protest, they too are shot. A few white farmers are struggling on, but life is made impossible for them; they have always relied on the local men and women to work with them. It hasn't taken long for the farmers to realise they can no longer stay in Zimbabwe. The worst part is that after years of hard work, they are leaving with nothing, unable even to withdraw their money from the banks.'

The silence that followed seemed endless, and Chloe was relieved when Laurie began once again to speak. He was like a dog with a bone; she knew full well that he wasn't going to leave this problem alone.

'Without cultivation of the land, there is no food, and children are dying from starvation. All the big charity organisations are sending food and supplies, but without proper supervision at the other end, it's not getting through to the people who need it.'

Chloe couldn't bear to look at Laurie's face. His tone of voice had told her how angry he was. 'Shall I put the TV on? If all the papers have picked up on this subject, then I'm sure the BBC will have regular news bulletins.'

Laurence went on talking as if she hadn't spoken.

'There will always be some people who have no conscience, who will connive to make a fast few quid, never mind the trail of misery they leave behind.'

His expression said it all. It was a challenge, just what he was used to, and Chloe knew that he was about to get involved again, and that nothing she could say or do would make the slightest bit of difference.

It was the first week in May. The evenings were now lighter for much longer and a watery sun was still shining as the four adults settled down to what was supposed to be a friendly get-together. Peter, having read the newspapers earlier in the day, started the ball rolling.

'It doesn't seem feasible that a country so rich in diamonds and gold can allow small children to die from starvation,' he said, sadly shaking his head.

'That in itself proves a point,' agreed Laurie. 'The white farmers knew how to get the best from the land and they provided work for the local men and women. Without that local labour the land is not being developed.'

'Words alone won't help,' Peter said slowly. 'I'd like to assist in any way I can. If you have any ideas, you can count me in.' He paused for a moment. 'First off I feel I ought to apologise. I have been holding the cards close to my chest for far too long when really I should have been more open and discussed matters with Dorothy. When my wife and child died, I thought life was over for me. It takes a long while to move on from something like that and get back to normal.'

'We do understand,' Laurence was quick to reassure him, 'You needed to grieve, it can't have been easy for you.'

'As a matter of fact, until Tommy invited me on board ship that Christmas, every single day had been hellish. Dorothy saved my life. It was she who gave me the will to go on living.'

Peter heard himself come out with this admission and was amazed that he had found the courage to say the impulsive words. The moments when he had reached rock bottom had never been acknowledged or admitted, even to himself.

'I have been clinging on to Dorothy like a drowning man for all these years, and that has to change. I did go up to London last week, but the fact that I wasn't offered the job was my own fault: my heart wasn't in it. You must have been wondering how I stand cashwise. Over the years I have made some damn good investments. When Marion died, I sold our lovely house for a vast sum of money, which I have never touched, and I do receive an excellent pension from the Merchant Navy. So financially I am absolutely fine, but the need to work is making me desperate.'

'Thanks for being so frank,' Laurie said. 'Nobody knows better than I that the urge to work can be great.'

Dorothy was amazed at her husband's impulsive words, but she was truly grateful that he had brought his feelings out into the open. Beyond any doubt she loved this gentle man. After the disgusting way her first husband had behaved towards her, Peter had been heaven-sent.

The fire that Laurence loved to light when they spent an evening at home snapped and crackled, little flames leaping as he threw yet another log into the grate before coming to settle beside Chloe on the settee.

'It's pretty disgusting.' Dorothy pushed aside the newspaper. 'Every man and woman in this country will always contribute to the Red Cross, and when the lasses from the Salvation Army walk into a pub there is never a man that doesn't put his hand in his pocket to find coins to drop into their collecting tins. There's dozens of charities more than willing to make sure that what Zimbabwe is most in need of is either shipped or flown out to them, but to read that somewhere en route the consignments are being hijacked is abominable.' This had been a long statement for Dorothy, but she felt better for having made her feelings known.

'I'll fetch the cheese board and the finger food that Chloe has prepared if you will open that bottle of wine on the sideboard Laurie said, nodding at Peter.

With the men out of the room, Chloe looked at her sister-in-law, sitting there in her black polo-necked sweater with her make-up and glossy hair immaculate, and was filled with curiosity. 'Are you happy with the way your life has turned out, Dorothy?'

'Yes Chloe, I am. I adore being married to Peter, but I still find enough to do to fill my time. Teaching part-time is perfect for me. I must say I'm pleased that it sounds as though Laurie is thinking of getting involved in charity work again. It would be good for Peter to join him; it would give him a sense of purpose and keep his mind occupied. He has never accepted the fact that I still work and he doesn't, although to be truthful, he does so much around the house.'

Chloe's thoughts were running along the same lines. Keeping busy and active would help them all to stay young. She felt she could face getting old when time really caught up with them, but she hated the idea of getting slovenly. She took great pains with her appearance, still bought expensive classic clothes and wore them well. When she looked into a mirror, she saw what Laurence still loved and admired about her. An erect, slim figure of a woman who was proud and indomitable.

The outcome of that evening saw Laurie and Peter travelling together on the eight fifty train to London the very next morning.

On arrival, Laurie suggested that they walk from the railway station to the City, because he believed that laziness caused heart attacks in men of his age. This concern with his health was foolish, for he still cut an upright, striking figure. Good clothes had always been part of his image.

Having made several phone calls last night, Laurie had finally been offered a piece of information that had brought his head up sharply and then put a smile on his face. He wasn't going to share the knowledge, but when the time came, as come it would, he would see that his informer was well rewarded. He always preferred to move in roundabout ways, leaving no trail, and if necessary he would move with stealth.

It had just turned eleven o'clock by the time Laurence and Peter were seated in the ground-floor office of the Save the Children Fund. Laurence made the introductions, explaining that he had telephoned for an appointment the previous evening, and after that nothing was too much trouble for Miss Gregory, a small woman in her thirties with curly hair.

'I will just see if Mr Harvey is free. In the meantime, would you care to take coffee?'

Miss Gregory was soon back, and the two men were invited to come upstairs, where the coffee would be brought to them.

David Harvey, a well-dressed but overweight man in his fifties, held out his hand as Peter and Laurie entered the room. They were soon joined by another man, who was introduced as Alan Freeman, the charity's chief accountant. Coffee was brought and served, then Miss Gregory sat down with a notepad and pen at the ready and the meeting began.

David Harvey seemed to suddenly come to life. Looking at Laurence, he said, 'I have been made aware of the telephone conversation one of my colleagues had with you last night, and I must say he was so impressed that he lost no time in checking your credentials. Such a generous gesture as you two gentlemen have made makes our work not only easier but so very worthwhile.'

Let's not be hasty, Laurie was telling himself. He wanted to decide where his aims lay before asking what the options were. There would be so much satisfaction to be gained if he could sort out this very tricky problem, but he needed to be sure that this was the best way to go about it.

Both Peter and Laurie gave their full attention to what was being said about the distribution of food being sent to Zimbabwe and the problems that had arisen. David Harvey was of the opinion that the trouble was at both ends. 'Cargo goes astray before it leaves the docks, and on arrival anywhere in the world there are always workers who think they are entitled to priority.'

When the room had finally gone quiet, Laurie stood up. He needed more time before he was ready to discuss what he believed was the solution to the problem. What he did tell these gentlemen was that making compromises work was his special talent.

Handshakes all round and a date set for another meeting in two days' time.

Out in the street, both Peter and Laurence

were breathing heavily. Peter was the first to move. 'Come on, Laurie,' he urged. 'Nothing ventured, nothing gained. All we have to do now is summon up some Dutch courage.'

Laurie didn't reply. He grinned at his brother-in-law and together they walked towards the nearest pub.

Each of them was asking themselves the same question. What the hell were they getting themselves into? Neither had an answer.

## Chapter 23

The last few days felt as if a whirlwind had blown into his life, Lawrence was thinking as he drove through the busy streets of London. He came to yet another junction on the interminable South Circular road and the light turned from green to amber. His first instinct was to push his foot to the floor and race the signal. He gave a weary sigh, flapped his arm out of the window like a fool, and came to a careful stop.

He should try not to worry; nervous people made mistakes. He ought to forget about Zimbabwe, think about something else. Easier said than done. He was in this matter now up to his ears.

The lights changed and he pulled forward.

Some good had already come of their visit to Save the Children: Peter had been introduced to some people at Oxfam, and the long and the short of it was that he'd been offered paid office work four days a week.

And Laurence himself? Well, there was no going back now.

He had several things to pick up from various places in London today, but his last stop, and the most important of all, was to pay a visit to the Home Office. He had made two telephone calls yesterday to ensure that those who needed to know that he would be travelling to Zimbabwe had been informed. Papers that might prove to be useful should his visit not proceed too smoothly would have been prepared and would be waiting for him to collect.

Why was he going to Zimbabwe? How many more times was he going to ask himself that very same question?

He was taking nothing of importance with him except his knowledge, which he was going to trade for another piece of information. If it worked, he would be back in England within days and once more his reputation would be covered in glory. But if all that were so, why did he have this feeling that for the first time ever he was deluding himself?

Up ahead and to his left he noticed signs giving directions to a multi-storey car park.

He made an instant decision. Ten minutes later he was parked up and using his mobile phone. It was time to call in a few favours, and if it all went to plan, he wouldn't even have to leave the country.

Three phone calls later, Laurie had an amused smile on his face. It wasn't always what you knew but *who* you knew that could make a difference in today's world.

It was midday, and Laurie was in the small office above the Bulldog Club in the heart of London's Docklands. It was a working men's club that catered for every form of recreation for these hard-working dockside labourers.

A surge of hot air had hit him as he'd entered the club, and he was glad when Danny Cole took his jacket from him and led him upstairs. Danny didn't change. He was well over six feet tall, broad-shouldered, built like the side of a house, and he took keeping fit to the full limit. Laurence had first met him about ten years ago, and Danny had proved to be a man who made a damn good friend but woe betide anyone who got on the wrong side of him.

Once they were seated, Danny opened the conversation. 'Laurie, my old mate, I know you must need my help or you wouldn't be slumming it down here on the Docks. First off, I've been waiting me chance to say thanks for raising so much money for the boys' club. It's up and running and is the biggest and best club for youngsters in the East End. Now, will you have a drink or shall I phone down for some coffee?'

Laurie laughed. 'No need for thanks, and coffee would be fine.'

It was brought up to them by a motherly-looking woman who plonked the tray down on Danny's desk saying, 'I 'eard Mr Walmsley was 'ere and you know me legs don't like me coming up and down your ruddy stairs, Danny, but I 'ad to thank 'im – 'e knows what for. Under that cover is some nice thick slices of toast, an' yeah, I 'ave put loads of butter on 'em.'

The two men exchanged amused glances, then Laurie stood up and gave the woman an affectionate hug.

'Get on wiv yer, Mr Walmsley, I'll make all the gals in the place jealous when I tell them I've bin in your arms.'

They could hear her laughter as she slowly made her way down the stairs.

Danny poured the coffee into two cups, and silence reigned as they ate and drank. When they'd finished, Danny gathered up the mugs and plates and put them back on the tray.

'Well let's have it,' he said. 'Let's see if two heads can be better than one.'

Laurie took out the page of the newspaper

that referred to the plight of Zimbabwe and handed it to Danny, looking quietly around the office while Danny read the article.

'All the papers carried much the same, but I was under the impression it was being taken care of.' It sounded as if Danny was talking to himself.

It was some time before he spoke again, and when he did, the anger in his voice was clear. 'Laurie, are you all right sitting there while I make a few phone calls, or would you rather go downstairs and have a look around the club?'

'If it's all right with you, I'm happy to stay here.'

Three phone calls had been short and sharp, and now Danny was making a fourth. 'Hatcher, it's me, Danny Cole. Which dock has been handling cargo to Zimbabwe?...Yes, it is a short question but I want a full answer.'

Minutes passed, Danny still holding the phone to his ear. Eventually he spoke. 'Okay, we'll meet at seven tonight. In the meantime, ask Bill Stevens to come up to my office.' Silence, and then Danny almost shouted, 'Yes, I do mean right now. Thanks for your help, Hatcher,' he added.

Fifteen minutes slipped by and Danny was standing sorting through a hefty pile of papers when there was a rap on the door of the office.

'Come in,' he called sharply as he shuffled

the papers into order and came around to stand in front of his desk.

A short, stocky labourer entered. His wispy grey hair was uncombed, flattened by the cap he'd been wearing. A shabby jacket was flung around his shoulders.

'What number dock are you working on this month?' Danny shot the question without any preliminaries.

'I'm not, I'm overseeing the gang that's working on the dry dock. Any reason why you need to know?'

'Yer outgoing cargoes of late, they've included wheat, barley, sugar and suchlike?' Danny had answered a question with a question and he waited impatiently for an answer.

Bill looked as though he'd decided to try and face Danny down. He was nervous, but he was also angry. 'What the fucking 'ell has it got t'do wiv you?'

'One hell of a lot,' was Danny's quick answer. 'My dad worked these docks for years until he was badly injured and forced to retire, but I still have two brothers who are dockers, as you well know.'

Bill seemed to recognise the underlying threat in Danny's words and said quickly, 'You're beating round the bloody bush. If you've got something to say, get on wiv it.'

'I've been given to understand that you've been using a strange sort of marking on some commodities as they're hoisted aboard. I am sure that several people will be very interested to find out just why these markings are necessary when the cargo is being shipped out as a whole specification, bought and paid for by various charities. There is no need for any part of a cargo to be separated.'

Bill Stevens was astonished and it showed. It was almost possible to read his thoughts: surely this bloke couldn't know what went on in the docks, couldn't be aware how many men were involved. He pulled back his shoulders and took a deep breath.

'I'm leaving right now. As I said, what goes on in my dock is fuck all t'do with you. You should stick ter managing yer boys' club.'

'Maybe I should.' Danny laughed, but his expression was not in the least bit jovial. 'Let me tell you something. I've learnt this morning that yesterday a whole truckload destined for Zimbabwe disappeared even before it left the docks.'

'We can't all be bloody do-gooders; some of us 'ave to earn an extra crust now and again. I bet your charity accounts for that posh boys' club wouldn't stand much looking into. Creamed it off the top, did yer? Still, I won't begrudge you a bit of fiddling if yer keep your bleeding nose out of my affairs.'

Danny drew his arm back, knuckled his fingers and punched the docker full in the face. As Stevens lay half unconscious on the floor, blood pouring from his flattened nose,

Danny bent down and unzipped the man's trousers. He wasn't finished with Bill Stevens. What he'd been doing was wrong in anybody's book. He grabbed Stevens' genitals in one huge hand, and squeezed as hard as he could.

Bill Stevens tried to scream, but he had no breath. His mouth gaped in a soundless howl as he tried desperately to suck air. He turned his face away, doubled up in agony.

Without so much as a smile on his face, Danny picked up the phone. 'Alec, it's me, Danny, I need a plain car or a van to take one of the dockers up to the hospital... No, he can't walk so you'd better send two men to carry him down my stairs.'

Laurie couldn't hear the response from the other end; what he did hear was Danny saying, 'He only got what he rightly deserved and I don't think the matter will end here. Some situations get out of hand and men have to realise that there are still limits as to how far one can overstep the mark. What a few wicked bastards get up to makes it look bad for everyone else. Stealing grub meant for starving infants is going too far.'

Laurence was locked in a great bear hug as Danny assured him that the matter would now be dealt with by men in high places. Laurie murmured his thanks and there were smiles of satisfaction all round as the two men said their goodbyes.

'Don't be a stranger. We don't mind a toffee-nosed git like yerself coming to the East End,' Danny assured Laurie as he playfully punched his shoulder. 'Oh, and by the way, when the boys' club has been up and running for one year, we're gonna 'ave a prizegiving and I expect you to be there.'

Laurie grinned. 'Let me know in good time when you need my chequebook.'

'Will do. See yer then, and give my regards to your gorgeous wife.'

Driving home, Laurence felt elated, but at the same time utterly exhausted. Today had proved a point, but at what cost? He himself had been saved from having to make the journey to Zimbabwe, but Bill Stevens' life was in ruins. All on account of his own greed. No one played by the book the whole time, Laurie told himself, but there had to be a limit.

Chloe was thrilled to see him walk through the door, and after he had lovingly kissed her, he said, 'Problem solved. No need for me to go traipsing abroad.'

'That is wonderful news,' Chloe declared. 'Is the matter truly going to be sorted out without you having to go to Zimbabwe?' The relief in her voice had Laurie smiling as she added, 'How the hell did you manage it?'

'Let's just say I've had a little help from my friends.'

# Chapter 24

Chloe leaned forward and looked out of the window. The British Airways aeroplane had been climbing steadily through the clouds and was now streaking through a sky so penetratingly blue, its shimmering clearness hurt her eyes. Momentarily dazzled by this early-morning brightness, she turned away from the window, rested her head against the back of the seat and closed her eyes.

A faint smile played around her mouth as she thought with a great deal of love about Laurence and herself, together with Dorothy and Peter. They still owned their lovely homes in Ditchling and life was not all work and good deeds. Both families travelled widely and saw what went on in other parts of the world.

Whenever Chloe felt regrets, she always turned her thoughts to Ditchling, to the house that Roger had never been given the chance to live in, but which she and Laurence had made their own. It was the place where she had found not only peace but love. True, lasting love. Thanks to Roger, and all that he had given her, this house had become a retreat. Her home.

Come her next birthday, she would be sixty-eight years old.

She still looked great, Laurie told her that all the time. Over and over he would say he couldn't believe it. 'Look at me,' he'd say. 'I've gained weight and my hair is slate grey. But you...' and then he'd smile that same old confident smile, 'you look exactly the same, though even more beautiful.' His eyes would shine with pride and he would take her in his arms, holding her tight, letting her know that she truly belonged to him and only him.

Of course her beauty was not maintained without effort. Since she'd turned fifty she'd had a personal trainer who came to the house twice a week during the winter months. She thought sometimes that his workouts were brutal. But the results were splendid. Her body was back to what it had been before she had given birth to their two sons, and that fact alone made her feel gloriously young.

She had been away for almost two months, the first time she had made such a long journey on her own. How many times during her stay in Australia had she wished she had never left home? The whole holiday had been a ghastly mistake. But in twenty-four hours she would be landing at Heathrow and her darling Laurence would be waiting for her.

This thought cheered her immensely and she relaxed in her seat and closed her eyes.

The tension that had built up over the last few weeks was diminishing a little. She was tired of the quarrels and raging battles that had repeatedly taken place in her brothers' homes, leaving her feeling exhausted. There had been times when she had regretted the fact that the Salvation Army had finally located her brothers' whereabouts in Australia. Laurence had urged her to go, telling her how thrilled they would be to see her after such a long period of time.

She had begged him to come with her, but his refusal had been adamant. She needed to meet her brothers on her own. If all went well, he had added, they would keep in constant touch and visit frequently in the future.

The truth had been vastly different. It wasn't that she hadn't liked Australia; just that the accusations that had been thrown at her had left her feeling worn out, lonely and so very far from home.

She had deliberately sent them halfway around the world just to be rid of them was her brothers' chief allegation. The fact that she had only been fourteen years old herself at that time never seemed to count. Even her brothers' children, her nephews and nieces, had been hostile towards her.

Nothing, however, had stopped her brothers taking her to the bank and waiting while she withdrew a huge sum of money for each of them.

I'm getting too old for gallivanting around on planes, she thought ruefully, and then quickly dismissed that thought. In all truthfulness, she did not feel old. Only tired on occasions, and especially when she was confronted by angry people.

She straightened her back and crossed her legs, her big green eyes wide open again now. She lifted one of her hands and automatically smoothed her hair. It was still thick and long, now mostly worn up in a French pleat. Though it was no longer such a fiery chestnut colour, her hairdresser encouraged her to let him tint the roots every now and again.

She reminded herself that it wouldn't be long now before Laurence would have her safely back home in Ditchling. Home to peace, tranquillity, her beautiful old-fashioned garden and her two fine sons, who with their wives and children both lived nearby. Not forgetting her gorgeous niece Amberley, who lived in Hove and was happily married with two daughters.

This thought cheered her immensely and once more she relaxed in her seat. The tension that had built up over the last few weeks was slowly diminishing, but she still found it impossible to relax completely.

'Would you like a drink, madam?' asked the smart young steward.

'Yes please, coffee would be nice.'

She sipped her coffee and nibbled at a biscuit, then picked up her briefcase and took out her glasses and the sheaf of folders that she had picked up from the bank in Perth three weeks ago. Laurence had transferred a number of reports for her to read because their yearly charity turnover had been so heart-warming.

Chloe slipped on her rimless glasses and opened up one of the folders. As she scanned the papers, there was a gleam of satisfaction in her eyes. Laurence had led them and their money through many different channels. Over the years, success had served to reinforce not just their bank balances, but Dorothy and Peter's too. As she marked symbols on the documents for future reference, she thought just how thrilled her sister- and brother-in-law would be.

Satisfied that the papers were in order, Chloe put the folders and her glasses back into her briefcase, settled back in her seat and buzzed the steward to bring her another cup of coffee.

The hotel in Singapore was charming, and Chloe was smiling as she walked softly across the bedroom and through the slatted doors that led out to the wide, shady veranda, where huge fans revolved above a table and comfortable chairs. She knew that she would spend most of the short stopover out here.

She had done enough sightseeing and travelling whilst in Australia to last her for a long time. It was very quiet; nothing stirred except the fragrant blossoms in the surrounding gardens as she walked the length of the veranda, the leather soles of her sandals slapping on the wooden floor. She let herself sink into one of the long cushioned chairs, her legs supported by a footrest.

Her mind again wandered back over the years and suddenly she felt a surge of resentment. Her parents had been hard-working, loving people, but where had it got them? And now that she had more money than she knew what to do with, why weren't they here? It would have been so nice to have been able to give them even a few of the luxuries that she herself now took for granted. Life could be very unfair. Her intention in going to Australia had been to extend her loving family with her two brothers. So often she had wondered whether they had married and had children, how their lives had turned out.

She sighed. She must have dozed. Around her, doors were being opened, folk were stirring. Siesta was over.

A rap on her own door, and to her call of 'Come in,' a smartly dressed waitress entered the room carrying a tray loaded with delicate china, a silver teapot, cucumber sandwiches and a glass stand holding small fancy cakes.

As she enjoyed her afternoon tea, Chloe

comforted herself with the thought that first thing in the morning she would be boarding the plane on the last leg of her journey home. Soon she would be in Laurie's arms again.

Had Laurie known that she would be walking into a disaster? Surely not. Neither of them had imagined that her brothers would be so envious of her. They had made no attempt to disguise the hatred they felt for her. Any attempts at reconciliation had been met with sarcasm and insults. Not a soul had come to the airport to see her off, and that fact had hurt. I shall put it behind me, forget all about them, she had vowed the minute she had boarded the plane on the first leg of her journey home. But dear God, it was easier said than done.

The evening did a lot to calm Chloe down, and the soft, warm air in the dining room made her glad that she had kept one low-backed evening dress with her. The band was playing soft music, the dancing girls in their beautiful lacy costumes appeared to float through the air, and the meal was perfection. Nevertheless, she was glad to return to her bedroom and for the last time repack her overnight case. She tried to read, but finally gave it up as a bad job and fell into a fretful sleep.

When she heard a tap on her door, and a charming young maid brought her a tray of tea, she sat up in bed and sighed with relief.

Just this last leg of the journey and she would be back in England, and in the future she would never again go anywhere without her beloved Laurence.

The long flight had come to an end. Chloe was trembling as she gathered together her belongings, and she had to stand still for a moment when she reached the open doors of the plane. The steps leading downwards seemed endless, and her legs felt wobbly as she began the descent, but eventually her feet touched the ground. She was back home in England.

She passed through passport control without any trouble and looked around for a trolley, which she loaded up with her luggage. As she headed through customs, and out into the arrivals hall, it seemed to her that half the population of England was gathered here at Heathrow today. She wondered how on earth she was going to find Laurence.

Then, glory be to God, he was behind her, his arms enclosing her, her back leaning against his chest. She let go of the trolley and turned towards him, and their lips met. It was supposed to be a quick kiss, a welcome-home kiss, but Laurie leaned in closer and the kiss lingered. Suddenly one of her hands was behind his neck and both his arms were around her, and they were clutching each other, merging their bodies as if trying to become one person. When they finally broke apart, both of them were breathless.

'Phew.' Laurence let the sound flow out from between his lips before saying, 'God, you'll never know how much I've missed you. But Chloe, my darling, I think I should warn you in advance that as soon as we get home, we might have to make some serious love.'

Chloe's laugh was a tinkling sound. 'I don't think there will be any question about it,' she replied.

It was seven o'clock in the evening when they arrived home. Chloe paused for a moment on the threshold, and stepped inside. Home at last.

Tired as she was, she came back to life as Laurie's mouth covered hers. When he finally lifted her up into his arms and made for the bedroom, she was glowing and breathless, and at that point she began to realise just how much they meant to each other. He laid her down on the bed, loosened the pins from her hair and buried his face in her silky tresses. It was Chloe who started the kissing; she wanted to let Laurie know of all the love and happiness she felt deep inside, and just how much she had missed him, wanting him to feel the same way. And when his kisses became urgent, she knew that he did – and more.

They made love like never before. Soft moans from Chloe's throat only served to drive him on as her muscles tightened, gripping him as she encouraged him to quicken the pace. Then came the point when she simply held him tight as he took her to the edge, and suspended her there until he took her over into a glorious free-fall that left them both dragging breath into their lungs.

Sated, she held him close, murmuring indistinctly as she rested in his arms.

It was an indisputable fact that they belonged together. She was his, as he was hers.

During the night, they several times again attempted to prove to each other just how deep their love really was. Then, close to six o'clock in the morning, Laurie wiped the moisture from their foreheads before they settled down. He pulled the bedcovers up to their shoulders and nestled Chloe in his arms, her head lying within the hollow of his shoulder. Lying together, they closed their eyes and finally slept.

Each of them wanting nothing more than to be granted many more happy years together.

The publishers hope that this book has given you enjoyable reading. Large Print Books are especially designed to be as easy to see and hold as possible. If you wish a complete list of our books please ask at your local library or write directly to:

**Magna Large Print Books**
Magna House, Long Preston,
Skipton, North Yorkshire.
BD23 4ND

This Large Print Book, for people
who cannot read normal print,
is published under the auspices of

**THE ULVERSCROFT FOUNDATION**

... we hope you have enjoyed this book.
Please think for a moment about those
who have worse eyesight than you ...
and are unable to even read or enjoy
Large Print without great difficulty.

You can help them by sending a
donation, large or small, to:

**The Ulverscroft Foundation,
1, The Green, Bradgate Road,
Anstey, Leicestershire, LE7 7FU,
England.**
or request a copy of our brochure for
more details.

The Foundation will use all donations
to assist those people who are visually
impaired and need special attention
with medical research, diagnosis
and treatment.

Thank you very much for your help.